BRIAN F¹

MURDER E¹

BRIAN FLYNN was born in 1885 in Leyton, Essex. He won a scholarship to the City Of London School, and from there went into the civil service. In World War I he served as Special Constable on the Home Front, also teaching "Accountancy, Languages, Maths and Elocution to men, women, boys and girls" in the evenings, and acting in his spare time.

It was a seaside family holiday that inspired Brian Flynn to turn his hand to writing in the mid-twenties. Finding most mystery novels of the time "mediocre in the extreme", he decided to compose his own. Edith, the author's wife, encouraged its completion, and after a protracted period finding a publisher, it was eventually released in 1927 by John Hamilton in the UK and Macrae Smith in the U.S. as *The Billiard-Room Mystery*.

The author died in 1958. In all, he wrote and published 57 mysteries, the vast majority featuring the super-sleuth Antony Bathurst.

BRIAN FLYNN

MURDER EN ROUTE

With an introduction by
Steve Barge

DEAN STREET PRESS

INTRODUCTION

"I believe that the primary function of the mystery story is to entertain; to stimulate the imagination and even, at times, to supply humour. But it pleases the connoisseur most when it presents – and reveals – genuine mystery. To reach its full height, it has to offer an intellectual problem for the reader to consider, measure and solve."

THUS WROTE Brian Flynn in the *Crime Book Magazine* in 1948, setting out his ethos on writing detective fiction. At that point in his career, Flynn had published thirty-six mystery novels, beginning with *The Billiard-Room Mystery* in 1927 – he went on, before his death in 1958, to write twenty-one more, three under the pseudonym Charles Wogan. So how is it that the general reading populace – indeed, even some of the most ardent collectors of mystery fiction – were until recently unaware of his existence? The reputation of writers such as John Rhode survived their work being out of print, so what made Flynn and his books vanish so completely?

There are many factors that could have contributed to Flynn's disappearance. For reasons unknown, he was not a member of either The Detection Club or the Crime Writers' Association, two of the best ways for a writer to network with others. As such, his work never appeared in the various collaborations that those groups published. The occasional short story in such a collection can be a way of maintaining awareness of an author's name, but it seems that Brian Flynn wrote no short stories at all, something rare amongst crime writers.

There are a few mentions of him in various studies of the genre over the years. Sutherland Scott, in *Blood in Their Ink* (1953), states that Flynn, who was still writing at the time, "has long been popular". He goes on to praise *The Mystery of the Peacock's Eye* (1928) as containing "one of the ablest pieces of misdirection one could wish to meet". Anyone reading that particular review who feels like picking up the novel – out now from Dean Street Press – should stop reading at that point, as later in the book, Scott proceeds to casually spoil the ending, although as if he assumes that everyone will have read the novel already.

It is a later review, though, that may have done much to end – temporarily, I hope – Flynn's popularity.

"Straight tripe and savorless. It is doubtful, on the evidence, if any of his others would be different."

Thus wrote Jacques Barzun and Wendell Hertig Taylor in their celebrated work, *A Catalog of Crime* (1971). The book was an ambitious attempt to collate and review every crime fiction author, past and present. They presented brief reviews of some titles, a bibliography of some authors and a short biography of others. It is by no means complete – E & M.A. Radford had written thirty-six novels at this point in time but garner no mention – but it might have helped Flynn's reputation if he too had been overlooked. Instead one of the contributors picked up *Conspiracy at Angel* (1947), the thirty-second Anthony Bathurst title. I believe that title has a number of things to enjoy about it, but as a mystery, it doesn't match the quality of the majority of Flynn's output. Dismissing a writer's entire work on the basis of a single volume is questionable, but with the amount of crime writers they were trying to catalogue, one can, just about, understand the decision. But that decision meant that they missed out on a large number of truly entertaining mysteries that fully embrace the spirit of the Golden Age of Detection, and, moreover, many readers using the book as a reference work may have missed out as well.

So who was Brian Flynn? Born in 1885 in Leyton, Essex, Flynn won a scholarship to the City Of London School, and while he went into the civil service (ranking fourth in the whole country on the entrance examination) rather than go to university, the classical education that he received there clearly stayed with him. Protracted bouts of rheumatic fever prevented him fighting in the Great War, but instead he served as a Special Constable on the Home Front – one particular job involved warning the populace about Zeppelin raids armed only with a bicycle, a whistle and a placard reading "TAKE COVER". Flynn worked for the local government while teaching "Accountancy, Languages, Maths and Elocution to men, women, boys and girls" in the evening, and acting as part of the Trevalyan Players in his spare time.

It was a seaside family holiday that inspired him to turn his hand to writing. He asked his librarian to supply him a collection of mystery novels for "deck-chair reading" only to find himself disappointed. In his own words, they were "mediocre in the extreme." There is no record of what those books were, unfortunately, but on arriving home, the following conversation, again in Brian's own words, occurred:

> "ME (unpacking the books): If I couldn't write better stuff than any of these, I'd eat my own hat.
>
> Mrs ME (after the manner of women and particularly after the manner of wives): It's a great pity you don't do a bit more and talk a bit less.
>
> The shaft struck home. I accepted the challenge, laboured like the mountain and produced *The Billiard-Room Mystery*."

"Mrs ME", or Edith as most people referred to her, deserves our gratitude. While there were some delays with that first book, including Edith finding the neglected half-finished manuscript in a drawer where it had been "resting" for six months, and a protracted period finding a publisher, it was eventually released in 1927 by John Hamilton in the UK and Macrae Smith in the U.S. According to Flynn, John Hamilton asked for five more, but in fact they only published five in total, all as part of the Sundial Mystery Library imprint. Starting with *The Five Red Fingers* (1929), Flynn was published by John Long, who would go on to publish all of his remaining novels, bar his single non-series title, *Tragedy At Trinket* (1934). About ten of his early books were reprinted in the US before the war, either by Macrae Smith, Grosset & Dunlap or Mill, and a few titles also appeared in France, Denmark, Germany and Sweden, but the majority of his output only saw print in the United Kingdom. Some titles were reprinted during his lifetime – the John Long Four-Square Thrillers paperback range featured some Flynn titles, for example – but John Long's primary focus was the library market, and some titles had relatively low print runs. Currently, the majority of Flynn's work, in particular that only published in the U.K., is extremely rare – not just expensive, but seemingly non-existent even in the second-hand book market.

In the aforementioned article, Flynn states that the tales of Sherlock Holmes were a primary inspiration for his writing, having read them at a young age. A conversation in *The Billiard-Room Mystery* hints at other influences on his writing style. A character, presumably voicing Flynn's own thoughts, states that he is a fan of "the pre-war Holmes". When pushed further, he states that:

> "Mason's M. Hanaud, Bentley's Trent, Milne's Mr Gillingham and to a lesser extent, Agatha Christie's M. Poirot are all excellent in their way, but oh! – the many dozens that aren't."

He goes on to acknowledge the strengths of Bernard Capes' "Baron" from *The Mystery of The Skeleton Key* and H.C. Bailey's Reggie Fortune, but refuses to accept Chesterton's Father Brown.

> "He's entirely too Chestertonian. He deduces that the dustman was the murderer because of the shape of the piece that had been cut from the apple-pie."

Perhaps this might be the reason that the invitation to join the Detection Club never arrived . . .

Flynn created a sleuth that shared a number of traits with Holmes, but was hardly a carbon-copy. Enter Anthony Bathurst, a polymath and gentleman sleuth, a man of contradictions whose background is never made clear to the reader. He clearly has money, as he has his own rooms in London with a pair of servants on call and went to public school (Uppingham) and university (Oxford). He is a follower of all things that fall under the banner of sport, in particular horse racing and cricket, the latter being a sport that he could, allegedly, have represented England at. He is also a bit of a show-off, littering his speech (at times) with classical quotes, the obscurer the better, provided by the copies of the *Oxford Dictionary of Quotations* and *Brewer's Dictionary of Phrase & Fable* that Flynn kept by his writing desk, although Bathurst generally restrains himself to only doing this with people who would appreciate it or to annoy the local constabulary. He is fond of amateur dramatics (as was Flynn, a well-regarded amateur thespian who appeared in at least one self-penned play, *Blue Murder*), having been a member of OUDS, the Oxford University Dramatic Society. Like Holmes, Bathurst isn't averse to the occasional disguise, and as with Watson and Holmes, sometimes even his close allies don't recognise him. General information about his background is light on the ground. His parents were Irish, but he doesn't have an accent – see *The Spiked Lion* (1933) – and his eyes are grey. We learn in *The Orange Axe* that he doesn't pursue romantic relationships due to a bad experience in his first romance. That doesn't remain the case throughout the series – he falls head over heels in love in *Fear and Trembling*, for example – but in this opening tranche of titles, we don't see Anthony distracted by the fairer sex, not even one who will only entertain gentlemen who can beat her at golf!

Unlike a number of the Holmes' stories, Flynn's Bathurst tales are all fairly clued mysteries, perhaps a nod to his admiration of Christie, but first and foremost, Flynn was out to entertain the reader. The problems posed to Bathurst have a flair about them – the simultaneous murders, miles apart, in *The Case of the Black Twenty-Two* (1928) for example, or the scheme to draw lots to commit masked murder in *The Orange Axe* – and there is a momentum to the narrative. Some mystery writers have trouble with the pace slowing between the reveal of the problem and the reveal of the murderer, but Flynn's books sidestep that, with Bathurst's investigations never seeming to sag. He writes with a wit and intellect that can make even the most prosaic of interviews with suspects enjoyable to read about, and usually provides an action-packed finale before the murderer is finally revealed. Some of those revelations, I think it is fair to say, are surprises that can rank with some of the best in crime fiction.

We are fortunate that we can finally reintroduce Brian Flynn and Anthony Lotherington Bathurst to the many fans of classic crime fiction out there.

Murder en Route (1930)

"As I see things, Inspector, everything's wrong. It's only by realizing that they're wrong that I begin to get them right."

PUBLIC TRANSPORT is a common setting for murder in classic crime fiction, but predominantly, that mode of transport is the train. The probable reason for this is the ease of committing such a murder – characters are inevitably travelling in six-seat compartments which allow a good degree of privacy for the foul deed to be carried out, leaving the hapless guard or a fellow passenger to discover the corpse after the fact. Examples of these include *Death On The Boat Train* by John Rhode, where a passenger "commits suicide" while alone in the compartment and *The Case Of The Three Strange Faces* by Christopher Bush, where the sleuth Ludovic Travers sleeps through the murder taking place. John Rhode also had a penchant for the train as murder weapon, using it both in *Tragedy On The Line* and *Dead On The Track* – at least his police character, Inspector Haslet, has the common sense in the second book to recall the first incident.

Other modes of public transport are less common. The primary instances that spring to mind are *Death In The Clouds*, where Poirot sleeps through a poisoning in an airplane cabin crossing the channel, and *The Tragedy Of X*, where a poisonous murder device is dropped into the victim's pocket on a crowded tram. The double decker bus, however, is a very rare location for murder, with only two examples of murder committed while the bus is in motion that I am aware of. The first is *The Man Who Killed Fortescue* (1928) by Jonathan Stephen Strange *aka* Dorothy Stockbridge Tillett, where a body is discovered, stabbed in the neck, on the top deck after a mysterious figure ran down the stairs and off of the bus. Brian Flynn went one better two years later, with *Murder En Route*, when a man is strangled on the top deck, but no-one else was with them.

Flynn has dabbled in impossible crimes before, in *The Case Of The Black Twenty-Two* and *Invisible Death*, but it was not a recurring theme of his work. The later book, *The Spiked Lion*, also deals with a locked room murder, but these are the exceptions rather the rule. As is often the case with such mysteries, the reader may have to leave their cynicism at the door, especially when asking if there was an easier way to achieve their goal, but if every Golden Age villain resorted to more prosaic methods, the world of mystery fiction would be a much duller place to visit.

Bathurst once again stumbles into the case, rather than being recruited. He drops into a Glebeshire church when he hears the Reverend Parry-Probyn's organ practice and, as ever, proceeds to do everything he can to show off his general knowledge. When it transpires that the vicar is acquainted with the medical examiner on the case, Bathurst finds himself assembling a band of helpers, with the reluctant help of Inspector Curgenven, to get to the bottom of a most perplexing case.

Something should be said about the narrative structure of the book, as a large part of it is narrated by the good Reverend. This is the first time that Flynn has adopted a first person narrator since his opening book, *The Billiard-Room Mystery*, and it is a slightly odd choice, given that, once the Reverend begins his narration in Chapter Four, he has to relate some incidents where he was not present, whereas other chapters on such events are written in the third person. As I said, slightly odd, but it does not distract from the tale which is, on a relative scale, one of Flynn's better known works.

In part this was due to the fact that it was released in both the UK, by John Long in 1930 and the US by Macrae Smith in 1932 alongside *The Crime At The Crossways*, a retitled version of *The Creeping Jenny Mystery*, and also received a rare paperback release for Flynn as part of the John Long Four-Square Thriller range in the 1940s. However since then, it has been nearly seventy-five years since *Murder En Route* saw the light of day.

Steve Barge

CHAPTER I
THE NIGHT IN NOVEMBER

IT WAS a cold, wet and unutterably cheerless night in mid-November—a night when the mordant dog of Lear's enemy would have found shelter beside the blind king's fire. The thick fog that had held possession of the coastal line for several hours had given way at last to heavy rain—rain which positively seemed to revel in its falling. The last motor-bus at this particular season of the year was due to leave the seaside town of Esting at 8.33. It ran to its destination of Raybourne in the scheduled time of one hour and five minutes, and, in addition to a number of small villages, passed through on its way the coast towns of Lanning, Northlynn, Sladenham and Kirve, all of which were on the regular route of the Southbrooke Motor Services Company. Whereas from the beginning of April to the second week in October, in due allegiance to Summer Time, an augmented service was in being, with a last journey from Esting at five minutes past eleven, at the time of the year when this history opens the service along the coast to Raybourne was restricted to a mere dozen motor-buses per day.

On the night in question the exigencies of the English climate were the primary cause of the vehicle being almost empty when it left Esting and commenced its fourteen-mile journey. It was an open-decker, and the few people it carried huddled together inside. Frederick Whitehead, the conductor, joyless and cadaverous, gave his driver the necessary signal on the bell at the back and solemnly entered the inside of his bus for the purpose of collecting the fares. He was carrying, he discovered, only five people, two of whom were comparatively well known to him. They were a Mr. and Mrs. Jupp, of Sladenham. The remaining three people were strangers. Two of these three, a man and a woman, booked for as far as the bus travelled—the Tower Square terminus at Raybourne; the other, a young girl somewhere in the early twenties, asked for Northlynn. When questioned later on by the coroner who conducted the inquest, Whitehead was able to remember these particulars perfectly. At this stage of the journey there was nobody on top whatever, which was, as has been stated, entirely uncovered and completely exposed to the savagery of the elements.

Whitehead passed a melancholy remark to his two passengers who had booked to Sladenham Corner, and returned disconsolately to his platform. Thank heaven it was his last journey that night! He crouched against the bend of the staircase as much as he comfortably could, for by this time the rain had come on even worse than before and was beating on to his face and shoulders with pitiless severity. The bus made good pace from Esting, and as they approached the dark arch of the railway bridge half a mile or so from Lanning, Whitehead temporarily forsook his inadequate shelter and went to the extreme edge of his square platform. He did so from no whim or chance movement, but from an intention born of habit. He peered out into the almost impenetrable darkness. The rain lashed his face, but for a moment or two he was content to endure it, for he was looking for somebody—a passenger—a man who had caught this 8.33 motor-bus from Esting at this particular spot every night for a month or more. Whitehead did not have to look out for very long. His customary passenger was waiting as usual in the shelter and shadow of the bridge. Whitehead gave the signal for the bus to slow down, and the man who had been waiting in the rain, with the collar of his heavy overcoat turned right up to the ridge of his jaw, swung himself alertly on to the platform.

"No bon for you on top tonight, sir," called the conductor.

"The man addressed laughed and shook his head as he put his foot on the second stair and stood there for a second or two. His voice travelled down to Whitehead:

"Did you ever know me care two hoots for weather? They wouldn't call this rain in the country where I've come from," he declared; "they'd only call it 'heat-drops'. I'll ride tonight, conductor, where I always ride—in the open air." He ascended two more steps, and then he called down again: "Inside a bus? Me? Not yet awhile, my man. Not while I'm hale and hearty. It's only fit for old women—of both sexes."

Whitehead grinned to the occupants inside in appreciation of the last allusion, and jerked his head in the direction of the man as he ascended. "He's mustard, he is, and no mistake. But it's a solid fact he's consistent—I'll say that for 'im and give 'im 'is due. Always on top, no matter what the elements is like. In fact, the worse the weather is the better it seems to suit 'im. I never knew 'im so talkative as 'e is tonight."

What the conductor said was certainly true. For the passenger of our notice that had gone upstairs had never been known to ride inside. Whitehead clattered upstairs to take the fare.

"Who is he, Fred?" inquired Jupp, when he returned. "I've been seein' 'im a lot lately. I'm an old inhabitant of these 'ere parts, and he's a stranger to me. Where's he to?"

"Gets off at the Tower Square every night," replied Whitehead, "and has done for four or five weeks now. That's all I know about him. I've been picking him up at the Lanning railway bridge every night. There's one thing: you could pick him out anywhere, couldn't you? There's no mistaking him."

Jupp nodded agreement. "You're right there, surely. Besides his appearance, there's the matter of his education." He nodded again sagaciously.

"Education's like murder—it will out. I've seen him half a dozen times on this 'ere bus. 'E's got the hallmark about 'im. Anybody can see that. You can always tell it, and there's more than one sign of it, if you want to know, Fred, my boy."

Mrs. Jupp nodded her head in vigorous corroboration of her husband's statement, although the action was by no means a habit of hers.

Whitehead smiled. "More than one?" he questioned.

"Ay, Fred. And it's not everybody knows the signs—either—come to that. But I'll tell you 'em, if you'd care to listen." He leant forward in his seat towards Whitehead on the platform in his eagerness to explain his meaning. "I've knocked about a good bit longer than you, Fred Whitehead, as you'd be the first to admit, and I've kept my two eyes open. When you're married you have to—take it from me, my boy! If you didn't your own share of what's worth having 'ud be less than nothing. There are *three* signs that mark the gentry out from us common folk." He proceeded to emphasize his remarks with the tips of his fingers. "First—the way they've got of pronunciation of their words. Second—the kind o' clothes they wear, and how they all blend together so to speak. For instance, to illustrate my point, you'd never see one of 'em in a bowler hat and open-neck tennis shirt. Or with brown shoes under black trousers. And third—their way of doin' the 'air." In his ardour of triumphant explanation Mr. Jupp lost his aspirate most flagrantly. He concluded: "Him as went upstairs just now is a *gentleman*, and anybody as can't recognize it has lived with his eyes shut, which I've never done."

At this point conversation in the bus slackened. At the parish church of St. Philip, Northlynn, one of the inside passengers alighted—the young girl, dark-haired and distinctly pretty, who had been seated opposite Mr. and Mrs. Jupp. As she left the step of the bus Whitehead looked ahead and murmured: "Fog now." He was right. From here the vehicle crept at a snail's pace through the narrow, twisting and winding street that did duty as the main street of Northlynn. Here the fog held sway, thick and impenetrable, for Northlynn lay in the valley of the Linner, and the gale had not reached it. The shops were closed and the street itself deserted save for a few shadowy figures hardly discernible in the blanket of fog. The bus made its customary halt a dozen yards or so from the "Blue Boar", and then after a few minutes' wait carried on in the direction of Sladenham.

It is worthy of record here that it picked up no more passengers until between this point and destination at Tower Square, Raybourne. Mr. and Mrs. Jupp were deposited at the foot of the hill that lay on the Kirve side of Sladenham, and faced the journey to their farm on the top of Pyloran Hill, that it was necessary for them to encompass, with an ill grace. There was no fog here, but it was raining hard. By this time it was exactly nine minutes past nine, and as Mr. and Mrs. Jupp ascended the hill to Pyloran Hill Farm, the rain and accompanying gale had reached a stage of almost merciless ferocity. The remaining two passengers, the middle-aged couple, to all obvious evidences man and wife, finished their journey at Droskyn Corner, Kirve, despite the fact that their tickets would have taken them to Raybourne. The time was now nineteen minutes past nine, and the bus, according to time-table, was three minutes late. But the roads were deserted of traffic, and people were only abroad in mere handfuls. The driver, in an attempt to recapture his lost three minutes, made good pace from the Kirve Public Offices, and, not being again hailed by anybody, succeeded in his desire and ran into the Tower Square, Raybourne, promptly to schedule at 9.38. Whitehead waited on his platform for his upstairs passenger to descend. He did this invariably before collecting his box, ticket-holder and journey way-bills preparatory to paying in his cash takings.

It was still pouring in pitiless torrents. To the conductor's intense surprise, especially when he considered the conditions of the weather, there was no descending step to be heard on the staircase after the bus had come to a standstill. Whitehead decided to call out. "Tower Square, sir!" he shouted up the stairway from his platform. To this elocutionary effort also there was no response. Muttering an impatient exclamation that embraced not only the English climate but the vagaries of passengers in addition, the conductor ascended five stairs. This eminence gave him a sight of the seats on the top. His passenger was there in his usual place—asleep, no doubt! Whitehead essayed a second warning shout: "We're there, sir," he called. "Raybourne! Tower Square. All change! And my kipper'll be proper spoiled unless you make a move, sir!"

But this delicate reference to the evening meal was as unsuccessful in its immediate object as his two previous efforts had been. Whitehead went up another step and stared hard at the man seated in front of him. Then for the first time since the bus had stopped and he had thought of this "fare" riding outside, a wave of doubt and suspicion engulfed him. He sensed something unusual—abnormal. He quickly ascended the remaining stairs and reached the top flooring. There was still no movement from the man at whom he looked. Whitehead walked quickly forward and placed a hand on the man's shoulder. As he did so,

"H'm," he muttered, as he bent down to the corpse on the floor of the deck. "There's no doubt he's dead enough. Is this as you found him, Conductor?" He looked at Whitehead intently.

The latter shook his head—nervously. "N-no, Inspector. When I came up first he was sitting, as it were, on the seat in the usual sort of way, you know. I called out to 'im to tell him where he was, but of course 'e give me no answer. Then something came over me all of a sudden, and I seemed to realize what was the matter with 'im. I can't tell you 'ow it was, Inspector—or even why—it just come over me, that was all. So I took a step or two forward to 'im and touched 'im on the shoulder. I think as how I wanted to make sure like. Like this 'ere." Whitehead made a suitable action of explanation. "As I did so, Inspector, 'e seemed to go all flabby like, and fair collapsed—slid down on to the floor as you see 'im now."

"Who is he—any idea?" The inspector put the question without hesitation.

"Don't know 'is name—if that's what you mean," replied Whitehead, "but I know a little bit about 'im. I should say he lives 'ere in Raybourne somewhere, and has come from abroad. How I know is because of this: 'E's caught this bus every night for a month and more. My mate, Bill Sturgess 'ere, can confirm that! That's so, Bill, wot I say, ain't it?"

Sturgess nodded. "Quite right, Inspector. We've picked him up outside Lanning regular. Just by the railway arch."

"Lanning," echoed Curgenven, with a frown. "Do you think he worked there or something and came home this way?"

Whitehead shrugged his shoulders non-committally. "I reckon 'e was a gentleman—so I don't know about 'im working there. Like as not 'e was retired. But 'e got on the bus every night just by the Lanning railway arch—same as Bill says."

Curgenven stared at the motionless figure in front of them. Then he came to a sudden decision.

"Well, men, I'm not going to ask you any more questions now. I'm soaked to the skin standing here as it is. I'm going to give you orders, Sturgess, to run the bus into the yard of the police station. When you get it inside run it straight under the drill-shelter. Then we shall be under cover, and I'll get the Divisional Surgeon, Dr. Wilcox, to come along and have a look at him. I 'phoned to him about it before I came over here. When he tells us what's what I'll start doing the questioning, and run through this chap's belongings. Personally, I'm not sure yet what has killed him."

"Very good, Inspector. I'll get her moving at once." Sturgess scuttled down the staircase, clambered to his driving-seat and quickly got the engine under way. Inspector Curgenven and Whitehead went downstairs in the wake of the driver and seated themselves inside. By this time the disconsolate conductor had resigned himself to the inevitable and comfortless truth that his supper was irretrievably ruined. Sturgess ran the vehicle into the station yard and under the covered space as Curgenven had directed him. Then he descended, and joined the other two men as they alighted.

"Go inside," said the inspector to Whitehead, "and find Sergeant Oliver. He can't be far away. Tell him to bring Dr. Wilcox down to us as soon as the doctor comes in. I'm going to stay here."

Whitehead buttoned up his coat and dashed across the station yard.

"Dr. Wilcox ought to be here within a few minutes," explained Curgenven to Sturgess. "I had the luck to find him in when I 'phoned just now."

The inspector's optimism proved to be well founded, for Whitehead's return to the omnibus was very soon followed by the arrival of Dr. Wilcox.

"Sergeant Oliver's busy for the moment, so I've come along by myself. What's all this about, Inspector?" he added. "It's a dirty night to drag me out, if ever there was one. Seems to me a Divisional Surgeon's life in this part of the country isn't worth living. It's worse than being an ordinary G.P. Now then, Inspector—what is it?"

Curgenven jerked up his head at the doctor's last remark, and the movement held a touch of obstinacy mingled with self-justification.

"A dirty night, as you say, Doctor, and at the same time some dirty work, too, I'm very much afraid. Come up on top of here, will you, please?"

As the doctor and Inspector Curgenven ascended the stairs, the latter gave the Divisional Surgeon a brief outline of the story that Whitehead had brought to him half an hour previously.

"When you've had a look at him, Doctor," he concluded, "see if the same thing strikes you as struck me directly I looked him over."

"Right," said Dr. Wilcox; "shine your torch on him, will you, Curgenven."

The inspector did so. Dr. Wilcox busied himself with the body for a few moments. Then he straightened himself and wiped his knees with his handkerchief.

"Get these two bus chaps to carry him into the station, Inspector, will you? There's no point in keeping the body here any longer, and it's next door to impossible to conduct a proper examination up here under these conditions. It's as cold as hell—er—you know what I mean. Tell them to do so at once."

Sturgess and Whitehead carried the dead man over to the station and laid him on a table in one of the inner rooms.

"I'll join you in a moment," declared Curgenven. "I'm going to have a look round on the top of this bus. I'll be over to you, I expect, before you've finished."

The Divisional Surgeon nodded in agreement with the inspector's expressed opinion, and followed Whitehead and Sturgess into the police station. The two men were ordered to wait in another room, pending Curgenven's arrival. Within a very short period Dr. Wilcox formed his opinion. The cause of death was plain. Turning away from the body he saw Inspector Curgenven entering the room, accompanied by the driver and the conductor.

"Well, Inspector," announced the doctor, "you're quite right in your assumption. It didn't take me long to discover that. This man has been murdered right enough. If you want to know more about it—he's been strangled."

At this announcement Whitehead's eyes nearly fell from his head. Dr. Wilcox wiped his hands with meticulous carefulness. "I've lived in India in my time, Curgenven, as you're probably aware, and during my stay in that country I ran across two or three 'Thug' outrages. Two of them were near Srinagar, in Kashmir. The Thugs, you know," he added by way of explanation, "are the 'stranglers' among the natives." He gestured towards the body on the table somewhat dramatically. "Curgenven, I never saw a case more like one of those than this poor chap we've got lying here." He walked across to the dead man to give point to his last remark. "Come here, Inspector, will you?"

Curgenven silently obeyed. He saw there before him the body of a man of average height and sturdy build. The inspector hastily judged him to be about five feet nine inches tall, and to weigh somewhere in the region of twelve stone. His age he assessed as being anything between thirty-five and forty-five. His hair, of which he had plenty, was dark brown in colour, and he wore a small moustache which was a little lighter in shade than the hair on his head, chin and cheeks, for he had evidently not shaved for at least a day or two. His eyes beneath his horn-rimmed glasses seemed to be of no particular colour at all. Whereas Dr. Wilcox mentally placed them as nondescript, Curgenven, for the time being, labelled them as hazel as he gave them his first quick glance; but as a matter of actual fact, and with deference to either man, a better description would have been "russet-brown". He was extremely well dressed—his wide-brimmed hat, dark overcoat, blue serge suit, brown shoes, socks, collar and tie being all of excellent quality, and, what was more, from the point of view of wear and tear, in almost perfect condition.

"Look at his throat, Inspector," declared the Divisional Surgeon, "and then you'll see better what I mean."

Curgenven looked carefully as Dr. Wilcox proceeded with his explanation.

"This man has been strangled—suffocated, if you prefer the word. He has died of asphyxia. In the Indian outrages that I mentioned the throat of the victim is encircled with a knotted kerchief or rubber band. Into this kerchief or band is twisted a small crowbar, which is manipulated to sever the vertebrae of the neck. Death is almost instantaneous. The appearance of this body fully indicates the cause of death. Besides the marks on his throat, which you can see so much better now that I have removed his collar, the veins of the skin and of the head and neck tell their own story. They're gorged, you see, with the darker blood. The face and head are swollen and turgid. See how purple they're already becoming? In a very short time they'll be almost black. Not at all a pretty sight, Inspector."

Curgenven nodded assent. "Right, Doctor. I hadn't much doubt from the first. I just wanted you to make sure, that was all, before I began to make a move. Now, tell me, sir, how long has the man been dead?"

The Divisional Surgeon bent over the body again and carefully examined the discoloration of the dead man's swollen tongue. Then he pursed his lips critically as he considered Curgenven's question.

"What's the exact time now?" he asked.

"Half past ten," replied the inspector. "I may be a minute or so fast, but that will be good enough."

"H'm!" proceeded Dr. Wilcox. "Half past ten—let me see—if we put it down at somewhere between two and three hours I don't think we shall be very far out."

"Thanks; I see." Curgenven turned instantly to Whitehead and Sturgess. "Now, Whitehead," he opened, "what time was it that this man boarded your bus?"

"About 8.46, Inspector."

"What do you say to that, Doctor?"

Wilcox thought it over.

"H'm—an hour and three quarters! Well, I might be half an hour or so out—it's hard to say."

Curgenven went on: "How many passengers travelled on top of your bus this evening—*for any part* of the journey?"

"Passengers!" Whitehead repeated the word after Curgenven with a note of complete incredulity. "On a night like this!" he continued, with the same almost contemptuous scorn of the idea ringing in the words. "Now, just ask yourself the question, Inspector. Is it likely, now?"

Curgenven brought his two hands together in a movement of sharp derision.

"No, it's *not*, Whitehead, and what's more I'm well aware that it isn't." He turned to Dr. Wilcox. "Now, Doctor, you remember what I said to you just now about something striking me in connection with this chap! Come here and feel his coat—feel his hat! They're simply soaked with rain. Look at his shoes, too, and feel his socks. The man's wringing wet—through and through to the skin. Now why the hell was that man riding outside—on a night like tonight? Tell me that." He paused for a moment, almost breathlessly, but before the doctor could reply went on again: "Where did you say he got on, Whitehead? The archway under Lanning railway bridge?"

"That's right, Inspector. And with regard to 'is ridin' outside— perhaps it ain't so strange in his case as you'd think." He shuffled his feet uneasily as he caught Curgenven's eyes upon him and realized that the time had come for explanation.

"You know something!" The inspector pounced. But if he expected to hear something startling that directly affected the adventure of the evening he was from the beginning of the incident doomed to disappointment. For Whitehead, rather frightened at his position in the matter, and also by the atmosphere that seemed to him to hang around Curgenven's question, shook his head violently.

"No, Inspector, I don't. I'll give you my solemn oath I don't. I mean something quite different. I'll tell you what I did mean. When I said it wasn't as strange in his case as you'd think— about 'im ridin' on top—I spoke fair Gospel, because I'm the one man that knows." Whitehead's eyes blazed in his eagerness to justify his statement. "For the very good reason, Inspector, that this gentleman wot's dead *always* travelled on top—every night—rain or shine. He fair laughed at what we call wet, 'e did. It had no effect on him at all." He swung round to Sturgess for corroboration, as he had done previously. "That's fact, wot I say, ain't it, Bill?"

"You can bank on that," interposed the driver; "it's absolutely as my mate says—word for word."

"H'm!" Curgenven bit at his underlip. This to him altered the complexion of the affair considerably. "How far does every night cover?" he asked, with a tinge of asperity.

"A month to five weeks, Inspector. If I were at home now, and 'ad the opportunity to refer to one or two things, I could tell you the exact night when I first picked 'im up as my fare."

"Good—I may want you to, later on—we'll see. Let's go back to my question. Nobody else, from your story, as far as your own knowledge goes, rode on top of your bus this evening—eh? You would be prepared to swear that, if necessary?"

Some of Whitehead's self-confidence returned to him and reasserted itself. "Yes, I would. *Nobody!* Take it from me, Inspector—not a soul went up my stairway after the dead man did, exceptin' me to take 'is fare. Never mind about puttin' in 'as far as my knowledge goes'—because it goes all the way. Because I never left my platform from the time I went to collect his fare to when I 'opped up at Raybourne to tell 'im it was time for 'im to get down. So that's that. I'd swear it on anything."

Whitehead's belief in the truth and justice of his cause brought a jauntiness to his manner that before had been entirely lacking. Curgenven, too, was conscious of it, and although he would have been hard put to it to supply an adequate explanation of his own feelings, he was just as conscious also that he found this new semi-exuberant quality of the conductor distinctly annoying and irritating. At all events he determined that he would attempt to test Whitehead's story, and, if at all possible, to shake its accuracy.

"Just a minute, man. That's all very well. But in a case like this every second of time has got to be sealed up, as it were, and absolutely accounted for. Perhaps you don't yet realize that. I can't, and you can't—if you think you can—content ourselves with generalities that would suffice, we will say, to cover an ordinary journey on an ordinary evening. But tonight every fraction of a second has got to be *combed* out and examined, Whitehead. So make your mind up for that."

Whitehead was sufficiently master of himself to produce a look of indignation. At the same time he stuck doggedly to his previous point.

"I *can* account for every second of the journey. I've not been off my platform—except to go inside and on top once—for one second for the whole of the time of the journey, and I'll swear that *nobody* went upstairs—either before or after the dead man—they couldn't ha' done."

"When did you take his fare?"

"Directly he went up—say 8.47."

Curgenven regarded him shrewdly. "What about the time, then, when you were inside collecting fares? *Before* this man got on the bus. Wouldn't it have been possible for somebody—shall we say to have boarded the bus when your back was turned and your attention temporarily distracted? Think, now."

The conductor refuted the idea with scant ceremony.

"No, Inspector. I should ha' spotted him. And heard 'im too. You get used to doing so on my job. You'll never get it into my head otherwise. You get eyes in your—"

"You feel certain of that?" Curgenven interrupted him before Whitehead could finish his sentence.

"Certain."

"Well, then, suppose I am willing to concede you that point—there's still another very important possibility that we must consider—or so it seems to me. What about stoppages?"

"What do you mean by that—exactly?"

"How often do you stop between Esting and Raybourne—according to actual time-table arrangements—I don't mean you to include haphazard stoppages for—say—picking up passengers—but actual definite stops—when you pull up and wait?"

"Once, and once only at this time of night, Inspector. That's in High Street, Northlynn."

Curgenven nodded, as though the statement found favour in his sight. "I thought so. By the 'Blue Boar', isn't it? I know it used to be."

"Near enough—a few yards the Sladenham side of it. We stop there three minutes, *and I stood on my platform the whole time,* if you want to know. As a matter of fact, it was so foggy as we fetched up there that I was glad to crouch under the stairway for shelter; a fair choker it was, I can tell you."

"Which way did you face as you crouched?" The inspector's question was crisp. "Facing the step?"

Whitehead shook his head vigorously, and then proceeded:

"Dismiss the idea, Inspector, for I can tell you what you're after—what you're harping on; nobody could have boarded my bus tonight and gone upstairs without me knowing. The fog at Northlynn was thick, granted. But no man could have got on without me seeing 'im as I stood there. I'm certain of that as I am that my name's Fred Whitehead."

Curgenven made a curious clicking noise with his tongue. "But that's manifestly absurd, Whitehead. For, if what you say is true, it places you yourself in a rather awkward position. Can't you see that? I certainly wouldn't like to stand in your shoes."

Whitehead paled as he caught the drift of the inspector's meaning. "Why, how do you make—"

"Look at it for yourself, man! Here's a man strangled on your bus, and on your own admission you're the only person who's been near him—and the last person to see him alive. It's more than an admission. It's a vehement assertion."

The conductor's mouth half opened to reply as he caught the inspector's drift, but the weight of Curgenven's remarks was an effective barrier to his speech. Instead he shook his head rather helplessly and turned for succour to his driver, Sturgess. The latter, however, gestured his inability to render assistance to the appeal. After all, he had his own point of view to consider.

"Sorry, Fred, and all that," he said, "but you must know I can't give no evidence as to what went on at the back. I 'ad my own part of the outfit to see to."

Inspector Curgenven walked across to the telephone. Evidently he had made up his mind.

"I'm going to get things moving," he announced.

"First thing we shall have to get is an identification. We must. You two fellows leave your full names and addresses and clear off home. I'll see you again in the morning. Report here at nine o'clock. I'll make it all right with the Company. Perhaps we shall have some more definite news by then."

Whitehead and Sturgess nodded and withdrew.

Just as the inspector had finished the last of his 'phone messages, the quiet voice of Dr. Wilcox called him back to the table on which lay the dead man.

"Come here a minute, Curgenven, will you?" said the Divisional Surgeon. "Come and tell me what you make of this."

Chapter III
THE DEAD MAN'S WRISTS

"What have you discovered, Doctor?" queried Curgenven, as he walked back to where the body lay. "All I could find when I went over to him was two pounds four shillings and ninepence halfpenny in money, a gold watch and a racing programme. So it's evidently not murder for robbery. What else is there?"

Dr. Wilcox beckoned again with his hand. "Come and look at his wrists, Curgenven. There's something here very peculiar." As he spoke, the Divisional Surgeon pushed back the dead man's coat-sleeves and laid bare the two wrists. There was a kind of jagged tear on the inside of each. The blood had dried on the carpal end of the ulna on each of the murdered man's arms, and although to all appearances there had been no artery or large vein wounded, there had at the same time been a fairly strong flow of blood from the fine capillary vessels.

"There's been a struggle of sorts," declared Curgenven; "that's what those marks mean. He didn't go under without putting up a fight—that's very evident. And that conductor chap is prepared to swear that the man's been on top alone for the whole of the journey and that, I suppose, if tackled over it and forced to a definite opinion, a ghost did the murder. A spook that struggled. A likely story, isn't it, Doctor?"

"Seemed pretty sure of his ground, though, Curgenven, didn't he? Nothing you put up to him shook him at all. You must have seen that for yourself. No papers on the dead man, I suppose, Inspector?"

"None, Doctor. As I said, only his money, his watch and a racing programme. Here it is—the Cambridgeshire day at Newmarket, dated Wednesday, October the thirtieth."

Curgenven passed the programme over to the Divisional Surgeon and walked over to where lay the dead man's hat. It was a soft grey felt with an abnormally wide brim—almost a sombrero.

"American, I fancy," declared Curgenven. "Whitehead said he fancied the man had come from abroad somewhere—bet your life he's from the States." He turned the hat over carelessly and then gave vent to a sudden exclamation. "Hallo, Doctor, here's a clue to his identity at last. His initials are here inside his hat, 'C.S.'—look here!"

The doctor took the hat the inspector held out to him and looked inside it as Curgenven had directed. The two letters "C.S." had been stamped in gold on the leather band that ran round inside of the hat. "This is better, Curgenven," he exclaimed. "You shouldn't have any difficulty in tracing your man now."

"Yes. I ought to have seen it before. I suppose I missed it out there in the dark."

The inspector went to the telephone again and passed through to the Press, and the other channels that he had previously used, this additional and important piece of information.

"Do you know, Curgenven," said Dr. Wilcox meditatively, "I can't make up my mind with regard to these marks on his wrists? I am not satisfied that your explanation is the right one. I don't know—but I am not sure that they were not . . ." He walked back to the body and lifted up the sleeves again for a further examination.

"Not sure that they were not what, sir?" inquired the inspector curiously.

"Well," replied Dr. Wilcox, "when you saw them you mentioned a struggle, didn't you? I admit it's a possibility, but there's a condition of laceration present here that wasn't made, for instance, by the fingernails of the assailant, which I presume is something like your idea. The cuts are too deep for that by far. Against that, however; Curgenven, I'm pretty confident the wounds weren't made by any weapon of the knife or dagger variety, because they're quite different in appearance. Frankly, Curgenven, and to be perfectly candid, I'm rather puzzled over the point."

Dr. Wilcox walked up and down the room with his hands in his pockets. The inspector crossed him and began to examine again the dead man's clothes. After a time he spoke:

"I'm going to leave him dressed entirely as he is until the morning, Doctor. I think it might prove to be a mistake not to do so. Look at the back of the overcoat, sir."

Across the dark coat, close to the buttocks, ran a dirty whitish-grey mark. It was a smudge, as though the coat had been rubbed by something.

"There's another mark on the lapel of the jacket, Curgenven," pointed out the Divisional Surgeon; "look here." He placed his thumb under the lapel in question and pushed it up for Curgenven's inspection.

"Something's been spilt there, Doctor," agreed the inspector, as his eye caught the creamy stain. The doctor nodded acquiescence, bent down and sniffed at the dead man's lips, face and clothes. Then he removed the glasses and pulled down the lids of the eyes. He straightened himself with a puzzled expression on his face.

"Seems to me I can detect a faint odour about him somewhere—and familiar at that. But I'm blessed if I can place it at the moment. See what you think, Curgenven."

The inspector imitated the doctor's actions. Then he looked up with a smile that betokened success.

"I'm not a doctor, sir—but I think I can explain what it is that's been puzzling you. About the smell of the clothes, I mean."

Dr. Wilcox smiled back in expectant anticipation. "Yes? That's quite likely, Curgenven. Tell me, then, what is it?"

"Fried fish," declared Curgenven semi-triumphantly. "Nothing more romantic or mysterious than that. I'm open to bet that we shall find that this man is connected with a fish shop somewhere in or near Raybourne. A shop where they 'fry', as they call it. The smell of the frying gets in the clothes of the people that live in the place where this frying goes on, and hangs about them for ever. It seems impossible to get rid of it. Take it from me, Doctor, that is so. I had a young cousin that worked in one for three or four years. We always knew when he was about, for, by Jove, he did tiddley-wink! His name was Dick, and my old dad nicknamed him 'O Dick Alone'."

The doctor smiled.

"You may be right, Curgenven. The smell certainly does suggest what you say. But, all the same, he seems to me to be a superior sort of man for that game. I should put him down as a gentleman."

Curgenven shrugged his shoulders.

"Whitehead put him down as a gentleman, too. I remember him saying so—but he may have come down in the world for all we know. Education and poverty generally go together, so I've noticed. Or he may have lost his money betting—putting two and two together from the racing programme I found in his overcoat pocket."

"His clothes don't suggest to me that he's come down in the world. Anyhow—whatever he is—we ought to get some news in the morning—when the papers have got round a bit. Then we shall know if your theory's correct. By the way, did you say that you had examined the top of the bus thoroughly? You might be able to pick up something from that."

"As well as I could, Doctor, under the conditions. It's very dark. I am going over it again very thoroughly first thing in the morning. I shall also have to obtain from those two bus chaps the descriptions, and the names, if possible, of all the passengers who travelled inside the bus tonight. Very often on these routes they know most of their passengers—because they're regular and get on and off at the same regular spots. If they're all strangers tonight I shall be very much surprised, Doctor. More than that, I shall be very disappointed. Good night. Doctor."

CHAPTER IV
THE NARRATIVE OF THE RECTOR OF KIRVE ST. LAUDUS

I HAVE been requested by more than one responsible person to contribute some information in respect of the strange occurrence which so suddenly touched our lives in this remote but delightful corner of England, that we so proudly call our own. I have consented to do so because I was very close to it in its final stages—but I must make it clear at the outset that I do so with a certain amount of diffidence, for I don't know that I can truthfully say the task is one after my own heart. I am a man of peace, of restfulness, tranquillity and of slowly moving ways. The crowded arena is not, and never has been, for me. I feel that in it I should cut a sorry figure. The Puck of adventure has never touched me lightly on the shoulder with his magic wand and beckoned me to feel the scorching heat of a whirling escapade, and for the last twenty-two years I have been content to live here in Glebeshire with my church, my people, my books, my music and my garden, supremely happy and (to my mind) divinely content. I will leave the divinity of discontent to others, begging old Will's pardon on the way.

It was, therefore, by a strange whimsicality of Fate that I, of all people, should have been selected by Providence to take some definite responsibility for the solving of the sensational murder that took place on the 8.33 motor-bus that runs from Esting to Raybourne and passes the back gate of my Rectory a few minutes after it has passed through Kirve—a murder, the mystery of which staggered the whole country for a considerable length of time. For it was my lot to impinge upon the affair at two points. The first of these falls naturally into the category of ordinary, everyday occurrence, and there is nothing at all remarkable or abnormal in its happening. My niece, Suzanne, daughter of my only brother, Charles Parry-Probyn, of "The Crofts", Mosforth Park, in the county of Shropshire, had married Wilcox, who was now Divisional Surgeon over at Raybourne, upon his return from service in India nine years previously. That fact explains something. Raybourne is fourteen miles from Esting and about three and a half from Kirve St. Laudus.

The second point where I and the murder collided was much more obscure. And I don't think I can do better at this stage of my narrative of the whole affair than to make it plain immediately. It has been my habit after Evensong, let me tell you, ever since I lost my wife nineteen years ago on the next Feast of St. Andrew, to sit in my church, emptied of its congregation, and amuse myself for a little while on the organ. On the Sunday evening in question I was following my usual practice—it was "Stir up" Sunday, as a matter of fact, and in view of what transpired subsequently, I shall always remember the text from which I had preached half an hour previously.

For it has come home to me since that the text that I had chosen, all unknowingly on my part, epitomized so splendidly the amazing man whom I was so shortly afterwards destined to encounter. I had preached from the sixth chapter of the Gospel according to St. John, part of the twelfth verse: "Gather up the fragments that remain, that nothing be lost"; and although it may be a far cry from the apostle whom our Lord loved to the science of deduction and the general methods of a brilliant investigator, nevertheless I am going to stick to my point in the face of any opposition that I may be called upon to face.

For Anthony Lotherington Bathurst—the man of whom I write—solved this most baffling case out of the veriest fragments that remained for him as data upon which to work. The fact that he also saved the life of a charming young lady towards the termination of the inquiry, almost solely by the exercise of his inimitable powers, will help you who read this narrative of mine to understand my previous allusion all the more clearly and. I hope, more sympathetically.

Anyhow, I had finished my little sojourn at the organ with first a portion of a Mass and then with a "Magnificat" of which I am passionately fond, and as I came back into the chancel I espied the tall figure of a stranger standing by the font at the west end of the church. Something about him seemed to attract me instinctively, and as I walked towards him I noticed that he was wearing an Uppingham tie. It is always a pleasure for me to talk to a stranger of this kind, so that I expect that I approached him with more than ordinary eagerness. I am a Charterhouse and Oriel man myself, and down here in Glebeshire we are very few and far between. To illustrate this—at the Bishop of Polchester's dinner last year to all Old Carthusians in his diocese there were but seven of us.

"Good evening, sir," was the tall stranger's greeting to me. "Permit me to thank you for your exquisite rendering of that 'Magnificat'—Bunnett in F, I fancy. The 'Mass', I think, was Schubert in B Flat."

Now, I'm a musician—my worst enemies would admit that—and, had I chosen, could have been Precentor of Fillsbury earlier in my career; but I am also human and of like passions to my fellow-men, and I was tremendously pleased that this tall, lithe, athletic stranger was able to appreciate the quality of my music. I murmured some inadequate reply, I'm afraid.

"I'm sorry I missed your service tonight, sir. But I'm staying some little distance away, and it took me a great deal longer to walk here than I contemplated. The directions my hostess gave me were somewhat imperfect. In fact, as I arrived at the lych-gate, I ran into your people coming away." As he spoke he walked up the aisle in the direction of the hymn board, and I followed him. I admit that I did so with some curiosity. He looked at the numbers of the hymns that we had sung during the evening service, and turned to me with something like a twinkle in his grey eyes. "Ancient and Modern?" he asked.

I nodded assent.

"Let me see," he said reflectively, "if my memory prove equal to the task of telling you the titles of those hymns." I smiled, I'm afraid, at the idea, but my smile was soon transformed to a stare of astonishment, for this amazing man correctly named every hymn numbered on the board! There were five of them, and by this time I have forgotten the names of three of them, but I can remember two. One was a comparatively unknown hymn and very seldom sung—No. 631—and the other, No. 172—"Praise to the Holiest in the Height", to which Bathurst gave the additional and, of course, ecclesiastically well-known description of the "Preposition Hymn".

I confess I was impressed by the effort.

"You have a good memory," I contributed, "and are no doubt a keen Churchman."

At my remark there came another of his irresistible smiles. "If by that you mean what I think you mean, it may interest (and possibly distress) you to know that I haven't attended a church service, save a Eucharistic one, for several years."

I was frankly surprised, but I made certain mental reservations, and our conversation developed on varied lines. We began to talk and we went on talking. In the space of an all-too-short hour we touched on football (both codes), rowing, church architecture, ancient monoliths, the susceptibility of the turquoise to polish, sclerosis of the posterior columns and degenerative arterial change, the Black Mass and the Medea of Euripides. His knowledge of intimate detail in every instance was positively astounding. He was a man who had husbanded his learning. To quote examples: in connection with football I happened to mention a very fine side of Old Carthusians—all contemporaries of mine and led by the inimitable "G.O."—that had carried almost everything before it in the amateur game some twenty-five to thirty years previously. Bathurst gave me the names of the entire side from goal to outside-left. I wonder if Sir Farquhar Buzzard would remember them all.

Then he went from Steve Fairbairn and the unorthodoxy of the "Jaggers" style, to a minute discussion of an aumbry at the side of our altar, to the original bringing of the turquoise from Persia by the Turks, to Professor Venner and the inner meanings of the Druidical remains, to atheromatous aneurism and calcareous degeneration and then finally to L'Abbé Guibourg and the French diabolists of 1848, and a comparison of the Medea of Euripides with Alcestis, of all of which subjects, mind you—in the original instance—I was more or less responsible for mentioning. Finally we came to crime and criminals, in which and whom I have been interested since a small boy. I laughingly told him that when I murdered a man the crime would be so perfect that it would be unsolvable.

When we parted he gave me his card—and even then I must admit I was little the wiser, for the name conveyed nothing to me. But later on in the evening, however, I found—when I showed it to him—that my son Michael was! Very much so! He had read one or two of Bathurst's earlier cases whilst he had been up at Oxford, and remembered the name well.

On the following Wednesday—by one of those strange and baffling strokes of Fate that do come our way sometimes— there occurred the murder between Esting and Raybourne, and Michael, reading that Jack Wilcox was involved, bethought himself of the approximate presence of Anthony Bathurst. Inquiries amongst a few of my congregation—for there are few secrets in a village like mine—soon elicited the address at which he was staying, and the afternoon but one following upon the murder, Michael ran Wilcox and me round in his car to Bathurst's temporary residence—a farm on the outskirts of Kirve. He had been staying there, it appeared, since the early weeks of October, having been immensely caught by the undeniable charm of Kirve itself and the surrounding country. I reintroduced myself and presented the other two. Of course he recognized me at once, and listened very attentively and courteously to the doctor's story.

"You know, Mr. Bathurst," I interjected, Michael prodding me vigorously the meantime, "I must inform you that this is not an entirely disinterested call on our part. I may as well be quite frank and make that clear from the start. My son Michael here is, I am afraid, excessively anxious to be a close spectator of one of your investigations, with which enthusiasm he has also infected me just a—er—trifle, shall we say, and Dr. Wilcox has come to tell you that up to the moment the inspector in charge of the case—Inspector Curgenven—has been able to make very little headway at all. A man has been murdered, and nobody seems to have gone near him."

I flattered myself that I had put the case to him very neatly, and I fancy that Anthony Bathurst realized that I was thinking so, for there came the twinkle in his grey eyes that I had seen before. I believe that he used it upon me as a chastening influence.

"I have, of course," he said, "seen something of the case from both the London and local Press." He walked to a side table in the room under the casemented window, and after a short search selected a newspaper from the pile that it held. "The fullest account of the affair that I have so far encountered is this in the *Raybourne Packet and Advertiser*. Tell me all that you found, Dr. Wilcox, will you please?"

Bathurst nodded his head once or twice as Jack Wilcox told his story. "A most remarkable case," he observed at the conclusion of it, "and one that I am bound to say I find distinctly attractive. As you've approached me, and also as I'm entirely free from similar work at the moment, I'll wire the Commissioner at Scotland Yard, so that he can pull the strings for me at this end. Excuse me just a moment, if you will."

He was soon back, and I could see from the light that had now taken possession of his eyes that he was eager to strike the trail.

"Now, Doctor Wilcox," he said, "just a question or two before I get to work properly. Can you tell me what steps Inspector Curgenven is taking in the primarily important matter of identification? Is he taking any beyond the natural and ordinary appeal through the channels of the Press, do you know?"

"Oh yes. So far, the ordinary channels, as you call them, have yielded nothing. He's been hard at work on the possible connection of the fish-shop. Curgenven himself is positive that the odour on the dead man's clothes that I mentioned to you just now emanates from this—er—source. Personally, I'm not so certain, although I admit that I can't put forward any alternative suggestion. My difficulty is to associate the man, as I saw him, with an occupation of that kind."

Bathurst paced the cosy room. "The question of quick and satisfactory identification depends so much on whether the murdered man is an inhabitant of the locality or a comparative stranger here. If the latter, the wheels of tracing him may naturally revolve very slowly. But the conductor, you say, describes him as a frequent and regular traveller from Lanning to Raybourne. If that be so, I'm rather surprised that he hasn't been identified by this time. You see, he has been missing close on forty-eight hours now. *Somebody*, surely, must be aware of that fact."

At this moment I put my first question—my first contribution as it were to the investigation into which I had been so curiously drawn.

"Is the inspector already at work on this fish-shop clue?"

"He was—all day yesterday and again this morning. But there are, I believe, between thirty and forty fish-shops in Raybourne alone. So you see it will take time to visit each one of them." Wilcox smiled at me as he replied. "We have been told, you know, sir, for some time now, to eat more fish. The fishmongers have followed the fruiterers."

Bathurst stopped his pacing and looked curiously at the doctor. It struck me at the time how every word of a sentence was always carefully considered by him and never lightly passed over.

"Why do you say in Raybourne *alone*, Doctor? Do you imagine, then, that this man may not have lived in Raybourne? If so, to where would you assign him?"

Wilcox looked a bit surprised, I thought, at Bathurst's question, but answered it quite promptly and without any hesitation at all. "I meant nothing in particular. After all, we have only the story of Whitehead, the conductor, that the man was in the habit of getting off the bus at the Raybourne terminus—haven't we?"

Bathurst nodded. "I see. I wasn't quite sure how you were looking at things. Seems conclusive, I think, that he should be found to have resided either in Raybourne or on the outskirts of Raybourne. He would hardly have been in the habit of travelling back to Lanning each night, I should say, although I admit that we must, for the moment, regard it as a possibility." He turned suddenly towards the group of us. "What time is the last bus back from Raybourne to Lanning? Any of you gentlemen happen to know?"

Michael was ready on the instant. "The last bus to Esting leaves the Tower Square at 9.57—I mean on the Southbrooke system. That was what you meant, wasn't it? There are local buses—the smaller ones—no doubt you've seen them; they're chocolate-coloured. They run as far as Northlynn on the inland road as late as eleven o'clock. They cater for the theatre people, you see."

"Thanks, Mr. Parry-Probyn. I wasn't referring to the South-brooke buses only—I was thinking of the possibility of the man's regular return to, say, Lanning, or to any place other than Raybourne. Not a probable contingency, by any means, but from what you have just told me it certainly *was* possible." He turned to me particularly. "So you see, sir, Curgenven may be starting his investigations at the wrong end. However, we shall know, no doubt, before very long."

My son's eagerness urged him to the discussion again. "I should think, Mr. Bathurst, that it would be impossible to face a more bewildering case—if the conductor's story be true, that is. Personally, I can't see a point about it where you can make a definite starting—"

Anthony Bathurst shook his head. "It's a case where the evidence of so many people—apparently *outside* the affair—will have to be very carefully sifted and combed out. What each one of them saw—what each one of them heard—anything which came to any one of them down the avenue of any one sense—may eventually prove to be a vital and decisive factor, and perhaps the starting-point in the investigation which will bring it eventually to a successful termination."

I thought I saw his point. "You allude, in the first place," I said, a little diffidently perhaps, "to the people that were—"

"In the bus, sir," he answered; "one of them may possess more knowledge than Whitehead—surely it is quite on the cards?" He turned to Jack Wilcox. "If you will sponsor me, Doctor, pending Sir Austin Kemble's intervention from Scotland Yard, I'll come over to Raybourne with you gentlemen now. For every minute that I lose at this stage of the inquiry may make my task very much more difficult. Perhaps the Rector would share my car."

I intimated immediately that I should be delighted.

CHAPTER V
THE LETTERS ON THE PROGRAMME
(From the Rector's MSS. Continued.)

IT WOULD be, I suppose, about ten minutes to four when Bathurst and I alighted in the yard of Raybourne police station. Michael—with Wilcox—was seven minutes or so behind. His car was unable to maintain the pace set by Bathurst's powerful Crossley, and we had soon left them a long way in the rear. Curgenven, whom I had met previously in connection with a case that involved the father of one of my choirboys, came at once to greet the doctor, and Wilcox explained the position to him. The inspector was affability itself.

"Ah, Rector," he said, with a pleasantness that made you think such things as murder cases were myths, and violent deaths no more than nightmares, "and how's that chorister of yours in whose welfare you were so concerned? Got over his father's trouble? Still with you?"

"Gone, Inspector—gone! And the consequence is that my *decani* side has never been the same since. His leaving was a contrapuntal tragedy! Some places, you know, Curgenven, are very hard to fill." He laughed lightly. "Only some, Rector! I reckon they'll fill mine all right when the time comes. Especially after this last case that has dropped into my lap." Turning to Anthony Bathurst, he extended a friendly and welcoming hand. "I fancy I have heard of you, Mr. Bathurst, and I know also the extent to which you enjoy the confidence of Sir Austin Kemble. No doubt you will inform him that you're having a look round here. And, if I hadn't heard of you, any friend of the Rev. Parry-Probyn's here would come to me carrying the very best of guarantees." As he said this the smile in Curgenven's eyes intensified the sincerity with which he spoke. I know that it afforded me extreme pleasure. I saw the gratified gleam in Michael's face and I caught, at the same time, the ready response that sprang from Bathurst himself.

"That's very nice of you, Inspector Curgenven. But you flatter me. I only hope that I shall be able to help you. Dr. Wilcox here has told me that up to now you haven't made much progress with a particularly nasty case. Is the man identified yet?"

The inspector smiled. "Almost. Not quite."

Mr. Bathurst knitted his brows. He was puzzled. "You mean—?"

"I mean this. I had a 'phone message about twenty minutes ago from one of my men that's working the shops in the neighbourhood. He covered the whole of our own town of Raybourne yesterday—with no success whatever. Called at thirty-eight places. Nothing doing! Nobody missing and nothing suspicious in any one of them. This morning I instructed him to do Kirve, Kirve St. Laudus, and Verrinder. Verrinder is, of course, the village to the south of Raybourne—beyond it—in the opposite direction to Kirve and Kirve St. Laudus. Curtis—that's his name—thinks he has struck oil this afternoon. There is a little fish-shop in the main street of Verrinder, so he tells me, that's kept by an elderly widow, who does the 'frying' herself in the evening. The name's Martha Nuckey. I think I remember her husband as having formerly worked in the dockyard here." Curgenven swung round on to the doctor. "I'm pretty positive, Doctor Wilcox, this information will prove that my fish-shop clue was sound. For this Mrs. Nuckey, Curtis informs me, has a lodger—*who hasn't been home for two nights*. His name, I may say, is Claude Sutcliffe. Taking into account the initials in the dead man's hat, the identification looks authentic to me. What do you think yourself, Mr. Bathurst?"

"I can see no reason to doubt it, Inspector. The facts seem to tally all right, so far. When is this Mrs. Nuckey coming along? Moreover, why hasn't she been before? That latter question seems to me to require a little understanding, and certainly some explanation."

The same thing had occurred to me—in fact I had been on the point of mentioning it to Wilcox when Bathurst spoke—and I therefore watched Curgenven's face intently to see what line he would take in the disposal of Bathurst's question.

"The explanation will have to come from Mrs. Nuckey, Mr. Bathurst. I shall have to question her about it." The inspector looked at his watch. "Our anxiety should be short-lived, anyhow. Curtis and Mrs. Nuckey should be here very shortly—according to my reckoning. He's bringing her along in a car."

Bathurst nodded approvingly. "If that be so, I'll postpone my examination of the dead man and the bus on which he was found until after I've heard this woman's story."

"Very well, Mr. Bathurst. It's all the same to me. While you're waiting you might care to have a glance at that. Beyond his gold watch and his money—two pounds four shillings and ninepence halfpenny—that was the only thing that I found on him."

Curgenven passed over what was, I was enabled to observe from the words on the outside of it, a racing programme. "May I look?" I asked; and at Bathurst's consenting gesture, Michael and I crossed over and looked over his shoulder. It was the programme of the Cambridgeshire day at the last Newmarket meeting—Wednesday, October 30th. As I looked at it I couldn't help experiencing a stab of poignant remembrance, for my thoughts went winging back to Michael's mother—my dead wife.

Horse-racing, as such, has naturally little charm or interest for me, although, born in Leicestershire, I have always loved a good horse. My father, indeed, followed the Quorn with an enthusiasm that was a household word in the fox-hunting county. Daisy, my wife, as befitted a West Country girl, had also hunted with the Cattistock, and I fear at times found the position of wife to a parish priest over-disciplinary, although she would have burned at the stake before letting me see it. In the early years of our marriage my stipend had been totally inadequate for our proper support, and if my wife and I had not been helped by our respective private incomes I fear that our struggle to live satisfactorily and to educate our children fittingly would have taxed our resources far beyond their limit. Anyhow, on two occasions in succeeding years, my wife had secretly "invested" a little money on "Christmas Daisy" to win this race—the Cambridgeshire, the programme for which I saw in front of me—for very obvious reasons (her birthday, I may say, was December 24th, and her name I have told you)—and the horse had gallantly obliged her and proved successful.

As I looked at the programme that Anthony Bathurst held in his hand I well remembered the laughing confession that she had made to me after the race. I'm afraid she knew how easily success obtains forgiveness, and how seldom failure. I could see that there were pencilled notes and figures scattered over the programme—in most instances beneath the entries for the respective races. On the outside page there were two columns of figures—one headed "Down" and the other "Up". There was a curious ornamental flourish about the capital letters in each instance that gave the handwriting a most distinctive individuality. One felt that one would be able to recognize it again—anywhere. The "D", for example, had a sweeping circular stroke at the top of it—of a kind that I couldn't remember ever having seen before. Bathurst raised his eyes to us questioningly as we bent over him.

"'Up' and 'Down', I take it, are synonyms that refer to 'wins' and 'losses'." The inspector heard what he had said and signified his agreement. "Not much doubt of that, I think. I formed that opinion myself. Doesn't tell us much, though, does it?"

Bathurst turned over the thick, stiffish pages and stopped at the entries for the big race itself. "Our man evidently backed 'Caiaphas' and 'Doctor Laputa'," he observed, "judging from the notes he has made here. 'Doctor Laputa' ran third—he seems to have got twenty-five to one about it."

Once again the initial letters were characterized by a disproportionate ostentatiousness. There were no other marks on the programme save on the back. Here there were four columns of figures headed respectively "S.", "T.", "D." and "M."—all in the same handwriting previously described. The capital "D" was unmistakable.

"It might repay a little careful study," remarked Anthony Bathurst, "when we know more. As it is, ignorant as we are of so many points that may—"

"Here's Curtis," broke in Curgenven, coming from the direction of the window. "He's got Mrs. Nuckey with him. Good man! We may shortly hear something interesting."

The woman that entered, ushered in by the man Curtis, was to all appearances in the early sixties. She was plump, happy-looking, short-sighted, and motherly. She took the chair that Curgenven placed for her and peered at us as we sat round her with a good deal of curiosity and certainly a little nervousness. Nevertheless, she was not entirely without a courage of her own. I could see this in her eyes, as she blinked at us through her large spectacles.

"Good afternoon, Mrs. Nuckey," commenced the inspector, in an attempt to put her at her ease. "I'm Inspector Curgenven, as you doubtless know, and this gentleman here is Dr. Wilcox, the Divisional Surgeon. The other gentlemen are friends of mine, and you can speak quite freely in front of them. I'll just outline what I've got to say to you. Now, I understand that a lodger of yours hasn't been home to your place for a couple of nights. Is that so?"

Mrs. Nuckey half raised herself in her chair, and then seemed to bump herself down again as she suddenly found the words to reply to Curgenven's question.

"Yes, sir. A Mr. Sutcliffe—Mr. Claude Sutcliffe, his name is. And if he's been murdered, as this gentleman that brought me along here this afternoon seems to think he has—all I can say is that I'm not surprised."

She folded her arms in emphasis of her statement. Curgenven seized on the remark with avidity. "Oh! Why is that, Mrs. Nucky?"

She lowered her voice and looked almost furtively round the room.

"Because that's the very thing he went in fear and trembling of. I know that for a certainty, because he told me."

CHAPTER VI

THE FIRST IDENTIFICATION
(From the Rector's MSS. Continued.)

BEFORE I could gauge the full effect that her remark had had upon Curgenven or Bathurst, the former broke in with first a question and then an order. 'Is that so, Mrs. Nuckey? Well—that's very interesting. You'll have to tell us all about it but before you do that, describe your Mr. Sutcliffe to us, and also the way he was dressed when you last saw him. If it's our man you can then come along and identify him."

"He was mostly always dressed the same," said Mrs. Nuckey; "dark overcoat, blue serge suit, brown shoes and a wide-brimmed grey soft felt hat. I don't think I've ever seen him in anything else—since he walked into my shop the first time."

"Did he wear glasses?" It was Curgenven again. It was a question that I may say that I was awaiting, or I had anticipated that this fact would have been one of the first of Mrs. Nuckey's descriptive items.

"Always, sir." She nodded vigorously in support of what she said. "I never saw Mr. Sutcliffe without them."

"What kind?"

"Them American kind, such as Harold Lloyd always wears on the pictures. What is it they call 'em—horn-rimmed?"

The inspector nodded. "I see. You're quite certain that—"

Here the lady interrupted him abruptly. "It's a funny thing, Inspector—but in a manner of speaking this has come as no surprise to me, as I hinted to you just now. Mr. Sutcliffe's been extra worried these last two or three days. I am sure of that. He ain't been at all what you might call himself. When I inquired one morning if there was anything particular troubling him he told me no—he'd only got a rather bad turn of his rheumatics, or the screws, as he called it. That was quite true—he's had it in his right arm and shoulder. So bad he's had it that he hasn't been able to shave for three days. Couldn't get his arm up high enough." Here Mrs. Nuckey paused and shook her head doubtfully. "But

I'm sure there was worse things on his mind than that, and that he was worried over them wicked people that was trackin' him down. I believe that's the very expression 'e used to me soon after he first came to live over my shop—trackin' 'im down."

"Just a minute, Mrs. Nuckey. Hold on, will you?" Curgenven turned to Dr. Wilcox. "It's our man, without a doubt," he remarked. "What she just said clinches it. Remember the growth on his face and chin?"

The doctor nodded. "Just what I was thinking. She can see him in a moment or so, at any rate, and settle it. But you're quite right; our man is her man all right."

It was at this juncture that Anthony Bathurst took a hand. Perhaps that statement is just a trifle beside the point, and I should have written "attempted to take a hand". For what exactly happened was this: Bathurst leant forward in the direction of Mrs. Nuckey, looked very shrewdly at her, and then turned again towards Inspector Curgenven. "Do you mind if I ask Mrs. Nuckey a question, Inspector?"

"All in good time, Mr. Bathurst, if you don't mind," replied Curgenven. "There are several that I desire to ask her. Then you can have your turn. Order and sequence are great things to regard, I always think, when one's trying to get at the bottom of a case of this kind."

The vestige of a smile flitted over Bathurst's face, but that was the only indication beyond a slight bow of his reception of the inspector's remark. I saw Michael toss his head with angry annoyance, but these things made little impression on a man like Curgenven.

"Now, Mrs. Nuckey," he commenced, "how long has this Mr. Sutcliffe lived with you?"

"Let me see, now. Mr. Sutcliffe came to take a room over my shop on the sixteenth of October—last month—which is a little different way of putting it, if you don't mind me saying so, Inspector. You must see that for yourself. I've always been a respectable widow woman, although perhaps I say it that shouldn't."

"Mrs. Nuckey, Inspector," interposed Bathurst quietly, "differs from you a trifle. She believes in 'order', but evidently not in 'sequence'."

Curgenven paid no heed to the sally. "Go on, Mrs. Nuckey. You know what I meant. Who were these people you say your lodger was frightened of? The people he told you of?"

Mrs. Nuckey screwed up her face, now that the inspector had deliberately brought her to the important issue. But she was able to state a case.

"The sixteenth of October," she said slowly, "was a Thursday, I fancy, and it would be about—"

"You will pardon me, Mrs. Nuckey, but you're a day out—the sixteenth of October was a Wednesday—it may or may not be of importance."

The interruption came from Anthony Bathurst, and the old lady immediately accepted it and its truthfulness.

"Yes—you're quite right, sir. I remember now. It was a Wednesday. I am a day out—I knew it was somewhere round about the middle of the week. Well, it would have been about the following Sunday week that Mr. Sutcliffe began to tell me things about himself. He said he had lived best part of his life abroad, that he'd lived in foreign parts ever since he was a young lad of fifteen or sixteen years of age. The country he said he'd been in was the Argentine and there was another word he mentioned when he used to talk about it—now, what was it? My memory's not what it was. Pat—Patter—"

"Patagonia?" suggested Anthony Bathurst hopefully, and Mrs. Nuckey nodded her head quickly and emphatically.

"That's the word, sir, you've got it in one. Well, Mr. Sutcliffe told me how he'd offended some of these natives out there, over some treasure-hunt that he'd been engaged in, and how they'd sworn to get even with him before they'd finished. That was the reason why he'd come down to these parts—to be well out of their way, as you might say. He said they was fair devils once they got their knife in you, so to speak, and although they was small and undersized compared with us English people, all the same it didn't make a ha'porth of difference to 'em when they was out to get anybody—they was fair terrors for their size, 'e said—like the late Lord Roberts."

Curgenven opened his mouth to speak, but Anthony Bathurst brooked no denial on this occasion and swept him aside very summarily. "Did he tell you that in those words, Mrs. Nuckey? Are you positive on the point?"

"Quite, sir. The words he used were those very words."

"Thank you," responded Bathurst. "I find the case growing very interesting."

Michael's eyes were now alive with excitement, but I for my part was at a loss to know what had occasioned it. Before I could speculate on the matter Curgenven took up the threads once more. "Did Sutcliffe ever refer to this matter of Patagonia again? About these enemies of his, I mean?"

"Yes—once or twice."

"Did he give you any more details?"

Mrs. Nuckey shook her head. "Never, sir—no more than what I've just told you."

"H'm, I see. Now answer me this." Curgenven spoke very slowly and quite lightly at first—but then suddenly changed his tone and almost shot his question at her.

"Why didn't you take any action, Mrs. Nuckey, when you knew your lodger hadn't been home for two nights? Why did you wait for the police to call upon you and make inquiries? If my man Curtis hadn't called upon you this morning, it seems to me that your lodger Sutcliffe might still be lying unidentified. Hadn't you heard of the murder? Hadn't you read of it in any of the papers? If you didn't—please tell me why you didn't."

This fusillade of questions came so rapidly from Curgenven, each one so hard upon the heels of the one that preceded it, that Mrs. Nuckey, had she wanted to, had no time to collect her thoughts. I watched her very curiously and carefully, to see how she would bear up under the battery. She blinked at Curgenven through her glasses, but otherwise gave no sign of discomfiture.

"I can answer all your questions, Inspector, in one. That is, if you'll allow me to, of course. But about a fortnight ago, somewhere about the first week of this month, Mr. Sutcliffe never came home all night. Next morning, when he turned up and I—natural like—asked him the question as to where he'd been and what had been happening to him, he just laughed at me and said he'd been stopping with a friend. He also said—and please listen to this, Inspector, because it will explain all you asked me—that if ever it happened again that he wasn't home all night, I wasn't to worry a little bit—he'd be in perfectly good and safe hands. So there you are—you can see for yourself."

Curgenven walked over to Wilcox and stood conversing with him for a matter of a few seconds. Then I was interested to see him cross to where Bathurst was sitting. "You can go ahead with your questions now, Mr. Bathurst, as quickly as you like, and I shall be pleased to listen to the answers."

"Thank you. Inspector. My questions to this lady will be very simple ones. Firstly, Mrs. Nuckey—this: when you were describing just now the first meeting you had with this Mr. Sutcliffe, you used the expression 'when he walked into my shop the first time'. At least, that is the form in which I've remembered it. Would you mind explaining to me *exactly* what you meant by that? In other words, would you mind telling me exactly what happened at your first meeting?"

I was able to see that Mrs. Nuckey was surprised by this question—although, on second thoughts, perhaps, "surprised" is not the best word for me to use. Let me say that she was more puzzled than surprised, for I don't think she saw immediately the. exact meaning of Anthony Bathurst's remark. But to do her justice she attempted to give him the answer that he required.

"Well, sir, I said he walked into my shop, because that's just what he did do. On the sixteenth of last month, in the afternoon, it was, Mr. Sutcliffe walked into my shop when I was serving and asked if I could let him have a room. Before I could recover from my surprise, as you might say, he'd offered me such downright good terms that I should have been a fool to refuse them. I've got to live, the same as the rest of us—as the years go by it doesn't get easier—and since Nuckey was taken—"

Here Bathurst interrupted her. "Why were you so surprised, Mrs. Nuckey? Surely a request for a room should not—"

"But I've never let rooms in Verrinder since I've lived there, sir. I didn't have a card hanging up or anything like that. Who would ever come to live in a fried-fish shop from choice?"

"I appreciate your point, Mrs. Nuckey, but I suppose Mr. Sutcliffe was very keen to come—eh? What were his terms? I'd like to hear them."

"He offered me five pounds a week, sir, for the room, and I was to find everything."

"Did he put forward any reason as to why he was so keen on your room—or your shop?"

"He did. For the view across the hills to the Linner Valley. He said it was perfect, and that you could see it better from my room than from any other in the village of Verrinder. He said he'd worked out the position."

"Is the view all that he claimed for it?"

Mrs. Nuckey shrugged her shoulders. "My sight's not good at the best of times. He said 'e could see it like that—that was enough for me."

I wondered how Bathurst would like this, but his ready smile answered me. Jack Wilcox and the inspector were smiling as well.

"Now for my second question." As he spoke, Bathurst's smile broadened appreciably, and I believe that even Mrs. Nuckey warmed under its influence. "What night was it that Mr. Sutcliffe failed to come home to Verrinder? Do you think you could remember the exact date?"

She shook her head a bit doubtfully. "I'm not quite sure, sir. But it was about a fortnight ago, I know. It was the very foggy night of the week before last." At this, I think the whole of Mrs. Nuckey's audience, to use one of those modern colloquialisms, "sat up and took notice". Curgenven turned round to her, his face betraying the keenest interest; Jack Wilcox looked mystified; Michael almost enraptured, whilst in Anthony Bathurst's eyes there shone a gleam of excitement. And he rubbed his hands—a mannerism of his that I was destined to see very much more of during the next week or so. "Two foggy nights, eh, Mrs. Nuckey, and Mr. Sutcliffe doesn't come home on either occasion? Very, very interesting. Don't you think so, Inspector?"

"Perhaps I don't attach the importance to it that you do. Lots of fog in these parts at this time of the year, Mr. Bathurst," replied Curgenven. "Very likely a mere coincidence."

But Bathurst had returned again to the lady who had brought the information to the Raybourne police station. "This night that your lodger stayed away—had he been in the Verrinder district during the day, can you tell me? Did you see him at all during that day, for instance?"

"No, sir—not all day. I can remember that fact quite well. He had breakfast at half past nine and then went out. I usually got his dinner for him—but he told me not to bother that day. I didn't see him again till eleven o'clock the next morning." Bathurst thought hard for a moment and then took over to her the racing programme that had been found in the dead man's pocket. "Look carefully at this writing, Mrs. Nuckey, will you, please? Are these words and figures in Mr. Sutcliffe's handwriting?"

She shook her head with emphasis. "You're wasting your time asking me that question, sir. I've never set eyes on his handwriting all the time he's been with me."

"Bad luck, Curgenven," he declared, handing back the programme. "All the same, we can't expect the ball to run for us all the time, can we?"

He plunged his hands into the pockets of his trousers and sat there silent and contemplative. I found myself wondering as to what his next move would be, for, candidly, we seemed to me to have reached something of an *impasse*. Suddenly he looked up from his brown study.

"Any correspondence come for this man during the time he lodged at your place?"

"One postcard only, sir. I can answer that because I remember it so well. It came about ten days, I should think, before he was killed. It was a plain postcard, not a picture one, and had only two letters on it; they were 'O.K.' I couldn't help seeing them when I took it up to his room the day it came. There was no name at the bottom—or signature. Not even initials."

"Notice the postmark by any chance, Mrs. Nuckey?"

"Yes, sir, I did that. It was Poole—or so it looked to me."

"Poole—eh? We must remember that, Inspector. Now—one last question. Has this lodger of yours left much behind? Clothes? Belongings?"

"I haven't had a search round yet, sir—but I shouldn't think so. I've never noticed much in his room when I've gone up to set it tidy. All his luggage was in one suit-case when he came."

"Then the inspector and I must have a look round ourselves. Thank you very much, Mrs. Nuckey. That's all, Inspector—thank you."

Bathurst rose, seemingly more satisfied, and came towards Michael and me.

"We shall want you now, ma'am," said Curgenven, "to identify the body just as a matter of form. There's no occasion for you to be scared. He's not knocked about or anything. He's just as he was when you knew him—because I've been particular to keep him just as he was found. I'm going to try an experiment before the inquest. Come this way, Mrs. Nuckey, will you? If you like, you other gentlemen can come at the same time."

I determined to take advantage of the offer, now that I had been in the case for so long, and motioned to Michael to follow me. He needed no second bidding. Passing out of the room behind Curgenven, we crossed the yard and entered an outbuilding that served as the mortuary. The body of a man fully clothed lay on a flat board that had been placed across three trestles. His hat lay at his side. Save for that and for the fact that his overcoat was unbuttoned and his collar partly undone, he was exactly as he had been found. Mrs. Nuckey put her hand to her heart, and, without coming very close to the corpse, gave a suppressed sort of scream.

"Oh—that's him!" she cried. "I'd know his hat and overcoat anywhere—and those spectacles. Yes—that's Mr. Sutcliffe without a doubt."

She covered her eyes with her hands, as though to shut out the unpleasant sight.

Chapter VII
BATHURST GOES OVER THE GROUND
(From the Rector's MSS. Continued.)

Within a quarter of an hour of the identification Mrs. Nuckey was on her way back to Verrinder.

Curgenven had made arrangements with her to the effect that he would call at her shop within a very short time for the purpose of examining the room that Sutcliffe had occupied. As I looked at Bathurst I thought that I detected signs of something like impatience showing in his features. I do not wish to be misunderstood. I do not mean that Bathurst showed impatience at anything that had transpired, or at the way in which Curgenven had conducted the examination of Mrs. Nuckey. Far from it. Let me explain. What I intend to convey is that he evinced signs of a great desire to be up and doing. I think Jack Wilcox noticed this, too—because he immediately came forward to Curgenven with a suggestion. "Perhaps Mr. Bathurst would care to have a more intimate glance at—"

Before he could finish his sentence Bathurst turned quickly to the inspector. "Thanks, Doctor. There are two things at which I should like to have a look, one of which I have already seen but not examined. A big difference! I should like to examine the body of Sutcliffe very carefully, and also the bus on which his body was found. I presume the vehicle is still here?"

It was exactly what I had been expecting, and I flattered myself on the accuracy of my judgment.

"Very well, then," returned Curgenven; "the bus is where Sturgess drove it on the night of the murder. It hasn't been moved. Which do you want to look at first?"

"I'll have a look at Sutcliffe himself first—if it's all the same to you, Inspector."

We returned to the mortuary, and this time Bathurst walked straight over to the dead man. I saw him look carefully at the ugly and almost black marks on the throat and then shake his head. Then, suddenly, "Hallo—-what's this? What have we here?" He had caught sight of the bloodstained wrists. From the twin lights of excitement and wonderment that shone in his eyes I could see that he had happened upon something that he regarded as being of the highest importance. "What have you got to say about this, Doctor Wilcox?" he asked, wheeling round to him with rapid insistence.

"Well, Bathurst, they're cuts of some kind, as you can see. Done with something jagged, I should say—like, for example, a—"

Bathurst interposed quickly. "Just a minute, Doctor. Let me see whether you're thinking as I am. Wouldn't you agree with me that they resemble *tears* rather than cuts? Look here, Doctor; they're pretty deep, but so uneven—your word jagged certainly applies to them—they look as though some-thing's been wearing away at the inside of the two wrists rather than cutting them. Do you follow what I mean?"

Wilcox nodded, and I saw Michael look at the marks and move his head quickly, as though thoroughly agreeing with what Anthony Bathurst had said. As the doctor bent down again, I heard Bathurst mutter to himself: "The inside of each wrist— the *inside* only. Could it be a case of . . . ?" Bending quickly, he whipped out his magnifying-glass and proceeded to examine minutely the dead man's clothes. The smeary stain on the left lapel of the blue under-jacket appeared to interest him considerably. Much to my surprise—for I will frankly admit that I *was* surprised at the time—I saw him move his head as though in complete approval of its presence on the coat. The whity-grey mark on the back of the overcoat next arrested his attention. But, judged by the expression that momentarily flitted across his face, he had neither approval nor understanding of this. He rubbed his finger gently across it and then placed the finger to his nostrils and sniffed at it. Curgenven watched him and smiled.

"You've got to where I got, Mr. Bathurst. To the fish-shop. Fried fish!"

Bathurst shook his head decisively. "Not quite, Inspector, although I know what you mean. I get it on the clothes, it's true, and I must congratulate you on a smart piece of work in that

must admit in doing so that I held a preliminary advantage over you, Doctor. Which makes a difference, doesn't it?" The smile became a laugh.

"An advantage? I'm afraid I don't follow you. Surely the advantage should be on the—"

Bathurst shook his head. "No, Doctor, not that. I can see that you do not follow me. I will explain myself. I think I know what caused the mark on the mouth, because the presence of the mark itself did not surprise me. Now do you get me?"

"Did not surprise you?" repeated Wilcox after him. "How do you mean?"

There was no mistaking Anthony Bathurst's delight now, for his grey eyes held it as well as his lips. "I have the best of reasons, Doctor, believe me. It didn't surprise, because I looked for it—which is the best of all reasons, isn't it?"

I saw Curgenven toss up his head in evident impatience and with more than a suggestion of incredulity. "You must have second sight," he growled. "I haven't been blessed with it myself, so I'm handicapped." It was impossible to miss the sarcasm that the remark contained. But Bathurst showed no sign that he realized it. He could always, so I discovered afterwards through my intimacy with him, pass over things of this nature with entire imperturbability. He was always extraordinarily magnanimous with regard to them. He turned again to Wilcox, obviously determined to change the line of the inquiry.

"Would you agree with me, Doctor, that this man Sutcliffe was what we should term an out-of-doors man? A man who spent a considerable amount of his time in the open air?"

"Undoubtedly. Although dead for some hours, his skin is still well tanned, and his hands are quite brown. Extraordinarily so for the season of the year and considering the weather that we've been having recently."

"Good! Then let me try the glasses again." Bathurst replaced the glasses on his face, and then to my astonishment made no further reference to them. It was as though he had completely forgotten that he had put them on. He addressed his next remark to me. "I am in your debt, sir, more than ever. I have to thank you for introducing me to a most fascinating problem—one which will require *all* my powers of second sight, to use the inspector's own words." His eyes twinkled merrily through the glass of the spectacles as he spoke. But Curgenven remained silent—his eyes centred fixedly on Bathurst himself. The latter thrust his hands into his pockets and paced the room three or four times in rapid succession. "Where is there a mirror, Inspector? Does there happen to be one handy?" he inquired suddenly.

"You'll find one in the next room," replied Curgenven. "But take my tip, Mr. Bathurst; you look much better without 'em. They don't improve your style of beauty."

Bathurst paid no attention to this last remark, but turned off into the room that the inspector had indicated. Within a minute he was back again with us. He held Sutcliffe's horn-rimmed glasses in his hand. Pointing to his face on each side just above the cheekbones, he caused us all to rivet our attention on him.

"Well, gentlemen," he cried, "what do you see—here and here?"

The red mark made by the glasses from the corner of each eye to each ear was plainly visible to all of us as our eyes followed the direction of his finger. Curgenven, by this time, had divested himself of his critical faculty, and his interest was beyond doubt fully aroused.

"You see what I mean," cried Anthony Bathurst. "I can tell that you do. Well now, come over here and look at this dead man Sutcliffe."

We all crowded round and did as directed. I could see nothing. The others of us seemed to be in the same boat.

"Look at the corners of his eyes as well," he ordered.

Once again I could see nothing.

"There'd be nothing to see in the dead man's case, Mr. Bathurst," declared Curgenven, with emphasis. "His skin is bronzed and tanned, as you yourself stated, and has begun to blacken. Your face is comparatively pale alongside his. The marks of the spectacles show on you where they couldn't possibly show on him. Red on a natural tan like his doesn't exactly thrust itself on your notice."

Mr. Bathurst rubbed his hands. "You think so, Inspector? You think that everything's as you would expect to find it, eh? Well, I don't, and I'll make you a present of the information. As I see things, Inspector, everything's *wrong*. It's only by realizing that they're *wrong* that I begin to get them *right*. Inspector Curgenven, I'm very much afraid that you and I are measuring our strength with an unusually clever and cunning criminal—one whom it will take us all our time to lay by the heels. It is essential that we should discover as soon as possible *how* this devilish crime was committed. If we find his method it may lead us to him. Take me to the bus at once, if you please. I'm very much afraid that I haven't a moment to lose."

Chapter VIII
WHAT THE BUS TOLD BATHURST

(From the Rector's MSS. Continued.)

BATHURST WAS now the embodiment of rapid and resolute activity.

"What have you done, Inspector?" he asked, as we made our way across the yard. "Tell me as quickly as you can. With regard to the murder itself, I mean, apart from the question, for instance, of the identification of the dead man?"

Curvengen was stolidity itself when he answered. "What could I do? I thought it best to find out first who the murdered man was. Look at the case for yourself, sir. This man was murdered on a bus somewhere between Lanning and Raybourne. Nobody can be traced to have been on the bus with him, with the exception of the conductor Whitehead. There were people in the bus, but not on it. Also, although there was a thick fog, I understand, along the Linner Valley—a fact which of itself merits a lot of consideration—Whitehead, the conductor, swears that nobody boarded the bus, or could have boarded it even, without his being aware of the fact. He's positive on the point."

"H'm—his story will have to be very thoroughly tested. All the same it's the starting-point. I'm going on top, Inspector. Coming with me?" He seemed by now to be totally oblivious of the presence of us others, and swung up the steps with Curgenven close on his heels. Jack Wilcox, Michael and I followed at a respectable distance and interval. It was now quite dark, and I heard Bathurst speak with a sharp note of annoyance in his voice. "I ought to have done this before. Still one can't foresee . . ." He whipped out an electric torch from his pocket and flashed it over the various seats. "Where exactly was the man sitting, Inspector?"

Curgenven pointed to the seat. "Here, Mr. Bathurst."

"Left-hand side—eh, Inspector? Ah, well, it might have been worse. I'm pleased to hear you say that. And in the middle—eh?"

I counted the seats in an effort to understand the real meaning of his remark. There were seven of them on the left-hand side, and, according to the inspector's statement, Sutcliffe had occupied the fourth from the staircase. There were, therefore, three seats behind him and three seats in front. But what was different about this seat from any of the others I found it impossible to imagine. What was the point attached to this middle seat? Bathurst's torch played round and about the seat. Curgenven produced another, no doubt in an attempt to help him, and the two circles of light flickered and stabbed at each other as it were, and gave to our party of investigators an eerie touch that blended well with the darkness and drabness of the November afternoon. And I mused on the swift passing of time, and remembered that the coming Sunday was Advent Sunday—that the Feast of Pentecost, now nearly six months past, seemed to me to be but a few weeks old—when I heard the sharp intaking of Bathurst's breath. His torch—or, rather, the light from it—had focused upon the top rail of the bus just in front of where Michael and I were standing watching. I looked at this spot, upon which his eyes were intently fixed, and saw that it was just above the seat immediately in the rear of that on which Sutcliffe had been found, that is to say, above the third seat from the rear.

"Mud, Curgenven," cried Bathurst; "black mud! See it?"

"It was a muddy night, sir—plenty of mud everywhere. It had rained for a matter of some hours. If you look on the bus windows you'll see splashes of mud everywhere. Our country roads do chuck it up, you know, sir. They're not all Class One, and there's more than one pot-hole knocking about. Ask the average motorist about them."

From the way that he spoke I could see that Curgenven was unimpressed, and there was a dryness in his tone that could not possibly be mistaken. Without replying Bathurst pulled an envelope from his breast-pocket, and with his finger carefully removed a little of the mud from the rail into the envelope, which he held underneath. As he did so, once again I was reminded of the way in which his ever-alert mind was ready to dart off at a tangent.

"Sutcliffe's underclothes, Inspector. Had a good look at them?"

"Naturally. But nothing much to work on there. No name, no initials. Just ordinary gent's underwear, sold in their thousands all over the country."

"New, by any chance?"

"Well, yes—I should say they were, like the other parts of his wardrobe."

"H'm!" He went back to his inspection of the rail. "One mark only—nothing else—unless . . ." He went on his knees and flashed the electric torch all round the floor of the vehicle.

"The fragments that remain," I murmured to myself, "that nothing be lost." After all—come what may—the direct superintendence of the Creator is, and must be, over everything. The warping of one creature's mind results in a brutal murder. The exquisite balance of another leads to the apprehension and execution of the murderer. The Infinite Power that directs the solar system in absolute safety through the mystery of space adjusts at the same time the length of the insect's proboscis to the exactitude of the depth of the treasure-holding nectary, and of His infinite understanding the blind soul, bereft of a sweetest sense, develops yet a sweeter spirituality and with it the ear of an angel.

Bathurst rose from his examination of the floor.

"Nothing, Curgenven, nothing at all! About photographing the body. I should like you to . . ." He broke off into details. "Beyond that I don't think I need detain you any longer. I have formed certain theories about the case which will necessitate the most careful and painstaking investigation. You might let me have the address of Mrs. Nuckey; of Whitehead the conductor; and of Sturgess the driver, will you, Curgenven? Also, I should like a list of all the passengers who travelled on the bus that night, and their addresses. Thank you. We must find out who this Sutcliffe is—and his business—where he comes from—all his antecedents—and *why* this murder was staged as it has been. Then we can hope to move. But I'm afraid not till then. For my opinion, Inspector, is still the same. This murder has been carefully planned by a criminal who has studied the tiniest detail. But, careful though he has been, and ruthlessly cunning as he has proved himself to be, he has made one mistake. That mistake, Curgenven, will hang him. That's another piece of information with which I'll present you here and now."

There was no braggadocio in his voice—you were conscious only of his definite purpose. He looked at me as he spoke, and I shivered. The air was growing colder and damper, and this talk of dead men, murders and hangings had crept its chill course into my bones. I had no mind to talk with Richard the King of graves and worms and epitaphs. I knew where we were, but I wondered where we should finish. Bathurst turned towards my son: "Can you drive a Crossley? Yes? Drive me home, Mr. Parry-Probyn—do you mind? I want to sit and think." Michael assented readily. He was much younger than I, and no doubt was feeling far more pleased with things as they were than I could possibly feel.

Chapter IX
THE PROBLEM
(From the Rector's MSS. Continued.)

I am indebted to Michael for most of the substance of this chapter. He drove Bathurst back to the farm where he was staying, and his companion maintained an unbroken silence throughout the whole of the journey. But he made his apologies, however, for this at the very outset.

"I'm very much afraid, Mr. Parry-Probyn," he volunteered, as they entered the car, "that I am going to prove far from an entertaining companion on our journey home. I shall be much more of an infliction than an entertainment. But I am sure you will forgive me—I wish to think, and think long and hard." Michael laughed an acquiescent rejoinder, and thus they came to the farm at Kirve St. Laudus. Here Bathurst brightened a little and invited Michael into his cosy sitting-room. You may guess that the offer was accepted very gladly.

"Take a pew, Parry-Probyn, while I fix up the lamp, and we'll gnaw a bone together, and during the period that we shall thus spend so felicitously, there shall be no mention of crime in general or of the Raybourne tragedy in particular. Agreed?"

Michael smiled an assent, and it was not till nearly an hour later, when the fowl on their plates had turned the latter into twin Golgotha, that the topic to which he had referred was mentioned. Michael has just come down from Magdalen, and Oxford reminiscences for a time ruled fast and furious. But when Bathurst filled his pipe and lighted its tobacco, and then pushed his pouch across to Michael, the latter was privileged to hear his first "summary" of the case. My boy has told me since that they drew their chairs up to the fire, and Bathurst gazed steadfastly into the flames as he made his points plain *seriatim*.

"What are the features of the case that impress you? Tell me—it would interest me to know," he said.

"Well," replied Michael, "first of all, undoubtedly the fact that nobody seems to have gone near the man between the time he got on the bus and the time that he was found to be dead. Also the—"

"Except the conductor. Don't forget that."

"Can't we rule him out? Surely you don't—?"

Bathurst smiled. "I rule nobody out—until I know that I can—safely. I can't forget my investigation of that strange affair of the 'Peacock's Eye'. But go on."

"Well, besides what I said, the news that Mrs. Nuckey brought us that Sutcliffe had enemies—enemies, too, from whom he was evidently hiding."

Bathurst nodded. "Anything else?"

"Nothing that stands out perhaps like the two points that I have mentioned. Of course, we can find quite a collection of—"

"Care to hear my opinion?"

"Oh—rather! Afraid I've been eagerly looking forward to it. Do you agree with me?"

"About what you've just put forward?"

"Yes."

"I don't—to be absolutely frank. You know, Parry-Probyn, the extraordinary thing with regard to affairs of this nature is this: the seemingly insignificant things are the factors that invariably count the most. That has been my experience always. Just as the one particular straw spells disaster to the camel, and at the same time gives us our geographical direction when the wind is getting up, so it is in investigations like this. The little points are those which must be most carefully watched. Now you, when I asked you, picked on two of what I may very well describe as the main details. I am going to differ from you."

"I think I understand," returned Michael. "I've very often felt the same idea myself. You mean that international spies and Russian countesses are not so important in a *story* of crime, for instance, as—"

"A split infinitive, possibly, in the mouth of an archbishop. Exactly! Just my point."

"Yes—I see. I think that I follow you *very* clearly now. As I said, the same thing has struck me many and many a time. Now in this case you attach the greatest importance to . . . ?"

Michael let his sentence stand unfinished to mark his query.

Anthony Bathurst regarded him gravely. "I expect I shall occasion you some surprise when you hear what I have to say. But these are the points with which I am concerned most." He proceeded to tick them off on his fingers with the stem of his pipe. "One—the dead man's singular infatuation for drenching rain as a panacea for muscular rheumatism; two—the fact that he has no bus-ticket anywhere about him—most significant that; three—his unshaven face and chin; four—the strange coincidence of the two foggy nights; and five—that little question concerning his myopia. I am willing to concede that there are perhaps twenty-eight or twenty-nine other remarkable features, but the five I have named are the five which unquestionably stand out as the most prominent, in the sense that they are so informative."

One of the five points immediately caught and fired Michael's imagination. "By Jove! That question of his bus-ticket! Now that's jolly funny. Do you know it never occurred to me before, whereas, of course, it should have done. Shows what a hopelessly drivelling ass I am. It wasn't on him, you say?"

"You heard what Inspector Curgenven said, the same as I did. But in a degree I am to blame. I neglected to do something that I had intended to do."

"You have formed a theory?" demanded Michael, in an excess of enthusiasm. "What do you think, then, happened when the bus—?"

"Not so fast." Bathurst laughed gently. "I have formed a theory, it is true, which, if correct, may lead us almost anywhere. Perhaps that's the worst of it."

"When will you test it, Bathurst? Immediately?"

"Why not? Care to come with me?"

"Where?"

Anthony Bathurst referred to a slip of paper that he took from his pocket. "Before we came away, Curgenven let me have several addresses for which I asked him. They are addresses of various people who touch the case. My first place of call is going to be 14 Richmond Terrace, Raybourne—it happens to be the residence of Frederick Whitehead, the conductor of the tragic bus." He looked at his wrist watch. "It will be close on ten o'clock when we get there, so we ought to catch him all right. At the worst we shouldn't have long to wait. I'll drive the Crossley this time."

"Right-oh," returned Michael. "I'm game." He looked at his companion curiously and then decided to put a question to him. "I say, Bathurst, I've been thinking over what Mrs. Nuckey told us. When you said just now that your theory, if correct, might lead us anywhere—were you by any chance thinking of Patagonia?"

Bathurst shook his head. "I was not. In fact, I think I can assert with some confidence that Patagonia is the *last* place to which we shall be called." He started the engine running. "Yes—I think that's one of the facts upon which we *can* bank. Thundering good job, you know, Parry-Probyn, being sure of *one* thing."

CHAPTER X
MR. BATHURST'S FIRST THEORY
(From the Rector's MSS. Continued.)

WHITEHEAD was in. He had just come off duty, as Bathurst had calculated, and it seemed to Michael, as he came into his little front-room to greet them, that he rather welcomed the opportunity to discuss the case. I will not weary my readers with the incidents of the opening conversation. They dealt with the facts as we know them, and Bathurst explained his position. I will proceed at once to the initial unfolding of this first theory that Anthony Bathurst had formed.

"Now, Whitehead," he said, "I am so far clear upon all the facts that you have told me. I accept your statement unreservedly, because I can see quite well that you are sincere in what you say. You are prepared to swear that nobody went anywhere near the top of your bus with the exception of yourself and the dead man, allowing, too, for the fog that prevailed at Northlynn. Now think very carefully before you answer my first question, because I have very strong reasons for asking it of you. Do you understand?"

"Yes, sir; what is it?" The conductor's eyes protruded from his head at the seriousness that was evident in Bathurst's tone. Had the answer that he was to give affected his own life or bodily safety he couldn't have received the intimation of the query with greater solemnity. His eyes were fixed on, and never left, Anthony Bathurst's face.

"Would you be prepared to swear, Whitehead, that the passenger that boarded your bus on the night of the murder *was the same man who had travelled with you each evening before*? Think, Whitehead—for on the answer that you give me much depends."

The conductor received the question with more than a touch of incredulity. "Of course, sir! Yes, sir! Why not?"

"Did you speak to him?"

"Why, yes, sir."

"When?"

"When he first got on."

"And you recognized his voice absolutely? Be sure, man."

"Yes, sir. I recognized his voice. Not a doubt about it, sir."

"How many times had you spoken to him before? Did you know his voice well?"

"Half a dozen or so. Perhaps a few more even. I knew his voice *quite* well."

Bathurst rose, and stood thinking deeply. "Pardon me, Whitehead, if I appear to labour the question. I am not doing so without a very good reason. I want you to concentrate upon what I am going to say to you. Your usual passenger, the man of five or six weeks' acquaintance, who used to get on near the Lanning archway, habitually wore the collar of his overcoat turned right up. Yes?"

"Quite right, sir. He—"

"Wait. And listen again. He also wore horn-rimmed glasses and a very unusually wide-brimmed felt hat. Yes?"

"Yes, sir. Quite right again, sir. All those things that you—"

"Listen yet again, Whitehead. Are you absolutely *certain, positive,* without the shadow of a doubt, that the man who boarded your bus didn't merely *seem* to you to be your usual passenger, just because of these external and usual signs that marked him out so distinctively, and for which you had accustomed yourself to look? That you didn't recognize the style of the coat, the hat, the glasses—and *not* the man himself?"

Whitehead shook his head doggedly against the rain of Bathurst's questions.

"No, sir; I'm sorry, sir. I see what you're after. But your idea's wrong, sir. I give you my affidavit on it. It was my usual passenger all right. I knew his voice too *well* to be mistaken."

Michael could see by this time that Bathurst's theory had sustained a severe shock. Whitehead stood his ground and stuck resolutely to his guns. Nothing that Bathurst had so far said had shaken him. He leant toward his questioner with an unusual light shining in his usually expressionless eyes.

"Could I prove it to you in another way, sir? Because I can. At least I think I can."

"How? I should like you to do so very much. If you can do what you say, it will clear the air for me considerably. Tell me."

"Well, sir, the gentleman 'ad a very funny little habit with regard to his ticket. Us conductors learn to notice little things like that about our fares."

No sooner had Whitehead mentioned the final word than Bathurst was all attention. His eye caught Michael's, and back to the latter came the memory of their recent conversation.

"Oh—what was that, Whitehead?"

"He used to push the ticket into the turn-up of his trousers—and 'e did so on the night 'e was murdered. I saw 'im do so with my own eyes when I punched it for 'im and 'anded it to 'im. In fact, before now, sir, I've seen 'im take three or four old tickets out of his trousers when he's put a new one in—tickets that 'e'd forgotten."

Bathurst considered this latest piece of information very carefully. As he had feared, the thing he had neglected to do was coming home to him. If the conductor's story were true, it would certainly help to clinch matters. He made up his mind to put it to immediate test.

"There's a 'phone at the first big dairy-farm along the road to Kirve. I've used it two or three times since I've been down here. We'll run up there at once, and I'll get on to Curgenven. Come along, you two."

Ten minutes' journey brought them to the farm, and Bathurst quickly got through to the police station at Raybourne.

"Is that you, Inspector? Did they tell you who it was? Good. I want to worry you. There's a little thing I want you to do for me. See if there's a bus-ticket, or even, perhaps, tickets, in the turn-up of Sutcliffe's trousers, will you? Yes—I'll hold on. What? . . . You have. . . . How many? . . . One . . . of course . . . yes, I agree with you there. . . . Well, that seems to settle it. . . . Very many thanks, Inspector." He replaced the receiver, and turned to Michael and the conductor. "You are quite correct, Whitehead; Inspector Curgenven had been over Sutcliffe's clothes again, and found the ticket in the turn-up of the trousers, just as you described. He has also been into your depot and has proved from your journey way-bill that it is a ticket issued by you on the night of the murder—the number and series tally with your way-bill return. So that's that." He spoke somewhat despondently.

"You are disappointed?" suggested my son.

"In a way—yes."

"Why? What does it mean exactly?"

"It means that it looks as though I've got to start all over again. Which is always a thought that tends to induce depression in me. Care to come for a short spin? It's a lovely night now."

The two men agreed, and for some time Bathurst drove in silence. Suddenly he turned to Whitehead. "This is an extraordinarily good road, Whitehead. I can't make it out. The surface is excellent. Very different from the usual run of roads in this district. I haven't struck a pot-hole for quite three minutes."

"Yes, sir, it is. But you see, sir, there's a reason for it—or two, even. The Mayor of Raybourne lives one side of it, and the Borough Engineer on the other."

Anthony Bathurst laughed. "Really? Now that's most interesting. I suppose your job helps you to . . ." He checked himself swiftly, and Michael, leaning forward to look at him, saw a light of excitement come into and take possession of his eyes. "Tell me, Whitehead—can you remember a foggy night about a fortnight before the murder?"

"Very well, sir. Very thick it was, too, I—"

"Was Sutcliffe on top that night, can you remember?"

"He was, sir. I joked with him over it—some yarn he'd got about pea soup."

Bathurst rubbed his hands, and Michael turned to him.

"You've thought of something, Mr. Bathurst? You can see light?"

It was when Whitehead had gone that Bathurst answered him.

"Perhaps it's just on the cards. Something has just occurred to me that I was a fool not to think of it before. At any rate, it's worth testing. And we'll test it as soon as we can. All the same, though, I must get more confirmation of a lot that Master Whitehead has told me."

Chapter XI
EILEEN TREVOR BEGINS TO WONDER

"TELEGRAM for you, Miss Trevor." Gladys, the maid-of-all work at Freyne House, popped her somewhat untidy head round the schoolroom door and handed over the thin envelope with due solemnity. As always—she scented romance! The girl who took it, pausing from her tea to do so, was slim, dark-haired and boyish. Her tall, shapely, lissom figure was that of an athlete, and her dark-blue laughing eyes bore eloquent testimony to the fact that all her life was an enjoyment to her—not only physically, but mentally also. Work and play came alike to her, and she eagerly welcomed the glorious effort that each one in turn demanded of her vitalities. Her mother was dead—had died in giving her birth—and her father had lived abroad ever since she could remember. She had not set eyes on him for seventeen years. She herself had been born in the United States, and at the age of five had been sent to England to be educated, eventually to this very academy for young ladies—Freyne House—where she now held the position of junior classical mistress and dispensed small quantities of Latin and Greek to such pupils as scorned the modernities and enrolled themselves on the classical side.

On the afternoon in question Eileen Walsingham Trevor (to give her her full patronymic) was feeling very cheery with herself. She had played centre-forward for the South against the North in an International Hockey Trial that afternoon on her own home turf at Freyne, and had pleased herself immensely by putting up a really good show, a show that must have impressed several of the *cognoscenti*. On the winning side by a margin of five to two, she had not only scored three beautiful goals off her own stick, but had held her wings together in such masterly manner that it had caused one influential critic round the ropes to remark in her hearing that "that girl playing centre for the South was more like S.H. Shoveller than any woman centre he had ever seen". Although she had coloured to the roots of her hair when the remark floated over to her, it had bucked her no end, nevertheless, and she could almost feel her cap against Wales nestling on her head.

She dexterously patted her hair on each side of the same head and opened the envelope of the telegram that Gladys had handed to her to read its message. Reaching almost mechanically for another section of buttered crumpet, she read it again. An interested observer would have noticed a frown come over her face as she did so—a frown that, unlike most of Eileen's frowns, stayed there for some time. The telegram was worded as follows:

Liverpool. Expect me 9.30 tonight. Most important news.—Mallinson.

Eileen tapped the floor impatiently with her foot. Then, rising suddenly from her hassock by the fireside, she crossed to her desk in the centre of the schoolroom and unlocked a drawer. From the drawer she took two letters. Locking the drawer again, she returned to her seat of comfort in front of the fire and to her pile of hot crumpets. Smoothing out the first of the letters that she had been to obtain, she puckered her brows and read it through very carefully and thoroughly. It was dated August 4th and headed "Effingham Farm, near Tacoma, U.S.A."

My dear Eileen,

What I am about to say to you will doubtless come us a great surprise. But I am coming to England after an absence from the old country of close on twenty-four years. I never told you anything about myself during your early years because I did not wish to, and even if I had I do not suppose for one moment that you would have remembered it, for you were only a few months over five when I sent you to England to school. They told me you were too young, but there was no real home for you then where I was. Anyhow, something has just come to my knowledge that is of the greatest possible importance. It affects not only me, but you, after me, and in my experience the hand of Fate has never worked more strangely.

It is because of this that I am coming to England before the autumn. I nearly wrote "fall". My arrangements are not yet completed, but I shall in all probability cross some time about the end of October or the beginning of November. I shall not write to you again until I land. Then I shall communicate with you at once, but in the meantime I think that I can promise you this: before Christmas you will he something more than an assistant mistress, or whatever it is you are at Freyne House. Don't write to me in reply to this, but if anything should happen to me between now and October—you never know in this transitory life of faiths, hopes and fears; see how the old Prayer Book sticks—communicate with Harold Forsyth, Esq., 5 Garnock Chambers, Swithin Old Lane, near Liverpool. Mark the envelope "If away, please forward", but don't worry him unnecessarily.

I remain, my dear Eileen,
Your affectionate father,
Roland Walsingham Trevor.

P.S.—It may interest you to know that I am twenty-three years older than my name "Trevor". That should give you a clue. Surprised?

Eileen wrinkled her nose at the epistle and considered it critically. The writing was not the writing of a man who seemed to have habitual use of the pen. The letters were well formed, but there was a stiffness about some of the strokes that was unmistakable. The writing of an educated man who had changed the manner of his life! Eileen put the sheet of paper down with something like a sniff, and proceeded to pick up the other letter that she had previously taken from the drawer of the desk. This second one was much shorter. It read as follows:

Crosby's Commercial Hotel, Gulliver Street, Liverpool.
Nov. 8th.

Dear Miss Trevor,

I am instructed by your father to write this letter to you, as he himself is not in a position to write to you. I regret to inform you that since arriving in Liverpool he has had rather a serious accident, and is at present in a hospital in this city. He begs me to tell you not to worry and to make no attempt to see him, as he is in no actual danger at the moment. I will keep you posted as to his condition as well as I am able, and will let you know immediately he is well enough to see you. But remember that "no news" will be "good news".

Faithfully yours,
James B. Mallinson.

Eileen wrinkled her nose for the second time that evening. It was a fortnight exactly since she had received this letter from Mallinson, and the telegram that she had just taken from Gladys had to a certain extent relieved her mind of some anxiety. "Any news", she argued to herself—certainly in some circumstances—

is better than "no news". "No news" may be euphemistically described both historically and by Mr. James B. Mallinson, but all the same it means anxiety, suspense, doubt. This telegram, even though it might mean disaster when the time came for its translation, would at least resolve itself into something like certainty. It would put an end to her vague forebodings. All through the piece, from the time of her receipt of the first letter from her father, Eileen had—for reasons of her own—kept her own counsel, although at times the self-imposed silence had been a sore trial to her. She looked at the big clock on the wall. There were still three hours to go before the time of Mallinson's announced arrival.

Mallinson! Who was this man Mallinson, by the way? She racked her brains in an abortive attempt to connect him with her father. But in no way could she recall the name. Her father's letters over a period of seventeen years had told her very little beyond the fact that his farm had weathered a bad time and had gradually begun to prosper. She failed to recall the mention of the name "Mallinson" in any one of them. Her father had paid the bills that came along periodically in respect of her education, and after that had acceded quite willingly to the suggestion from the Principal of Freyne House that Eileen should be appointed to the vacancy that had conveniently arisen on the teaching staff of that academy. It was, therefore, with a very definite feeling of doubt and wonderment that she advanced to meet Mallinson upon his arrival some three hours later.

CHAPTER XII
THE WALSINGHAM INHERITANCE

MUCH TO her surprise, for she had had no intimation of such a visit, Mallinson was accompanied by two others. As he advanced to greet her—his right arm in a sling—she deliberately lifted her eyebrows in a question that was so insistent that it was impossible for him to overlook it. Mallinson attempted to explain the unexpected position.

"Good evening, Miss Trevor. . . ." His voice held emotion, but he quickly pulled himself together and mastered it. "I am James Mallinson—the man that you were expecting. You have received my wire, of course. I ask your pardon for troubling you . . . and also for having brought these two other gentlemen to see you—without—er—warning or asking your leave. But there is ample justification, believe me, for my having done either."

His idea, no doubt, was to watch the effect of his words upon her. Eileen's answer came quickly.

"Good evening to you, Mr. Mallinson. There is no need to apologize. I am sure of the truth of what you say. And these two gentlemen who have come with you are . . . ?"

Mallinson beckoned the two men forward. "Miss Eileen Trevor . . . Mr. Bartholomew Savory . . . and his son, Mr. Hector Savory." The two men obeyed Mallinson's invitation and bowed to the girl they saw in front of them. Mallinson proceeded with some haste. "These gentlemen would be, perhaps, better known to you if I gave them their proper professional description. I guess you'd identify them more easily. They represent the firm of Savory, Son, and Savory—Solicitors, of Lord Street, Liverpool."

Eileen acknowledged the bows that the two men accorded her and waved them towards the chairs.

"Won't you please sit down?—although I'm afraid you won't find the chairs too comfortable. But you have come some distance, and I'm sure that . . ." She paused, hardly knowing what to say. It was a situation the like of which she had not previously encountered, and which she now found herself at a loss to meet.

"Thank you, Miss Trevor." It was the elder man who spoke. His voice was pleasant, crisp and cultured, although it held at the same time a slight touch of the North Country accent. Eileen looked at the two of them closely. The elder, Bartholomew Savory, was a man, she judged, somewhere round about sixty years of age. But she admitted to herself that he carried his years well. His shoulders were broad, and his whole frame well knit, and although he showed some signs of approaching corpulency, his five feet ten inches or thereabouts tended to take it off somewhat and make him, for his age certainly, a very presentable figure. His dark hair was tinged with grey at the temples, and his light-blue eyes held a keenness and a general alertness the measure of which would not have disgraced a very much younger man.

Hector Savory, the son, was not quite as tall as his father. He seemed to Eileen to be somewhere in the late thirties. But he had inherited his father's strength. His hair was fairer, but he was clean-shaven like his sire, and he wore a pair of rimless pince-nez that gave his face an air of acuteness, or, better still perhaps, legal wisdom, that was rather noticeably absent from that of the older man. Mallinson was a person of about the same height as Bartholomew Savory, and appeared to be a few years older than Hector. His bronzed features spoke eloquently of life in the open air, and, added to his healthy tan, there was an engaging frankness about his face that caught Eileen's fancy and rendered him distinctly attractive to her. His tawny yellow hair and blue eyes contrasted sharply with the black scarf that formed the sling in which he held his right arm, and every now and then a fugitive shadow would cross his face that evidently told of a twinge of pain. Like Bartholomew and Hector Savory, he accepted the invitation that had been given him, and he took a chair sitting on the girl's right, with the solicitors facing him on her left.

"I think, Mr. Savory," said Mallinson, coming to the business in hand, "it would be as well if you took upon yourself to . . ."

Bartholomew Savory nodded his approval and produced a bundle of imposing-looking documents from his breast pocket.

"First of all let me introduce myself a little more fully. I am the senior partner, Miss Trevor, of the firm of Savory, Son, and Savory, practising at Lordship Chambers, Lord Street, Liverpool. My son, here, Hector Savory, is the junior partner. My brother, Ernest Savory, who was in partnership with us, died seven or eight years ago, so that my son and I are at this moment the sole surviving partners." He looked up from the array of papers that he had arranged, upon his knees with an air of pride. "We are, I think I can claim without fear of legitimate contradiction, the most highly respected firm of its kind within the city of Liverpool. I mention that fact, Miss Trevor, not—er—vaingloriously, but in order that it may explain to you more fully what is about to follow. For I believe that I am right in my assumption that you are ignorant of most of the facts. That is so, is it not, Mr. Mallinson?" He looked at Mallinson for corroboration.

"As far as I understand . . . yes." His light-blue eyes caught the girl's for a moment as he answered, and Eileen found herself wondering rather at the expression that they held. At the same time, had she been taxed she couldn't have explained why.

"I will continue," proceeded Bartholomew Savory, "and Miss Trevor will, I hope, correct me where and whenever I am inaccurate. One of my most influential clients was Sir Joshua Walsingham, of Effingham Grange, near Loxteth, in the County of Lancaster. For a long time—in fact for the greater part of his career, by far—Sir Joshua was a comparatively poor man, and it taxed his ingenuity very considerably, and his actual resources even more, to keep his large house in tolerably decent repair and himself in a moderate degree of comfort."

Savory spoke strongly and well. He held his words on his lips with an undoubted sense of command. It was evident to all of them that he could handle a situation—awkward or otherwise. But the name "Walsingham" had burned its way into Eileen's brain, and she heard the rest in a strange buzz of excitement and emotion. What had her father meant when he wrote . . . ? But Savory was speaking again.

"The Great War, however, of 1914-1918 changed all that, and Sir Joshua, like many others of his contemporaries, from a man of very moderate means became a very rich man. His ships, whose trade had dwindled tremendously until many of them had lain idle, acquired a new and immense value that the Government translated into very effective terms, and when Sir Joshua died three years ago last April he had amassed a fortune. But—since life is made up of compensations and balances, of deficits and embarrassments—there was a pretty substantial shadow on the old man's life. His wife had been dead, I may say, for many years. Of relatives he had none, and his only child, a boy, Roland by name, had left home in a fit of temper, after a bitter quarrel with his father over a young girl, some twenty years or so previously.

"Each swore to forget the other, and no communication, to my knowledge, had passed between them from that day to the day of Sir Joshua's death.

"A year or so after Roland's disappearance news was received that he and his young wife had perished in the terrible Californian railway disaster of 1909, but it was never actually confirmed, and in his declining years old Sir Joshua relented and clung to the hope that his boy was still alive and would one day return to him. I and my son here, in turn, pointed out to him time after time the extreme unlikeliness of such an event, but we were not altogether successful in dissuading him from nursing the belief. Old men, you know, cling tenaciously to their favourite fancies. For when he died, Sir Joshua Walsingham left his entire fortune of over two hundred and seventy-three thousand pounds to Roland Walsingham, his only son, to trace whom he directed every effort of human agency was to be made."

Bartholomew Savory paused dramatically and then proceeded to speak again with very heavy intentness:

"That man Roland Walsingham, of whom I have just told you, Miss Trevor, son of Sir Joshua Walsingham, was . . . and I hope *is*, your father!"

At his words Eileen sprang excitedly to her feet.

"Why, Mr. Savory, what do you mean? Why do you talk like that? What has happened to cause you to . . . ?"

Bartholomew Savory motioned her courteously to her seat again. "Hector," he said, turning to his son, "go on from where I have left off, for the remainder of the story concerns you perhaps more than it does me. And please relieve Miss Trevor's anxiety as much as you possibly can."

Hector took up the story, and his incisive tones, coupled with his deliberation, were as impressive in their way as his father's had been before him.

"My father has told you that we were left with instructions to spare no expense to trace Roland Walsingham. We did as the old man Sir Joshua had directed. All the usual channels were utilized and exploited as thoroughly as possible, but with no success whatever. There seemed to be no doubt at all that not only was Roland dead, but also had left no heirs. If not, he had disappeared into the bowels of the earth—which from our point of view was almost an equivalent. Our efforts ceased. But in July of this year—towards the end of that month, to be exact—we were greatly surprised and, of course, very naturally delighted, to receive this letter. It was, of course, addressed to the firm. I was the man to read it first, and I at once took it to my father. Read it for yourself, Miss Trevor. I take it that you can testify to its being in your father's handwriting?"

He passed the letter over to Eileen. She read it:

> *Effingham Farm,*
> *Near Tacoma, U.S.A.*
> *July 22nd, 1929.*

Messrs. Savory, Son, and Savory
Lordship Chambers, Lord Street,
Liverpool,
Lancashire, England.

Sirs,

I have much pleasure to acquaint you with the fact that I claim to be the Roland Walsingham, heir to the late Sir Joshua Walsingham, of Effingham Grange, near Loxteth, Lancashire, for whom you have been advertising, I understand, for some considerable time, as soon as convenient, from the point of view of leaving my work here, I shall attend upon you at your office with the necessary documents and certificates to substantiate my claim. I shall, however, write to you again nearer to the date of my leaving this country, giving full particulars as to when you may expect me.

> *I remain, very sincerely yours,*
> *Roland Walsingham.*

Hector Savory repeated his question. "Your father's handwriting, Miss Trevor—or perhaps I should say Miss Walsingham? No doubt of it?"

"None at all." Eileen shook her head decisively. "I can prove it—if you will only look at a letter I have here." She went to the desk and produced the letter that had come to her from Tacoma. "Look for yourself and compare, Mr. Savory."

Hector Savory examined the two letters and nodded his satisfaction at what he saw. "Good," he added. "Now let me read you this second letter that has come from the States, dated October. Usual address, and to the firm as before.

Dear Sirs,

Further to my letter of the 22nd of July last, and your reply thereto of August 8th, I beg to inform you that I am sailing per the SS. Gigantic, *on the 2nd proximo, accompanied by my manager Mr. James B. Mallinson.*

Very sincerely yours,

Roland Walsingham.

P.S—I have booked my passage in the name of Roland Trevor.

"Not many words wasted there, eh?"

Hector Savory looked at Eileen, then at his father and then at Mallinson.

"This is where you come in, I think, Mr. Mallinson. Take up the running, will you?"

The tawny-haired man nodded and showed his white, even teeth in something approaching a smile. When he spoke it was with an easy, almost nonchalant drawl.

"I'm not drifting back anything like as far as the elder Mr. Savory—because there's no need to. No, Miss Trevor, it's only about ten years in my case. But you've got to know that I linked up with Roland Trevor in the autumn of '19. I'd served overseas with the American Expeditionary Force and I was blowing back across the States in a casual kind of way, looking at a lot and seein' nothing to wave flags about, when I hit up against Trevor— the Roland Trevor you've been hearing about. We suited one another all along the line, and he finished up by offering me a job of work on his fruit farm in Tacoma. I took it—was darned glad of the opportunity, let me tell you, Miss Trevor and gentlemen—and Trevor and I have been hooked up together ever since Effingham Farm prospered. Moreover the boss and I got proper chummy. He was a white man right through—a 'pukka sahib'. He told me of his daughter way back in the old homeland, and often spoke to me of his dead wife.

"Well, to cut a long story short, all went serenely at Effingham till the July of this year. Trevor had been out for the day, up in the Puget Sound vicinity, I fancy, and came back in a mood that I don't think—speaking from memory—I had ever seen him in before. A sort of excitement—suppressed for best part of the time and then suddenly bubbling over and taking a mighty keen hold of him. Knowing him, and knowing his nature, I left him alone and said nothing, asked no questions, and didn't interfere in any way at all. I'd found from experience that that was always the best way with him. Well, I heard nothing from him till October. A clam would have been garrulous alongside him. For just on three months he kept his own counsel and his lips tight, and never let on a word.

"Then about the third week in October he told me he was coming to England on the second of November over an important matter of business and, of all things in the world, wanted me to accompany him. He said I had been a faithful servant, that he wanted companionship, hated being alone, and so on and so forth, and that the trip would do me the world of good. The farm—much to my surprise, for I knew it meant a tremendous lot to him—was to be left in charge of the second and third overseers—Aldbridge and Sharp by name. I know now why he didn't care! Two hundred and seventy-three thousand pounds kind of make a difference to a man's outlook. Or a woman's—come to that. It's like morning—it gilds the skies."

Mallinson broke off and looked quizzically at Eileen. If he expected her to reply to his glance he was disappointed, for something was hammering away in Eileen's brain that demanded explanation with a relentless persistence.

Mallinson, nothing daunted, went on as nonchalantly as ever.

"Well, being approximately human, you can guess that I wasn't exactly averse to a holiday under the conditions laid down, and Trevor and I sailed on the *Gigantic* on the second of this month, as he had foreshadowed. Trevor had booked first-class passages for us, and with the old pond on its very best behaviour, considering the season of the year, we reached Liverpool on the seventh of November. Now, Miss Trevor, I have to tell you a very strange thing—for this is where I come up against my problem."

He lowered his voice and, as Eileen looked at him, seemed to attempt to avoid her eyes. The younger Savory noticed it from where he was sitting and it puzzled him.

CHAPTER XIII
THE WARNING

"YES?" interrogated the girl. "Please go on."

Mallinson nodded his head in emphasis. "Miss Trevor—a very extraordinary thing happened. When we got into Liverpool, Trevor received a letter. I didn't see the contents of it so I can't describe them to you in detail. But, anyhow, I think it caused Trevor to spill the entire box of beans to me concerning this Walsingham business. At any rate, something must have done. He didn't tell me a lot, just told me who he was—who he claimed to be—and how he'd written to these two gentlemen here and, moreover, how glad he was now that he'd never before told a living soul a word about the business. *Because this letter which he had just received was in the nature of a warning, and was also anonymous.* That's all I know about it, and he urged on me the strictest silence at the time with regard to the entire outfit.

"I was a bit worried, because I couldn't pull my weight if it came to a rough house—I'd strained my shoulder, you see, at deck quoits one afternoon on the voyage over, and, as you can see, it's not right yet. Trevor was worried, too—I spotted that at once—and altogether the excursion wasn't turning out anything like we had expected. I'm speaking for myself, I know—at the same time I reckon I'm right as concerns Trevor. Well, we put up for the night of the seventh of November at a commercial hotel—'Crosby's', in Gulliver Street. If it turned out pretty decent, he said, he intended to stay a bit longer before he made a move, but on the eighth of November, Miss Trevor—the very next day—*your father disappeared*." Mallinson paused.

"Disappeared?" echoed Eileen. "Is that what you meant when you wrote to me and told me my father had met with an accident? Why couldn't you have told me the truth? I'm not a child. I hate that kind of treatment."

Her eyes flashed with her indignation. Mallinson appeared to be taken aback by her vehemence.

"What do you . . . ?" Then, after some hesitation, he seemed to recover himself. "What I did I did for the best. I thought it would shock you less if I described the affair as an accident than if I told you the truth." He frowned at the recollection. "Trevor disappeared and hasn't been seen since," he said hastily. "That's the position as it is at the moment—that's what these gentlemen and I have come to tell you and seek your advice about."

"I haven't seen my father for years and years, as you know full well, Mr. Mallinson, so I can't pretend that what I have just heard is a really terrible blow to me. Nothing like, of course, what it would have been had our relations been normal. It's just a shock—that's all." She sat still for a moment. "Just please tell me all you've done since you first discovered what had happened, for it's very obvious to me that no more time must be wasted. Too much has been already."

There was decision in her tone, and Mallinson, with the two Savorys, recognized it.

"You're quite right there, Miss Trevor. I agree with all you say and I am quite ready to give an account of my actions. I fully realize that it's kind of—up to me—to do so."

Mallinson settled down in his chair, carefully moving his injured shoulder. Before he could proceed with his story, Eileen intervened again.

"What do the police think about it, for I suppose they have been told?"

Bartholomew Savory nodded his entire corroboration of the question, but Mallinson shifted his body awkwardly and uneasily as he replied to it.

"No—I haven't been to the police, Miss Trevor. You may think it very remiss on my part not to have done so, but I promised your father, you see, not to say a word of his business to anybody, and I guess it's my job to keep faith with him as long as I can. It's worried me a lot, I can tell you, this past fortnight, to keep silent, but I gave my word and, you see, that alone means a lot to me. But leaving that for the time being, I'll tell you what I have done."

Eileen watched him very carefully, and Mallinson, catching the expression on her face, realized that this was indeed Roland Trevor's daughter. Unlike him physically, she nevertheless had inherited his strength of character and indomitable purpose. He proceeded.

"The last time I saw Trevor was at breakfast in Crosby's Hotel on the morning of November the eighth. He seemed in pretty good spirits, taking him on the whole, and gave me instructions to keep on my own all day and meet him in the smoking-lounge of the hotel last thing at night. He was going out, he said, and would in all probability be out all day. But he told me no more than that. I knew neither where he was going nor what business it was that was taking him there. I also knew better than to ask him. But of course I formed my own opinion, as was perfectly natural. I figured it out that his business was concerning the Walsingham inheritance and was with these two gentlemen here—all that is left of Savory, Son, and Savory." He stopped to moisten his lips with his tongue, and the elder Savory took advantage of the cessation to intervene.

"Quite a natural inference, in the circumstances, for Mr. Mallinson to draw. Don't you think so, Miss Trevor?"

"Go on," replied Eileen again, with grim earnestness. "Don't waste time."

Mallinson looked at her curiously and almost approvingly, but obeyed her directions.

"Well, I was there in the lounge that evening, waiting for Trevor, as he had ordered me, and there was no sign of him. He never showed up at all, and at last, after putting a few discreet inquiries round, I reluctantly gave it up and went to bed. I had a drink with the proprietor last thing, hoping, of course, that Trevor would materialize some time next morning. He didn't—to cut a long story short—and I haven't seen him from that day to this. As far as I am concerned, he's vanished. Mind if I smoke, Miss Trevor?"

"Rather like it, to be strictly truthful—but go on, please. I'm sorry if I seem to be frightfully impatient, but once again don't waste any more time than you need."

Mallinson produced his pouch and, handicapped as he was, slowly filled his pipe. He proceeded to light the tobacco just as deliberately, as Eileen tapped with her foot upon the rug.

"There isn't a great deal more for me to tell you, Miss Trevor. I knocked around Crosby's Hotel for eight or nine days or so, hoping against hope that Trevor would eventually roll up. I think anybody, considering all the circumstances, would excuse me doing that. When he didn't, and over a week had gone by, I decided, after a lot of hard thinking, to have a word with the firm of solicitors who I knew had Trevor's business affairs in hand. It struck me that I couldn't possibly do better. I thereupon blew right along to Lordship Chambers yesterday morning and had an interview with Mr. Bartholomew Savory. But I guess I barked up the wrong tree. My idea that he would be able to dispel the cloud of doubt and anxiety that had taken possession of my mind was doomed to early disappointment, for he was in no better position than I was.

"Your father *had not kept his appointment* with Mr. Savory, Miss Trevor—he had not been near the place. Mr. Savory himself had formed the opinion that he had missed the boat by which he had intended to travel and was crossing by a later one, but when he heard my story—how we'd crossed on the *Gigantic*, and how your father had walked out of the hotel in Liverpool and virtually vanished into thin air—he realized that matters were real serious." Mallinson stopped in his story here and puffed at his pipe very thoughtfully. Then he finished his statement: "I don't want to make things sound worse than they are, Miss Trevor, but we all thought that we should come to you at once. Here we are."

"It was my idea, that, Miss Trevor," put in Hector Savory impressively. "I thought perhaps it might be just possible that you were in possession of information that we were not—that your father might in some way have communicated with you. At least, it was a chance worth trying; but if I am any judge, and going entirely upon the way in which you have received both my father's statement and Mr. Mallinson's story, that is not so. I am right, am I not?"

"You are, Mr. Savory," replied Eileen very emphatically. "It has all been news to me. I am amazed. I am bewildered. Neither of which condition is going to get us anywhere, is it? The point is—what is the next step? What are we going to do? We *must* do something."

"There is only one thing that we can do," replied Bartholomew Savory. "Our course lies in front of us—plain to see. We must go to the police. Moreover, it is our bounden duty to do so."

"I agree with you, Mr. Savory," confirmed Eileen promptly; "and the first thing they'll ask us is why we have delayed doing so for so long. How will you explain that?"

She looked at the previous speaker, but it was obvious that her implied censure was meant for Mallinson. She proceeded: "It is certain at least that *somebody* must have seen my father when he left Crosby's Hotel, and we must take every step to trace that somebody. You must get back to Liverpool first thing in the morning, gentlemen, and I shall accompany you. I shall see my Principal here, Miss Price-Darrell, and arrange it. I shall have to get leave of absence, but I don't think there'll be any difficulty."

"Very well, Miss Trevor," responded the elder Savory, "we'll leave it at that and for the present bid each other good night. I don't think there's anything more that we can do at the moment. Beyond that I feel that I—"

Mallinson cut into him, his keen eyes alight with emotion.

"You'll pardon me, Miss Trevor, I know—but take care of yourself. Let me warn you—I don't like the look of things at all."

He turned on his heel hurriedly and left her.

CHAPTER XIV

MR. BATHURST AND THE CHORUS

(From the Rector's MSS. Continued.)

I DON'T think I shall ever forget the coldness of the room in the police station at Raybourne on the morning that Anthony Bathurst, assisted and supported by Inspector Curgenven, interviewed the various passengers who had travelled part of the journey that had been Claude Sutcliffe's last. Not only was the room cold, but dank, with November moisture and gloom. Mr. and Mrs. Jupp, of Pyloran Hill Farm, near Sladenham, were interrogated first. As the farmer and his better half took their seats with an uneasy reluctance, Bathurst took a letter from his pocket and handed it to Inspector Curgenven. The latter read it with something uncommonly like a frown, and I wondered what it was that had upset him.

"There was no necessity for Sir Austin Kemble to have written to you, Mr. Bathurst—no necessity at all. I flatter myself that I understood the situation thoroughly in the first place. Although I'm attached to a station in Glebeshire, I'm not altogether . . ."

A shrug of his shoulders completed the sentence.

Bathurst made no reply but came forward immediately for his questioning of Jupp. Michael, whom I, under the fervid onslaught of his enthusiasm, had allowed to come along with me, occupied the window-seat, like Eutychus, and was quick to confirm, from the early stages of this interrogation, the idea that he had formed of the line of attack upon the case as a whole that

Anthony Bathurst had determined to adopt. The first step was to test Whitehead's information through the Jupps.

"Mr. Jupp," he opened, "can you remember the dead man boarding your bus on the night of the murder? By that question I mean did you actually see him set foot on the conductor's platform?"

The farmer wagged his head with Socratic understanding and confirmation. "Yes, mister, I did that. He got on at the railway arch that you come up against just afore you run into Lanning. I see 'im get on right enough. So did my old woman. She's got sharp eyes, I can tell you." He chuckled.

"Good," said Anthony. "Was he a stranger to you, or were you acquainted with him?"

Jupp shuffled his feet. "I reckon I must be careful how I answer that, so's not to mislead you. I know what these inquest cases are. I had an aunt once who poisoned herself with cocoa."

"I can quite believe it," returned Bathurst. "I never run the risk myself."

"Put something in it, I mean," explained Jupp.

"I'm sorry I misunderstood you. . . . You were saying—"

"Well, it's like this. He was a stranger to me in the sense that I didn't know his name or who he was. See? But I'd seen 'im get on the 8.33 bus from Esting several times during the last few weeks or so. See my meaning, mister?"

"Quite," smiled Anthony, "and what you have told me gives me ample justification for asking you my next question. Listen. Would you be prepared to swear that the man that was picked up that night was the same man whom you had seen board the bus so many times before?"

He drummed carelessly with his fingers upon the surface of the wooden table that stood in the centre of the room. So much for him depended on Jupp's answer. I pressed forward and watched the latter. If the farmer corroborated Whitehead it would be necessary for Bathurst to fall back upon that second line of investigation that had suggested itself after he had come away from the conductor's house. The issue was not left long in doubt.

"Would I swear to it, mister? Ay—as many times as you'd like to hear me. Why, man, I heard the chap's voice, and there was no mistaking that. Putting aside his hat and his clothes, and all such like, never could I mistake his voice. I'd heard it several times in the past. Why, I mentioned it to young Fred Whitehead, funny enough. You know full well what I mean, mister—you could 'ear the education in his voice. What do they call it? I know—'culture'. Got the proper wireless touch. You know—a touch o' the Oxford College la-di-da."

Jupp caught the twinkle in my eye and hastened to make amends for his *lapsus linguae*. "Begging *your* pardon, Rector, of course, for puttin' it so blunt like. I was forgettin' who was here."

Bathurst interposed. "I take it, then, that you haven't the shadow of a—"

"Not the faintest glimmer of doubt, mister. He was the regular feller all right."

Bathurst turned to Amelia Jupp. "And you, Mrs. Jupp, are, of course, entirely in agreement with your husband?"

Amelia looked at him very shrewdly. "Well—if you want to know—and since you've asked me, I may as well tell you—it's very seldom that I *do* agree with him." She tossed her head. "I reckon I'm a fair-minded woman that can see both sides of any question—mine and the rubbishing rot the other woman tells me." Her eyes gleamed with set purpose. "But on this particular occasion I certainly *do* agree with Jupp—for the very good reason that he's right. And that's a reason you can't beat." She folded her arms defiantly.

Anthony Bathurst bowed. "Thank you, Mrs. Jupp. What you tell me sets my mind at rest upon the point." He turned again to Jupp himself. "Accepting what you have said, then, Mr. Jupp—let me ask you something else. Between Esting— that is to say the starting-point of your journey—and Pyloran Hill, Sladenham, where I am told you alighted, did you see any person *ascend* the steps to the deck with the exception of White- head the conductor?"

The farmer's reply was instant. "Not a livin' soul, mister." He paused, and then continued: "Nobody went up them stairs save Fred Whitehead himself—the once when he went up to collect the chap's fare." He laughed clumsily and immoderately. "Of course, I can't tell you what took place after me and the missus got off."

"I quite appreciate that, Mr. Jupp, and I'm not aware that I asked you to. One last question before you go. Do you remember a very foggy night about a fortnight before this affair? A particularly thick night, it was, in these parts, I am told."

"Yes, mister, I recall it well—somewhere about the beginning of the month it was. What about it?"

"Did you by any chance travel by the 8.33 bus that evening?"

Jupp shook his head. "No, sir, I did not. Me and the missus was by our own fireside the whole of that evening what you speak of, a-listening to the wireless. I mind the night well, because—"

"Then you can't help me. Very well, Mr. Jupp, and you, Mrs. Jupp, if I want to ask you anything more at any time I'll pop over to your farm and see you. Very many thanks."

Curgenven saw them out and ushered in a second couple. He introduced this latter pair as Mr. and Mrs. Monckton. I saw Bathurst look at them with a strong degree of interest. It will be readily remembered that these people were the two who had booked to Raybourne on the night of the murder but who had subsequently travelled as far as Droskyn Corner only.

"Mr. and Mrs. Monckton are not residents of these parts, Mr. Bathurst," explained the inspector, after his introduction; "they come from the North of England and happen to be spending a holiday here. That's how they came to be in Whitehead's bus."

Monckton was a pleasant-looking man of about forty years of age. He wore a neatly trimmed, fair moustache, and a pair of kindly looking eyes shone through his spectacles. He was decently dressed, and held an umbrella in one hand and a bowler hat in the other. The hat appeared to be a new one, judging from the gloss on the felt, but the umbrella was shabby and had long since seen its best days. His wife seemed to be three or four years younger than he and was dressed very simply. Although her dress was extremely unostentatious, there was no suggestion of either dinginess or dowdiness about it. On the other hand it was extremely neat and tidy.

Bathurst came to the point at once. He did not trouble to interrogate them in any way concerning Sutcliffe's identity. Evidently he considered that any evidence they could give on this point would be comparatively valueless. His first question touched the possibility of any unknown passenger or person having gone on top unperceived by the majority of those travelling inside. But directly he had asked it, both Mr. and Mrs. Monckton shook their heads emphatically in denial. The man went further. He put his denial into words. "The only other person who ascended the stairs during my journey, sir, was the conductor, when he went upstairs for the fare. I'm certain of it."

"Were you seated in a good position to judge?"

"Facing the staircase, sir, and only two or three seats from the door—I couldn't have been in a better."

Bathurst considered for a moment. Then he went over and had a few words with Inspector Curgenven. By the expression "had a few words" I am not meaning what one of my parishioners meant when she described to me a private vendetta of hers with a neighbour. My phrase is to be taken absolutely literally. When Bathurst returned he approached Mr. and Mrs. Monckton with something like a smile playing round his lips.

"I have two questions to put to you now, Mr. Monckton, and I fear that each of them trespasses on the personal. But you must extend me your forgiveness for that, and remember that an unfortunate man has been murdered. Firstly, may I ask you why you alighted at Droskyn Corner, which is near Kirve, even though you had paid the fare to the terminus at Raybourne? I must confess that your action, as it has been represented to me, puzzles me."

Monckton cast a sidelong glance in the direction of his wife. But if he expected succour from that quarter there was none forthcoming. Mrs. Monckton was not journeying into Macedonia for him and intended that the explanation which Bathurst sought should come from her husband unaided. Monckton's hesitation, however, was but momentary. I will attempt to reproduce his reply in the exact words that he employed.

"Well, sir," he commenced, "it was like this. The wife and I are on holiday, as the inspector here just informed you. We only came down to Raybourne the Sunday before the murder, so you can readily guess that we aren't too familiar with the place and the surroundings. On the day of the murder we'd been over to Esting to spend the day, and a lovely day it was too. A real champion. Couldn't ha' picked a worse one. We went by train in the morning, mooched round Esting for an hour or so, got properly soaked, the wife got her best hat spoiled and didn't forget to tell me about it, neither, and eventually—about half past two—we turned into the pictures." He smiled. "To keep dry, not for the dark. We're married—not honeymooners. Well, we came out and then went and had a meat tea in a little Italian restaurant on the front. Not too bad, neither, for the money.

"At a quarter past eight, just as we were thinkin' of making tracks for the station to get on the 'rattler', the rain was coming down in fair torrents. Now, sir, if you know Esting at all, you'll know that the railway station lays right at the back of the town—quite a tidy stretch it is to walk. Right along the main street you have to go and then turn round by the Town Hall. We were just settin' out for it when my wife spotted a motor-bus—*the* motor-bus as it turned out. 'Let's get this,' she said. 'It'll be worth the extra money to miss that walk to the station in this downpour.' Well, we jumped in and I took the two tickets to the Raybourne terminus—the Tower Square. You see, I wasn't thinkin' particularly—our 'digs' were in Raybourne, and that's all I thought about. I forgot at the time that they were on the outskirts of Kirve.

"When we got to what they call Droskyn Corner, the missus and I recognized it as being quite close to the Kirve Public Offices or, in other words, only about ten minutes' walk from where we are lodging. So I beckoned to her and we hopped out there and then. I'm afraid it seems a bit silly like on our part not to have thought things out better—but there you are, it's the Gospel truth, and I can't give you anything better. Sister Aimée McPherson herself couldn't."

Monckton mopped his perspiring brow with his handkerchief, and I looked away to avoid Michael's not too diplomatic smile.

But, before I realized it almost, Bathurst was already putting his second question of the "personal" type that he had foreshadowed.

"Thank you, Mr. Monckton. You have explained it excellently. I understand very well—quite a reasonable procedure on your part in the circumstances. Now tell me, what induced you to take your holidays so late in the year? One would hardly describe November as an attractive fraction of the calendar!"

Monckton grinned ruefully and rubbed the corner of his nose with the back of his hand. "Induced!" he repeated ironically. "Induced isn't the word, sir, believe me I could think of dozens that would suit the position better. But beggars can't be choosers. I had no option in the matter."

"You mean—?" Bathurst's question remained incomplete, for the man wearing glasses broke in again immediately:

"Just this, sir. I went to a new job last February, sir. Up in Birkenhead. I'm a Londoner—lived in London all my life as you might say, but I touched lucky last February, and got a job in the electricity department of the Birkenhead Corporation— shift engineer, to tell you everything. When the holiday list came round my name was mud *and* Wimpole—I was something like Mother Hubbard's dog—I had to take what was left—what nobody else wanted. In other words, I clicked for the middle fortnight in November—to say nothing of a murder in a motor-bus. Some holiday, I'm thinking."

He made a self-pitying gesture towards his wife, indicative evidently of the plight in which he and she found themselves. I saw Curgenven write something in his notebook before he raised his eyes to meet Bathurst's. The latter nodded, and with a murmured "Thank you, gentlemen", Mr. and Mrs. Monckton returned to their lodgings near Droskyn Corner, on the outskirts of Kirve. Close on the heels of their departure a sergeant of police entered. I recognized him at once as a Sergeant Millington. His young sister had once been in service at the Rectory at Kirve St. Laudus, prior to her leaving for the States to marry an American. She was an excellent girl and I had fostered quite an affection for her—so much so that I was quite upset when she left. Millington touched his forehead to me before going over to speak to

Inspector Curgenven. The two of them spoke in low tones. Then Curgenven broke away from him and came across to Bathurst.

"The other passenger in the bus, Mr. Bathurst—the young girl who booked to Northlynn and got out at St. Philip's Church—cannot be definitely traced. There were three likely contingencies that we were following up, although we had no reply at all to the notices we sent out. Nobody at all came forward on their own. Two of the three that we ferreted out have failed, and the third—the one that Sergeant Millington considered as the likeliest to bear fruit—has broken down in a rather sensational manner. I am sorry to tell you that we have just heard that the young girl in question, a Miss Lucy Somerville, of St. Philip's Terrace, Northlynn, has committed suicide."

CHAPTER XV
BATHURST PLAYS THE CORPSE
(From the Rector's MSS. Continued.)

BATHURST looked up at the news with undisguised interest. "When?"

"This morning, sir," replied the sergeant.

"How?" Bathurst followed up.

"Poison." Millington was laconic.

"Which—do you know?" Bathurst became more insistent.

"Lysol—getting quite popular with women down this quarter. This is the fifth since February. This girl drank a rare mouthful. Never saw a mouth burned worse."

"What was behind it, Sergeant—superficially, that is?"

"The usual, sir. The love business. Bet your life on that. It's always the same down this way. We haven't had over long to make inquiries, as you may guess, but there's a fellow mixed up in this case from Raybourne, so I understand. There was the usual tiff over another girl, and Lucy Somerville took it hard. Some do. People are different, you know, sir—we aren't all made alike. Some of us are easily consoled—others break their hearts."

Sergeant Millington shrugged his shoulders, whilst I cast my mind back to the philosophy of "The Miller of Hofbau". What Millington said was quite true. I always tell my flock that what we call "man" is only "male woman" and what we call "woman" is merely "female man". And it will always be the same, I suppose, as long as there are men and women. The hearts of some of us are on our sleeves, whilst with others they remain eternally inaccessible. Some of us worship one woman and one only; to others "one wench is as good as another". I saw Anthony Bathurst purse his lips.

"What put you on to this Miss Somerville, Inspector? Did information come from anybody?"

Curgenven shook his head. "Not what you would call directly. We went solely on the description of the girl in the bus. As a matter of fact, it was all we had to go on. Took Whitehead's and the farmer Jupp's. As a result of that we pushed a bill out, and two people from Northlynn came into the station here yesterday and informed us that the description of the girl we were seeking tallied very closely with this Lucy Somerville. Next thing Millington hears is that the girl's committed suicide. Of course," he concluded despondently, "we don't know yet for certain if it was the girl that we were after. All the same, it's damned funny."

"True," concurred Bathurst. "But I think we shall have to know as soon as possible. Get Jupp or somebody to go down to the mortuary or wherever the girl's body is and see what he says about it. Jupp would be the best, I think. He'd have observed her more closely than Whitehead. He travelled inside the bus with her for quite a period of time. I'd like to know about this girl as soon as possible." He rose and smiled across the room at Michael. "In the meantime, I'm going to try a little experiment. How long will it take you to get in touch with Whitehead and his driver—Sturgess, wasn't it?"

"I can 'phone the Company's offices, of course," returned Inspector Curgenven. "That won't take more than a minute or two. But I can't say how long it will take me to get the two men you want, can I? What's the idea?"

Bathurst turned first to me as he replied: "We will consecrate the plough. You, Rector, shall be Farmer Jupp." Then he turned to my boy. "You, Michael Parry-Probyn, shall be that worthy gentleman's good lady. The lilies of the field shall be considered. You, Inspector, with the sergeant here, shall enter the cast as Mr. and Mrs. Monckton, and for a super you can rope in another member of your Force as the young lady who got out at Northlynn, but don't let him have access to any Lysol. That just about completes us, I fancy—with Whitehead and Sturgess."

Curgenven stared. Then a light broke over his features.

"I can see what you're proposing to do, Mr. Bathurst. As a matter of fact, I had thought of it myself. You're going to—"

"What?" queried Bathurst.

"Repeat the journey from Esting to Raybourne as made by the bus on the night of the murder. That's what you mean to do, isn't it, Mr. Bathurst?"

"You've hit it, Inspector. You've got my idea exactly. When can you be ready, do you think?"

"As soon as I've fixed up with the Bus Company with regard to Whitehead and Sturgess. I don't anticipate any difficulty. But I'm still a little—I don't know how to put it." He paused and illustrated his problem "I'm not quite sure about one thing. What part are you going to play, Mr. Bathurst?"

"I," replied Bathurst lightly, "oh, I'm going to play the corpse. That is to say, from Esting to the scene of the murder. Cigarette, Curgenven?"

Chapter XVI
NEAR THE "BLUE BOAR"—NORTHLYNN

(From the Rector's MSS. Continued.)

IF THE inspector had stared in bewilderment before, to say that he stared now is to put it superlatively mildly. Possibly I approach an hendiadys if I say that his uniform swelled to the accompaniment of his indignation.

"The scene of the murder," he repeated alter Bathurst, with the vehemence of a certain species of incredulity; "what on earth are you talking about? Sutcliffe was murdered on the bus, as far as I know, somewhere on the journey—or as far as anybody else knows, come to that. Any other statement is just wild conjecture—or else an attempt at humour."

"Somehow I don't think it's either, Inspector," replied Bathurst, coolly and calmly. "Still, time will tell us, and then both you and I will be satisfied. To please you, however, I will discard my cloak of optimism for one of a more sober quality. You shall wear black, for I'll have a suit of sables." He smiled and threw a quick glance at me. "Let me express myself like this: I hope and expect that the journey we propose taking will help us considerably in the reading of the problem that has been set us. I'll lay a wager—and very confidently at that—that I shall be able to show you something. Are you fit, Rector?"

It was, if I remember correctly, exactly twenty-five minutes past three when Bathurst's Crossley landed Michael and me at The Plantation at Esting. Perhaps I had better explain that The Plantation is the place from where the Raybourne bus starts. Curgenven, Millington and a tall, raw-boned constable named Reid were already there waiting for us. As our car slowed down by the kerbside and I alighted with Michael, the inspector came towards us, and as he did so pointed a few yards up the road. I could see what he meant. There was a bus there waiting just on the corner of the next side-turning. Sturgess, the driver, was already in his place and had started the engine. When we walked up in a body Whitehead suddenly seemed to materialize to take his customary place on the conductor's platform. Bathurst went up and spoke to him, and I saw the conductor nod his head as though in understanding. Curgenven, Millington, the policeman—than whom I have never seen a more stolid specimen—Michael and I took our respective places within the vehicle under Bathurst's instructions. Whitehead arranged us in the exact manner of the passengers on the night of the murder.

"Now, sir," he said to Bathurst, "your place is on top."

To my surprise Bathurst refused the invitation. He shook his head and smiled, in fact.

"I am going to be Sutcliffe, Rector, all the way through. That means I'm getting on by the arch of the Lanning railway-bridge, just as he did. I'll be there waiting for you. I'm going on ahead in the car now. See you later." He entered the Crossley, waved his hand and was soon lost to our sight.

Curgenven gave Sturgess the signal to start immediately. I looked at my watch as we got under way. The time was now exactly thirty-three minutes past three, so that we were starting at the same time past the hour as the bus on the night of the murder. We ran for some distance in silence; that is to say as regards conversation. Millington and Curgenven held their watches in their hands—evidently bent on checking the detailed times of the run. The constable Reid watched them solemnly. When we reached the railway arch I could see Bathurst's Crossley drawn up by the side of the road. Bathurst himself was waiting under the shelter of the arch, just as Whitehead had told us Sutcliffe had done.

There was a man in Bathurst's car—a stranger to me, although I thought that I knew most of the people in the district. As Bathurst swung himself on to the conductor's platform and made his way up the stairs into Sutcliffe's seat, the big car followed on behind, the stranger driving it. Whitehead went up in Bathurst's wake, just as he had gone up behind the murdered man. A moment or two saw him down again, and the bus ploughed on again along the wet and muddy road towards the little town of Northlynn. I had, of course, done the journey upon innumerable occasions, and knew every twist and turn of the road. As we turned the comer by the Parish Church dedicated to St. Philip, I could not help observing how badly the old churchyard was in need of attention. But its fine sculptured plinth in Pentewan stone and the coupling together of its windows will always entitle it to unusual distinction.

While I was musing, the bus stopped. Reid, the constable who had accompanied Curgenven and Millington from Raybourne, alighted by the lychgate of the church. I remembered then whom he represented. From here the bus gathered speed and ran up the main street of Northlynn. The town itself has been described as the pick of the beauty-spots of Glebeshire, and if I may be allowed here to state that Glebeshire is universally acknowledged to be the most beautiful county in England, it follows therefore just as surely as day is followed by night that Northlynn must be the most beautiful part of England. The town itself is about a mile inside the Northlynn Estuary, within sight of the magnificent headland known to the world as Linner Head. The main street, in which we now were, turns, twists and winds—so much so that; in places, passing vehicles almost brush the arms and shoulders of the pedestrians on the side pavements. In fact more than once I have been struck on the forearm by the hastily opened door of a car that has stopped just in front of me.

There are a few houses intermingled with the many shops, and in the gardens of more than one of these I could see fuchsia, hydrangea and myrtle flourishing, although the month was November. No better testimonial can be given to the climate of Northlynn than the fact that the most tender exotics bloom there in the open air. Oranges, lemons and citrons reach perfection, the clianthus will be in full bloom by Saint Valentine's Day, or even at Candlemas, and snowdrops and crocuses have been known to flower as early as Christmas.

Eventually we turned and made for the "Blue Boar", or, rather, to be more precise, to the motor-bus stopping-place a few yards beyond that hostelry. As I had anticipated, we stopped. I was not quite sure what to do—and I think Michael was similarly placed—and neither Curgenven nor Millington, to judge by their immediate actions, seemed too sure of his ground or of the part he had to play. I expected Bathurst to come down from the top at once, but in this expectation I was disappointed. Just as Michael and I were making up our minds as to the course we should adopt, I heard a cry from the top deck. It came from Bathurst, and unless I was greatly mistaken there was a note of triumph in his voice. At any rate he was calling us upstairs, which was something definite at last. We went in a body, Curgenven leading. Michael's excitement communicated itself to me, and I found myself pushing forward as eagerly as in the old days when I played Soccer at Charterhouse and Oriel. I was amazed at what I saw, and I could see that all the others who were with me were just as astounded as I was.

The street here, just past the premises bearing the sign of the "Blue Boar", was as narrow as anywhere, and the bus had come to its ordinary halting-place just underneath the window-sill of a bedroom window. The window was the window of a room on top of an empty shop, and when I looked down at the shop, or better still, at what I could see of it, the thought flashed through my mind that I couldn't remember having noticed an empty shop hereabouts before. I mentioned this fact to Curgenven and the others a little later. The sill at which Anthony Bathurst was pointing was only about two feet above the side-rail of the bus.

"Look, Inspector!" he cried exultantly. "Look, gentlemen! Here—unless I'm very much mistaken, is one of the keys of our riddle. What do you think yourself, Curgenven?"

Curgenven nodded grimly.

"I think I see your drift, Mr. Bathurst, and I think also that I agree with you. A fog, the bus stops here as it was its habit to do, and Sutcliffe is murdered. A looped rope or something of that kind could easily be thrown and manipulated from that window. No need for us to look for the missing passenger. Neat—very neat. I congratulate you, Mr. Bathurst, and now I've done that we'll have a look round these premises, for there's no doubt we've struck the right nail on the head at last."

Anthony Bathurst regarded him quizzically, and I saw a light in his eyes that I hadn't seen before. He hesitated for a moment as though about to say something that Curgenven might be inclined to dispute. Then, evidently, he altered his mind. "Lead the way, Inspector," he announced gaily, "for we must certainly do as you suggest. Although I must admit that what interests me most at the moment is the nature of the shop itself! Have you noticed it, by any chance?"

My eyes followed the indication of his hand, and I saw Inspector Curgenven's eyes gleam with an intense eagerness.

On the front of the shop—in the usual place for such announcements—I could see an inscription: "James Chegwidden—Wet and Dried Fishmonger".

"Quite right, Rector," I heard Bathurst say, as he saw me read the words; "may I call your attention also to the card that still remains on the window? More to the point still, I fancy."

I looked, saw, and read again. "Fried Fish Nightly. Plaice, halibut, skate, haddock and huss."

"A shop where fish is *fried*, Inspector," continued Bathurst, twinkling-eyed and rubbing his hands. "Now what have you to say about that? Coincidence, or—?"

"Or what?" questioned Curgenven.

Bathurst suddenly became grave again. "Definite design. A very deep and baffling mystery," was his reply.

Chapter XVII
A PHOTOGRAPH OF TWO MEN
(From the Rector's MSS. Continued.)

THE INSPECTOR, keen on entrance, went at once to the door of the shop. He caught hold of the brass knob of the handle and attempted to turn it. I could see from the expression that flitted over his face that it refused to yield. The door was fastened—the shop was empty—shut up.

"I don't want to use force," said Curgenven, "unless it becomes absolutely necessary—neither do I want a crowd to collect. The latter especially. And that's what we'll find will happen unless I'm very—"

Bathurst smiled as he cut into his speech. "Somehow I don't associate crowds with the town of Northlynn, Inspector. Even its united population wouldn't be overwhelming. Look up the street now. How many people can you see?"

There were very few, as Bathurst had suggested, and I voiced the fact. However, Curgenven stuck to his point.

"That's all very well from your standpoint, Mr. Bathurst," he maintained; "all the same, I've a very good reason for saying what I did. And I'm going through next door. Wait for me outside here, and I'll let you in in a brace of shakes."

He turned on his heel quickly and went to the adjoining shop. It was a small hosier's, and the man who kept it was well known to me and had been established there for very many years. The rest of us cooled our heels on the pavement outside the shop that had once belonged to James Chegwidden, and waited for the coming of Curgenven. We hadn't very long to wait. Michael called me to the door.

"Come along. He's in, guv'nor," he said. "I can hear his footsteps at the back somewhere."

I put my ear to the door and listened—and heard what Michael had heard.

"He won't be long now," contributed Millington, "unless, of course, he had to—"

His sentence was cut short by the appearance in the shop of Curgenven himself. As he approached us he waved his hand in token of his success. It was the work of a moment for him to slip the bolt at the top of the door and pull the door open to us. We entered one by one, and as I did so the realization came home to me more vividly than ever before that I had plunged my feet deeply by now into an adventure such as does not come to everybody in his transitory life on earth. As we entered, Curgenven caught me unceremoniously by the arm. "Hist!" he whispered softly. "What the dickens is that? Can you hear?" His hand was elevated to enjoin silence. I listened intently. Then I heard a noise on the floor above where we were standing. There was no mistaking it. It was the sound of footsteps overhead. Somebody was walking about in the room directly on top of us. Michael clutched my other arm.

"We must look into this, Millington," cried Curgenven. "Come along with me—it's just possible that—"

The two policemen ran up the narrow flight of stairs that I could see in front of me a few yards away. Michael and I were quick to follow them; at least, Michael was, and I, in my generation, went behind him. At the head of the flight of stairs that we ascended was a room—the room with the window-sill that we had seen from the top of the bus. As Curgenven dashed towards it, the door of the room opened and I saw a tall and familiar figure framed in the doorway.

"Mr. Bathurst!" cried Curgenven in astonishment. "You in here already! How did you come to manage that?"

"It wasn't difficult, Inspector," Bathurst smiled back. "Quite the reverse! I got through the window, stepping on to the sill from the rail of the bus. I had an idea it could be done and, with the opportunity to try it, I tried it. It wasn't at all difficult for a moderately active man—believe me. Anyhow, come on in, gentlemen, all of you, and we'll have a look round." As he spoke he invited us to enter the room at the door of which he stood.

"It seems to me," he proceeded by way of further explanation, "that a good deal of useful information may be gained in here."

I should describe the room into which we came as ordinary. It was of the type commonly to be found directly over shop premises. It would have made an excellent living-room for a reasonable family, and the size of the table that was placed in the middle bore ample testimony to the size of the apartment. Of furniture there was but little. In addition to the table already mentioned, there were three chairs of the "bentwood" variety. They were chairs such as I have often seen in the kitchens of many of my parishioners. A broad band of elastic lay across one end of the table, which was covered by a strip of that ghastly commodity known in the trade, I believe, as American cloth. At the other end there were an enamel mug and a large earthenware plate containing a few crumbs of something. Drawn up at the side of the fireplace and close to it was an old horsehair sofa, the like of which I had not seen for many years.

Although the month was November the grate showed no signs of any recent fire. I cast my mind back, as I sit here writing, to that room as it was when I first saw it, and I think that I have been able to remember everything within it that may be fairly described as coming under the category of furniture. As I ranged myself with the others in the lee of the window, I heard an exclamation from Bathurst and saw him stoop suddenly below the table to pick up something from the floor. He tossed his find on to the table in full view of us all. Curgenven went swiftly forward and held it up for our inspection. It was a length of household clothes-line. As we gathered round it, Bathurst walked across to a cupboard to the left of the fireplace. I noticed that the button on the door was unfastened and the door itself ajar. He pulled it open.

"Not much here. Almost empty," I heard him mutter to himself, "but not quite."

I went and stood behind him. Michael came up on my right. Tiptoeing, I craned my neck over Bathurst's shoulder. The only article in the cupboard was an enamel jug. Bathurst lifted it from the shelf upon which it had been standing and looked carefully in it to see what it contained. "Milk"—he showed me—"about a teaspoonful, not more. Gone sour, too."

"The whole place is empty," declared Inspector Curgenven, "that's very evident—though I shouldn't say that it had been empty for very long—a week or so perhaps. However, I'll tell you what I do think. Whoever it was that was here cleared out in a hurry. Weren't expecting to go until the minute to do so arrived. I'm going to have a look round down below." He turned towards the sergeant. "Come along, Sergeant Millington."

"Do," responded Bathurst, "by all means. I'll join you later. Meanwhile, I'm going to do a bit more scouting round up here. I may be able to pick up something else."

Curgenven and Millington cleared out, and Michael and I were left in the room with Anthony Bathurst.

"Well, Rector," he addressed me, "this puts a somewhat different complexion on affairs, don't you think?"

Although I was by no means sure of his exact meaning, I intimated that I supposed that it did, and he went on:

"I've already seen evidence here that pleases me immensely. Certain half-theories that I had formed are becoming much less nebulous; there is so much here to support them and to assure me, almost, that I am at least on the right track, if nothing else."

Michael, much less diffident than I concerning the impetuosity of fools compared with the timorousness of angels, jumped gaily into the arena.

"What are they, Bathurst? Let me see if I can follow you."

"The piece of elastic, Parry-Probyn, the jug of milk, and—"

"The clothes-line," suggested Michael, with hopeful optimism.

Bathurst shook his head. "Its presence doesn't surprise me, but, to be fair, I can't say that I expected it. No. I referred more to the windowsill." He walked to the window again and pushed it up. I went and looked out. There was the bus directly underneath the sill, and I saw how easy it had been for an active man like Bathurst to enter the room as he had told us he had done. All the same, many things were mystifying me. Who were the people who had inhabited this room, and why had they murdered the man Sutcliffe? Bathurst was still prowling round, prying here, seeking there. He extended his long, lithe body along the floor and took out his magnifying-glass. After a moment or two he shook his head and rose to his feet again. The horsehair sofa next occupied his attention. He went all over it with the magnifying-glass, and a mark on the foot of it seemed to interest him considerably. But after careful investigation of it he seemed satisfied that it meant no more than the normal, for he left it and went over to the three wooden chairs which the room boasted. Picking them up in turn, he examined the legs of each under the magnifying-glass before replacing the chairs, one by one, in their original positions.

I heard him give an impatient exclamation before returning to the horsehair sofa. Upon this he lay at full length, just as he had done on the floor a few minutes previously. Pressing his nose into the portion of the sofa that I may describe as the head-rest, he sniffed at it hard, and then I saw him nod his head two or three times as though in corroboration of some idea that had suggested itself to him. Then he turned over and lay on his back. The attitude he adopted impressed me as being somewhat peculiar. I will let the adjective that I have employed stand, but perhaps "fantastic" is a better word for me to use to attain a more exact description. His arms crossed one another at the wrists, the wrists themselves being held so that they touched each other. He lay in this attitude for a few moments, his eyes closed and his brow thoughtfully furrowed. As he lay there I heard the step of Curgenven and Millington outside, ascending the staircase. The former came straight in to us.

"Nothing much of note down below, gentlemen," he announced rather solemnly. Catching sight of Bathurst on the sofa, his face changed. "Hallo, Mr. Bathurst; I didn't notice you were there at first. What's the game—having a siesta?"

For answer Bathurst swung himself adroitly into an ordinary sitting position, his head in his hands. I looked at him carefully, trying to fathom what was troubling him, for I was definitely certain that something was, and something of importance at that.

"What could the man have done? If it all happened as I fear it did, it's just possible that if he wanted to communicate with anybody he would have tried to do it by . . ." He spoke his thoughts aloud, but the last sentence embodying them remained unfinished. He toured the room again, Curgenven eying him with some amusement, I fancy, but Bathurst paid no heed to him, for his eyes were everywhere, and although they missed nothing that the room contained it seemed to be devoid of inspiration. Back he came to the horsehair sofa. There was the gleam in his eyes that I had noticed once or twice previously. He knelt upon the sofa and ran his eager fingers along the head of it.

"Looking for something, Mr. Bathurst?" inquired Curgenven. The man addressed smiled.

"In a way I am, Curgenven—but I don't know what it is, or even that it's here. It just might be—do you see?" He looked at the inspector. "That's why I'm of the opinion that what I'm doing is worth trying." The words had scarcely left his lips when the muscles of his face tightened. I craned forward to see exactly what he was doing. Michael at my side did likewise. Bathurst's fingertips were plucking at the space between the head and that part that I will call the bed of the sofa—where the two joined, as it were—and I saw him gradually pull out something that looked to me like a card of some kind.

"Hallo," he cried triumphantly, "what have we here? Bless my soul, Curgenven, but we're getting warmer and warmer. And the camera cannot lie!"

I shall never forget how we crowded round expectantly to inspect Bathurst's find. It was a photograph; something of the nature of a picture postcard in shape, style and size. The photograph was of two men; one of them was holding up an object that looked like a notice-board to my eye, and the other—in the foreground—was holding what suggested to me a weapon of sorts. On the board, which the man at the back was holding, was an inscription. It was easily readable, and its message was "The Lifting of the Ban". Each man was bare-headed and had been caught at a happy moment, for each was smiling. The man nearer to the camera was of good height and of good build. His companion was a little taller and, to my untutored mind in these matters, distinctly good-looking. He seemed, as far as one was able to judge from a photograph of this kind, to be about the same age as the other. On closer inspection, the thing that I had taken to be a weapon seemed to be more like a bird's body attached to a piece of rubber tubing. Across the bottom of the photograph was scrawled in an unscholarly hand, "The end of a perfect day. GeoDuck for ever".

Curgenven screwed his face up critically and looked at the picture very closely. He inclined his head this way and that, as though attempting to decide one way or the other a matter that was occasioning him some worry.

"Want any help, Inspector?" asked Anthony Bathurst softly.

Curgenven turned his head to the speaker.

"If you do, here it is." Bathurst took a pencil from his pocket and lightly and rapidly sketched a pair of horn-rimmed glasses round the eyes of the man holding the object that I had taken to be a weapon. On his head he sketched a broad-brimmed felt hat. "There you are, Inspector," he said, holding up the completed additions to the original; "our man, I fancy—Mr. Claude Sutcliffe. Recognize him, gentlemen?"

More than one of us that looked, gasped. I know this to be true, none better, for I heard the gasps distinctly.

"By Jove Mr. Bathurst," cried Curgenven, "you're dead right! That's Sutcliffe, sure enough. There isn't a doubt about it."

It was plain to all of us that it was so. Bathurst accepted the inspector's praise very quietly, although it was obvious that he was pleased at it.

"Thank you, Inspector," he said gravely. "What's your next move to be, then? Have you thought it out?"

"My next move?" echoed Curgenven. "My next move is to find this Mr. George Duck, whoever he is. And it shouldn't be difficult, working from this empty shop."

"Observe how the top of the photograph has been worn away, Inspector?" The question came from Mr. Bathurst.

"Let me look again, sir," returned Curgenven.

Chapter XVIII
LINKING UP
(From the Rector's MSS. Continued.)

On the evening of the day of our discoveries in the empty shop of the main street of Northlynn, I invited Anthony Bathurst to stop with us at the Rectory for a few days. But, *palmam qui meruit ferat*, and I will admit cheerfully that it was Michael who prompted me with the invitation. I was not so keen as he for more than one reason—although they may be difficult to explain. For one thing I was not sure that Bathurst would care about leaving his own cosy farmhouse—I happen to be very well aware, you see, of the standard of creature comfort to be obtained in one of our Glebeshire farmhouses—and for another I did not feel certain that Bathurst would desire to change his G.H.Q., if only from the standpoint of the continuation of his investigations. Into the other reasons that I had I will not delve at the moment, for in a way, perhaps, they were somewhat beside the point.

However, Bathurst very charmingly accepted the invitation that I proffered him, and the next morning at breakfast Michael considered that this suggestion of his received ample and satisfying reward. In fact, I have no doubt that he regarded it as having achieved instantaneous success. It came about like this: Bathurst had just helped himself to a goodly portion of a York ham that I had placed on the menu, when Emily brought in the morning papers. Owing to modern hustle we are able to get them nowadays about a quarter to ten, whereas in the old days we were distinctly lucky if we saw them by lunch-time. I nodded to Emily to give our guest his choice, for, without casting the slightest slur on Bathurst, I have always flattered myself that I realize the significance of the breakfast-table incident in *Mr. Perrin and Mr. Trail*. On this particular occasion I remember that I opened the *Morning Post* as Michael sampled his daily dose of "Beachcomber". Bathurst's discrimination exercised itself in favour of the *Telegraph*.

For a few moments, as may be expected, the conversation languished. It is, I am afraid, my bad habit to take large doses of my morning paper with my breakfast, and I can say without a single qualm of conscience that I like to see the bad habit reach the epidemic stage. Suddenly I heard an exclamation of surprise from behind the *Telegraph*. I cannot say that this was unusual, because I number many people in the circle of my acquaintance whom it affects similarly, but on this occasion the paper and its columns were the victims of my bad judgment, and I uttered a silent apology as soon as I discovered my mistake. Bathurst rose from his chair and came round to my side.

"Read this, Rector!" he said. It was easy to distinguish the excitement at work in his voice. "Tell me if anything about it strikes you as being highly interesting."

In some wonderment I read the paragraph that had aroused his attention. As far as I can remember at this interval, it ran as follows:

STRANGE DISAPPEARANCE OF AMERICAN
FRUIT FARMER

VISITOR TO LIVERPOOL VANISHES

IS IT FOUL PLAY?

These were the headlines that confronted my eye and I at once went on to read the text.

The Liverpool police have been requested to investigate the strange disappearance of an American visitor to that city by the name of Roland Trevor. Mr. Trevor is stated to have crossed on the S.S. *Gigantic*, which sailed from New York on the 2nd inst. He was accompanied on the voyage by a friend, Mr. James B. Mallinson. They travelled first-class and arrived at Liverpool on the 7th. On the evening of that day Mr. Trevor booked rooms for himself and Mr. Mallinson at Crosby's Commercial Hotel in Gulliver Street. On the following morning Mr. Trevor left the hotel, ostensibly on an errand of business, and nothing has been seen or heard of him since. Mr. Mallinson, after waiting some days in the hope that his friend would turn up, has placed the matter in the hands of the well-known solicitors. Savory, Son, and Savory, of Lordship Chambers, Lord Street, Liverpool. It is surmised that these gentlemen were, or had been at some time in the past, Mr. Trevor's legal advisers, for it is believed that the missing man was born in this country.

Our representative, who called on Mr. Bartholomew Savory yesterday afternoon at his offices in Lord Street, was informed by that gentleman that the rumours of Mr. Trevor's disappearance were substantially correct, and it was quite true that after a consultation with Mr. Mallinson and the missing gentleman's daughter he had placed the entire matter in the hands of the police. We understand that the lady mentioned is junior classical mistress at Freyne House School, Freyne, and is the well-known hockey player who recently represented the South against the North so successfully in the International Trial Match. Mr. Trevor, the missing man, was not on a pleasure trip to England. We are told on excellent authority that his presence here was dictated by urgent financial considerations and that further developments may be expected in the near future that may well prove to be highly sensational. His home in America is Effingham Farm, near Tacoma, where we believe he owned and worked an extremely prosperous fruit farm, in which activity he was assisted by his companion of the voyage across the Atlantic, Mr. James B. Mallinson. Up to the time of going to press we are not aware that the police have been able to make any movement towards a solution of Mr. Trevor's disappearance or discover any trace of his whereabouts. There is a persistent whisper, however, that foul play is strongly suspected.

I confess that I read the announcement with an interest that waned as I approached its conclusion, for Bathurst's meaning and intention were obscure to me. I think he saw that, for he took the paper from my hands and passed it over to Michael. I watched my son read it with no small amount of curiosity, and I will admit quite unashamedly that I was pleased to see that his appreciation of it was very much on the same lines as mine. Indeed, as he handed the paper back to Bathurst, he went a step further than even I had done. He showed his failure to understand its significance by a shake of his head.

'Well," asked our guest, smiling, "does nothing appeal to either of you gentlemen in connection with Mr. Roland Trevor's strange disappearance from a commercial hotel in the City of Liverpool?"

Michael pushed aside his plate with an impetuosity that rather surprised me.

"No. I don't see what you're driving at, Bathurst. I'm hanged if I do. I'll be quite open with you about it.

"But—there's one thing that seems to me to be very obvious," he blurted out in rapid continuation. "Our man Sutcliffe can't be this man Trevor—if that's what you're getting at; and I believe you are."

"Tell me why not, Michael," returned Bathurst gently; "and then I'll turn it over in my mind and see whether I agree with you. If your point is what I anticipate it will be, I don't know that you'll convince me. Still, carry on—let's have it. As a matter of fact you've said almost what I wanted you to say."

Michael regarded him with some amazement, and I think that he allowed the tone and gist of Bathurst's answer to disturb his usual serenity.

"Well," he urged—it must be conceded rather hesitant-ly—"it's an impossibility for Trevor to be Sutcliffe, isn't it? Look at it for yourself. I understand very well that Sutcliffe's people have never come forward to identify him, and that if it hadn't been for Mrs. Nuckey, the landlady, he would in all probability have still been unidentified—but, hang it all, according to the account in the paper, this man Trevor was in the States when Sutcliffe first turned up in these parts. Sutcliffe, as we know from Whitehead the bus conductor, Sturgess the driver, Jupp the farmer, all in support of Mrs. Nuckey's evidence, was knocking round about here for four or five weeks before the murder. Mrs. Nuckey gives the sixteenth of October as the date of Sutcliffe's arrival to stay with her, and she can tell us that, with the exception of one night, he was always—"

Bathurst leant forward and interrupted him.

"What you say is only too true," he said, almost musingly, "and I frankly admit that I may yet be forced to find satisfactory explanations for its disposal. All the same, and despite all that you've so logically said, I refuse to dismiss Mr. Roland Trevor." He carefully selected a cigarette from his case, and Michael and I followed his example. My son returned to the attack immediately.

"Tell us *why*! For it's obvious that you've been able to read more into this disappearance story—or, rather, out of it—than either my father or I have. And for the life of me I can't see what it is. I'm waiting, Bathurst," he concluded challengingly.

Anthony Bathurst blew a ring of smoke from his cigarette. I could see that he was thinking hard. Michael spoke again, and there was a tinge of mischief in his voice.

"Still waiting, Bathurst—and wondering at the same time."

"You want to know why I refuse to dismiss Roland Trevor from the case into which we three have been drawn? Well, that's a very fair challenge. I should be the last to deny that.

But I'm going to ask you to give your fullest consideration to three points."

"That's the stuff! I shall be only too pleased And they are?"

"Well, I'll take them in the order in which they have presented themselves to us. Firstly—what does the city of Roland Trevor's disappearance suggest to you? Anything—or nothing?"

"Liverpool," interposed Michael queryingly; "it's a seaport, if that's that you mean. But I don't see that—"

"I won't contradict you, Michael, but I'm afraid that you don't follow me—yet. Cast your mind back to a piece of our previous evidence. Evidence in connection with Claude Sutcliffe. Think!"

Michael wrinkled his brows before shaking his head. "Help me. Whose evidence? Whitehead's or—?"

"I'll help you with pleasure. Mrs. Nuckey's."

In a flash there came to me what he meant, but I have learned to triumph without inordinate exultation.

"I think, Bathurst, that I know to what you refer," I said quietly.

"Let's have it, then, Rector."

I told him. "Mrs. Nuckey informed us that Sutcliffe received a postcard some days before he was murdered. I will try to remember all that she told us in connection with that postcard. I believe it is the first duty of a detective to treasure detail, in all that he sees and hears, and not to be content with anything like vague impressions. She told us that it was a plain postcard and the message it carried had no signature attached to it. Nor were there initials, even, on it. The message was one of two letters: 'O.K.' And the postcard was postmarked 'Poole'. Your suggestion, Bathurst, is that it *was something that ended in 'Pool'* and may have been conceivably 'Liverpool'. Am I right?"

Bathurst walked across and playfully clapped me on the shoulder.

"Excellent, Rector, excellent. The battle is not always to youth, or the race to the feet of the young man. You have followed my train of reasoning flawlessly and exactly." Michael looked at him ruefully as he went on: "I admit that I've proved nothing from it or even established anything. Let me say merely as a first step that—arising from the matter of the postcard—I find the City of Liverpool possessing a certain amount of attractiveness for me. We'll leave it at that, and I will proceed to my second point. Although the fact itself implicates this man Trevor in no way at all, what is your explanation of what I will call the two fish-shops: Chegwidden's and Mrs. Nuckey's? The murderer used that room over the shop at Northlynn; I haven't the vestige of a doubt about it. And Sutcliffe walked into a similar shop at Verrinder and asked for a room there. *Asked for it—mind you!* Because he liked the view! Tut-tut! There was something else he liked and something else he wanted besides the panorama of Glebeshire scenery that he could see from his window. Now then, coming to our third point—inside the Northlynn shop, in the mysteriously deserted room with its easy access to the top of the motor-bus at rest outside—we find what?" He paused, and the points of light danced in his grey eyes.

"Several things," Michael took upon himself to answer.

"Mention one that impresses you as being of paramount importance."

"The clothes-line."

Bathurst turned to me. "Your turn, Rector. You're one up, you know."

I chanced my arm on this occasion. I had to. It was one of my lucky days, for again I scored. "The photograph."

The grey eyes that regarded me took on a keener interest. "Good! Go on, what about it? I want to know if you noticed what I did."

But here not only my powers of observation but also my native ingenuity failed me. "I noticed that one man was holding what I should describe as a weapon of some kind," I ventured.

"You're wide of the mark there, Rector, and also wide of the particular mark which I'm holding up to you. What I meant was this: where on the face of the earth was the photograph taken? Did you happen to notice that when you looked at it?"

I shook my head blankly, and I also saw from the corner of my eye that no help could be expected from Michael.

"I didn't notice any name of the photographer on it, if that's what you mean," I said at length. "It struck me as being a private photo, if you understand my meaning. I don't think, for instance, that it was taken at any studio."

Bathurst nodded agreement. "Neither do I. But although that is the case, even then I'm prepared to wager that I can tell you within a little where that photograph was taken. Especially when I remember what happened in July of this year."

"Tell me, then, Bathurst," I urged; "for I must admit that I haven't got to where you have. Where was the photograph taken?"

He threw away very deliberately the match that he had used to light his last cigarette. When his answer came it took my breath away, and I don't know that it left Michael in any better condition.

"I'm prepared to assert with confidence, my dear Rector, that that photograph we looked at yesterday, and which Inspector Curgenven now has in has possession, was taken either in, or very close to, Tacoma, U.S.A." He reached for the *Daily Telegraph* and prodded the Trevor column with his forefinger. "Tacoma," he repeated, "the home of the man who disappeared from Crosby's Hotel, Gulliver Street, in the City of Liverpool—Roland Trevor."

Chapter XIX

MR. BATHURST TESTS HIS THEORY

(From the Rector's MSS. Continued.)

"BUT HOW do you know the photograph was taken in Tacoma?" I asked.

Bathurst's eyes twinkled at the direct nature of my question. He parried it, however.

"I don't *know*, Rector. What I said was that I would assert so with confidence. That's a wee bit different, you know."

I returned to the attack. "That's true," I admitted, "and I'll take what you say at its exact face value. Why are you prepared to bank so thoroughly on the Tacoma connection with the photograph? You must have a very good reason for saying what you have done. What did you see in it that wasn't apparent to me?"

This time he definitely put me off. "Ah, Rector—for a short time at least you must allow me to keep my little secret. After all, if the men of the photograph excited your attention, it was only a natural occurrence, and I for one cannot blame you. All I will say is that what you called a weapon wasn't a weapon at all," he grinned, "although no doubt it had been very close to one. Have you such a thing as an *ABC* handy?" Michael got him ours. "I feel so strongly, Rector, about this strange disappearance of Roland Trevor, that I'm going to have a look into it personally. And the best place for me to do that will be in the before-mentioned City of Liverpool. There I can interview the missing man's daughter, his solicitors, and, best of all, I hope, this gentleman Mallinson, who has already filled two roles, it appears, in connection with Trevor—the role of farm-assistant and, after that, of companion-traveller. Who knows that he hasn't filled a third? I confess that I find Mr. James B. Mallinson a distinctly interesting personality. Then there is such a place as Crosby's Commercial Hotel. Let's find a train. I shan't go by car. I suppose I shall have to change at Polchester, shan't I?"

"You will," I returned. "Do you intend to go at once?"

"There's an eleven forty-four," he observed upon inspection of the time-table. "That will do me very nicely." He rose and flicked the knees of his trousers with his handkerchief. "Well, Rector, my stay with you hasn't been of very long duration, but I'm sure you understand. If I may, I'll trespass on your kindness again and come back."

"You will be very welcome."

"Many thanks, then—although I can't say to a day or so when it's likely to be. I'll leave it at this—expect me when you see me."

"Don't worry about that," I returned; "we'll be ready for you all right. Michael will accompany you to the station."

"Good! Tell him I'll be fit within a quarter of an hour."

Within half an hour he had not only left us, but Michael was back to the house again with the big Crossley. I am, of course, indebted to Bathurst himself for an account of what transpired upon his arrival in Lancashire. To use his own words—the words that he employed when he told me afterwards—he had to make up his mind quickly which of the three interests he should examine first. His decision was the same as I think mine would have been had I been confronted with a similar set of circumstances. The firm of Savory, Son, and Savory was a definite and tangible proposition, for he knew exactly where to find its offices. It was therefore to Lordship Chambers, Lord Street, that he betook himself first. The visiting-card that announced him bore a pencilled endorsement: "In the matter of Mr. Roland Trevor".

The youth that took it from him returned a great deal more swiftly than he had left him. "Mr. Savory will see you at once, sir. Will you please come this way?" Bathurst followed him for a comparatively short distance down a corridor, turned through a doorway, passed through what he took to be a general office for the staff of Savory, Son, and Savory, and was ushered into a spacious and handsomely furnished room. At a desk in the middle of the room sat an elderly man, florid-faced, broad-shoul-dered, and with greying hair. On the rug in front of the generous fire stood a younger man. He was fair, clean-shaven, and wore pince-nez. The youth who had conducted Bathurst from the inquiry office to where he now stood announced the caller, pulled the door to behind him, and made himself scarce.

"Come in," said the man seated at the desk.

"I rather fancy I have," replied Bathurst.

There was a brusqueness in the man's tone which was repeated in his second invitation. He frowned towards the visiting-card that he held between his fingers. "Take a seat, please—and kindly state your business. You will readily understand, of course, that in connection with Mr. Roland Trevor—about whom I understand you have come—I am only able to deal with *facts*. Do you represent the Press, may I ask?"

A fugitive smile flitted across the face of the man that he addressed.

"I am aware that I look far from my best in November," returned Bathurst, "but I had no idea that things were as bad as you suggest. I presume that lam speaking to the senior partner of Savory, Son, and Savory?"

"I am Bartholomew Savory, certainly. This gentleman is my son and sole partner, Mr. Hector Savory. And you—er—Mr. Bathurst?"

Bathurst pushed a letter across to him. Bartholomew Savory read it carefully, and a heavier frown than before settled on his brow. He called his son over. "Hector! Come here, please." Hector Savory read the letter without remark, and when he had done so a further silence fell upon the room. It was Bathurst who eventually broke it.

"That letter," he said gently, "must be my credentials."

For a moment or two neither of the Savorys replied. Then the elder man came to the point.

"That is as may be," he said. "The name of Sir Austin Kemble is, of course, well known to me. It would be idle for me to deny it. I fail to see, however, wherein his interest lies. That is to say, at the present juncture." He spoke slowly and quietly at first, but then his feelings became too strong for him. "My position in the matter is difficult—very difficult. It is hard to explain. The Liverpool police have instructed me to be the—er—acme of discretion. I am not versed in 'hush-hush', but I feel that the less I say will be the better. They have every hope, I believe, of clearing the whole matter up in a very few days from now."

Bathurst leant over towards him, his chin resting on his hands clasped over the handle of his stick. "And yet—whichever way we choose to look at it—Roland Trevor has disappeared, Mr. Savory. That is still true, is it not?"

Hector Savory broke into the conversation. "What do you mean by that, exactly, Mr. Bathurst?"

"Simply that Mr. Trevor has not been found. If he has not been found—he must be still lost. Nothing more than that, Mr. Savory."

"That's not to say he *won't* be found—men have been missing before today and turned up safe and sound. There have been dozens of cases." Hector spoke with decided emphasis.

"I will be perfectly candid," said Bathurst, "and no doubt you will extend a similar measure of frankness to me in return. Tell me this: why did Roland Trevor cross the Atlantic?"

Bartholomew Savory shook his head, and there was a strong hint of annoyance in his action. "Keep to the terms of your offer, if you please, sir. This question of yours is a complete reversal of that. Our frankness was to be in return for yours—whereas you start the ball rolling."

Bathurst shrugged his shoulders. "The 'quo' may follow the 'quid', surely, without an injustice being done to either. Still, I accept your conditions. I will tell you frankly why I have come to you, or, rather, the principal reason that has compelled me. I have reason to believe that Roland Trevor is in some mysterious way mixed up with a tragedy that has recently occurred in the south of England, in the county of Glebeshire, to be precise."

At Bathurst's statement the colour ebbed from the elder Savory's cheeks. There was no doubt that the news was by way of a shock to him. Hector Savory stood bolt upright in undisguised amazement.

"Explain yourself, please"—this from Bartholomew.

Bathurst took it upon himself to do so. "Do you read the papers, Mr. Savory?"

"Parts of them—I don't pay much attention to the sensational columns. I certainly haven't run across the case you mention. Give me the particulars, Mr. Bathurst."

Bathurst told the story of Sutcliffe's murder in bare outline.

"I've read some of it," put in Hector from his position on the hearthrug, "just the details—no more. Struck me as a remarkable case."

"It *is*, Mr. Savory. Very remarkable. In fact I—"

He was interrupted by the elder Savory. "But what I signally fail to understand, Mr. Bathurst, is your reason for connecting *Trevor* with this case. So far you haven't given me the least idea in that direction. What on earth caused you to make the statement that you did just now?"

Bathurst looked thoughtful. "Well—that's hard to say, perhaps. This man Sutcliffe had no friends. In fact, only his landlady has identified him up to the moment. When I heard that Trevor had disappeared so strangely and so suddenly up here I made up my mind to make inquiries. And there are one or two questions that I feel that I must ask you."

"Half a minute," intervened Hector; "refresh my memory on that Glebeshire motor-bus murder case, will you, Mr. Bathurst? One or two of its main points are beginning to come back to me. Hadn't this man Sutcliffe been living down in whatever place it was for some weeks? Am I wrong, or—?"

Bathurst shook his head. "No—you are quite right, Mr. Savory. That *is* so." He eyed his questioner shrewdly. "At least—the evidence that has been so far collected is to that effect."

"Well, then, sir," replied Hector Savory, somewhat contemptuously, "that fact alone disposes very summarily of our man Roland Trevor being mixed up in the affair. For Trevor was in America at the time. He didn't land in England here until the seventh of this month. That's plain enough, isn't it?" He wiped the glass of his pince-nez with his handkerchief, and the father with a movement of the head showed signs of corroborating the son's statement.

"It would seem so," said Bathurst softly, "and yet . . ." He paused.

"And yet what, sir?" demanded Bartholomew with a frown.

"And yet I am not satisfied."

"I think the time has come for you to be very frank, Mr. Bathurst. What is it that you are keeping up your sleeve?" Savory toyed with a paper-knife that he took from his desk and sat waiting for his visitor to continue.

"I will try to fall in with your wishes, Mr. Savory. Firstly, have you ever seen Roland Trevor?"

The question was weighed thoroughly before Bartholomew Savory answered it. "I have, Mr. Bathurst."

"Often?"

"Several times."

"So that you would know him at once?"

Savory furrowed his brows. "Hardly, but there are good reasons for that. It is, I think, over twenty three years since I set eyes on him."

Bathurst nodded. "I see. That, of course, makes an immense difference. To a certain extent I was prepared for something of the kind."

But Bartholomew Savory would have no more of it. "My dear sir," he almost expostulated, "I can give you no more information unless you come forward with what you know. You're far too one-sided for my liking. I must insist that you put all your cards on the table without any further waste of time." Bathurst raised a hand in protest. "I am afraid, Mr. Savory, that the strength of the hand that I hold is nothing like what you imagine it to be. In fact, I think it contains but one trump." He turned easily to find Hector watching him intently. "My picture cards, too, are few," he went on; "really, it would be better for me to speak of them—or, rather, 'it'—in the singular. Let us say, then, one trump—and one only."

"Let's have it, then, Mr. Bathurst—for I confess I'm completely puzzled." Hector became animated.

"Tacoma," murmured Anthony Bathurst, his chin on his fingers. "Tacoma—just that and nothing more."

The two Savorys became all attention, and Bathurst saw that he had at last succeeded in making an impression. He heard the elder Savory's words come clearly and crisply.

"Explain yourself as fully as possible, Mr. Bathurst. It is true that Roland Trevor came from Tacoma. How does Tacoma touch the other matter?"

Bartholomew looked a different man since Anthony Bathurst had played his card. The latter spoke very quietly.

"The Glebeshire police hold certain evidence definitely associating Tacoma with the motor-bus murder. Like you, I have been warned by them to be the last word as regards discretion. You will as readily understand the necessity for that in my case as in your own, but I think I may go as far as to say this: it looks very much at the moment that either the murdered man or the murderer links up with Tacoma. One of the two. We will leave it at that."

"What *is* the link?" snapped Hector.

"I appreciate your question, but you will forgive me, Mr. Savory, when I say that I am pledged to silence also as to the actual nature of this—er—link. Take it from me that this link is in existence and that the Raybourne police are in possession of it." Hector paced the room, and Bartholomew rose from his seat and joined him. For a moment or two neither spoke a word. Then Bartholomew Savory took up the running again.

"Mr. Bathurst," he argued, "while I admit that this Tacoma attachment is—er—extraordinary, and, of course, must necessarily be—er—investigated, after all it may mean nothing. The whole thing may very well be nothing more or less than a coincidence. They do happen, you know. It's a small world, and more than one person may have left Tacoma recently for the shores of the Old Country. You see my point, don't you?"

"Undoubtedly. What you say may be perfectly true. Only careful investigation will clear the air. Hence my visit to you." Bathurst stopped to consider the situation. "I will repeat a previous question, then, Mr. Savory. Why did Roland Trevor cross the Atlantic?"

Hector came forward as though about to speak, but with uplifted hand and with a look of extreme annoyance on his face, his father checked him.

"Mr. Bathurst," he said pompously, turning to Anthony, "I regret to repeat myself, but I am not prepared to give you that information. I repeat to you that, while the problem of Trevor's disappearance is being investigated by the police of this city, I am keeping my own counsel. I have been advised and even instructed to do so. I see no reasons to—er—disregard those instructions." He bowed stiffly in extenuation of the course that he had outlined.

"Very well, Mr. Savory," said Bathurst, rising from his chair, "you must, of course, please yourself, for you naturally know your own business best." He picked up his hat. "There is nothing to prevent me approaching the police myself, for that matter. I have no doubt they would find my story interesting."

"Nothing whatever," asserted Bartholomew almost cheerfully; "as you said yourself just now, you know your own business best. Each of us does."

"There are also two other avenues," went on Bathurst consideringly, "that I may be forced to explore—unless, of course, I'm satisfied beforehand that the theory which I have taken some pains to build up is toppling down. Then I shall abandon it and find another. But not before. That is the lesson of history, Mr. Savory. When we find that—"

The telephone bell on Savory's desk rang sharply and insistently. "Pardon me a moment, Mr. Bathurst," said Bartholomew. He walked to the desk and picked up the receiver. "I'm engaged now," Bathurst heard him say; "yes, yes, so is Mr. Hector . . . What? No—not for very long. I'm sorry, but he can't . . . it's impossible. Ask him to wait . . . Oh yes, I understand why you rang through—that's all right. Tell him I'll ring through to you as soon as I'm disengaged. By the way, Durrant, don't leave him in the general office—take him into Mr. Nixon's private room. Ask Mr. Nixon to entertain him till I'm ready to see him, and tell Miss Briston to hold herself in readiness." Bartholomew put down the receiver. "You were saying, Mr. Bathurst . . . ?" Bathurst bowed to him. "I really forget. Goodbye, Mr. Savory. I realize your position better than you think I do, perhaps. On the whole you have been very kind and helped me considerably. Very many thanks, and good-bye to you, too, sir." He bowed to the two men again in turn, and made his way out. On the pavement outside he hesitated for a moment before turning back whence he had come. After glancing at his wrist-watch he retraced his steps into the office again and towards the Savorys' private room. Knocking on the panel of the door, he entered quickly.

"You will pardon me," he explained, "for my carelessness, but I find that I have left a silver match-box on your table. Ah—here it is! I should have hated to have lost it. It was a Christmas present from a favourite aunt of mine. Good morning, gentlemen."

There was a man—a third man—seated in the room. His right arm was in a sling, and during the moment that he had stood there Bathurst had caught a glimpse of his face. What he saw astounded him! For the face was the face of one of the men in the photograph from the sofa in the empty shop in Northlynn. The *other* man—Sutcliffe's companion! Mr. Bathurst rubbed his hands with the utmost satisfaction.

"The end of a perfect day. GeoDuck for ever," he murmured reminiscently.

The hunt was up.

Chapter XX

THE USEFULNESS OF MALLINSON

(From the Rector's MSS. Continued.)

It was at least half an hour before Bathurst's patience was rewarded more tangibly. The man for whom he had waited so diligently came out of the offices of Messrs. Savory, Son, and Savory and turned quickly to the right. "When you want a good wife, M. de Marsac," quoted Bathurst, and followed him. Within a few strides he overtook his quarry. As he passed him, Bathurst turned sharply and took a good look at him. There was no doubt about it—it was the man who had been photographed with Sutcliffe right enough. For a moment or so Bathurst was undecided as to which was likely to be the best course to adopt. He quickly made up his mind. Slowing down, he allowed the man to come abreast of him. This accomplished, he stopped and suddenly accosted the other.

"Pardon me, sir," he opened; "but am I right in assuming that you are interested in the disappearance of Mr. Roland Trevor?"

The man hesitated, and Bathurst was quick to see a look of something akin to fear come into his eyes. If it were not fear he assessed it was something perilously like it. However, the man recovered himself and seemed to square his shoulders, as it were, as though determined to face whatever might be coming to him.

He stopped in his tracks and faced Bathurst resolutely, and the latter became instantly aware of the attractiveness of his face.

"You have the advantage of me, sir," he said. "I guess that you've—"

"In one respect, perhaps," interposed Bathurst; "in other respects, however, I should say that the boot is on the other foot. But give my first question proper consideration, and we'll discuss the matter." The man eyed him shrewdly and then evidently came to a decision. Dropping his voice to what was almost a whisper, he gave Bathurst a half-answer to his question. "What if I am? At all events, I have a right to be."

"I won't contest the point," returned Bathurst cheerfully, "because it gives us a common basis of companionship. Where can we talk?"

The man shook his head. "Who are you, and whom do you represent? I have particular reasons to exercise care; especially at the present moment."

"Come in here," urged Bathurst, "and in the privacy of a corner of the saloon-bar I will endeavour to explain myself. I will make no attempt to 'hocus' your drink, I promise you, and I give you my word of honour that I will pass on to you information that will interest you tremendously."

The man looked him up and down and then allowed himself to be persuaded by Bathurst's eloquence. The two of them entered the hostelry that Bathurst had indicated. He gave an order and seated himself with his companion at an unoccupied table in the corner.

"I approached you," he continued, "for the very good reason that I am convinced that you and I are in a position to help each other. Going a step further, you may even prove to be the only man in the country who can help me. I may occupy a like position towards you. My name is Anthony Bathurst."

"Representing?" queried the man dryly. Bathurst hesitated before replying. "Let us say—Law and Order."

"The police—do you mean?"

"I have no official connection with that body—but all the same—"

"You work with them?"

"Let me rather put it like this. I can be the personification of discretion, and if I ever feel that circumstances or conditions call for an excess of—"

"Tact?" suggested his companion.

"How do you define that?" countered Bathurst.

The man shrugged his shoulders. "*Savoir faire*—that kind of appeals to me to be as good a definition as any. How do you?"

"I would go just a little further than that. I would call it something like a sixth sense, which at the same time is the life of the other five." Bathurst warmed to his subject. "It translates the open eye, the quick ear, the discriminating taste, the keen smell, and the sensitive touch. If I may say so, the undiscerning are apt to confuse it with what is after all mere opportunism. That is certainly the modern temptation."

"I think I follow you," said the recipient of Bathurst's opinions; "and I guess you've got something more to say to me than this. I guess, too, that I'll take you at face value. Spill it, then. What's the colour of your information that's going to tickle my ear-drums so irresistibly?"

Bathurst leant forward over the table and told the story of the murder on the bus that plied between Esting and Raybourne. When he had finished, he thrust a rapid question at his companion. "A strange case—don't you think so, Mr. Mallinson?"

A look of surprise shot into the man's eyes. Bathurst told me afterwards that the chap looked so really and truly scared at the mention of the name that he followed it up with another question. "I am in order in addressing you by that name, am I not?"

Mallinson drew a sharp intake of breath as he yielded his position to the force of the assault.

"I suppose Mr. Savory must have—"

Bathurst declined the suggestion.

"Crosby's Hotel?" queried Mallinson.

"No—haven't been there yet. Going later."

"Miss Trevor, then?"

The third string was of no sterner stuff than the first and second.

"How, then—the police?"

Bathurst smiled. A fourth denial. He proceeded: "It is quite a simple matter, after all. I knew of a Mallinson's connection with the case from the newspaper reports. I had been fortunate also to have held your photograph in my hand very recently, and when I saw you with the Savorys—"

"My photograph?" cried Mallinson, leaping to his feet. "Explain yourself, Mr. Bathurst, please. Where the hell could you have . . . ?" His face was ashen—white and trembling with emotion.

Bathurst was amazed at the sudden transformation in the man. "Sit down, Mr. Mallinson, and I will endeavour to clear up your doubts. There's no occasion, I assure you, for your agitation."

He told the story of the finding of the Tacoma photograph.

"When I saw you in that room just now," he concluded, "I recognized you at once. And the other man in the photograph, with but slight alteration to his face, *was Sutcliffe* (or Trevor, shall we call him?) *the man who was murdered at Northlynn!*"

Mallinson trembled violently. "What do you mean, Mr. Bathurst? What do you mean by alterations to his face?"

"Oh—ordinary things. A hat on his head; his glasses on—"

Mallinson thumped the table. "Trevor never wore glasses. Besides—what you're trying to tell me is impossible—think of the time question."

"Waiving that for the time being," said Bathurst, "can you recall the particular photograph that I've described to you?"

There was just a semblance of hesitation in Mallinson's reply. "Yes—very well. It was taken away back in the summer. Say—it was real smart of you, Mr. Bathurst, with only that to work on, to freeze on to Tacoma."

Bathurst brushed aside the compliment with a wave of the hand.

"Now, Mr. Mallinson, it's my turn to ask for your information. Mr. Savory wouldn't give it to me when I asked him, and I don't know that I can in all fairness blame him. After all, he's a solicitor, and I quite understand that the interests of his clients must be protected. Integrity is a growth of years and, once it flourishes, must be carefully tended. Nobody understands that better than I. But I'm optimistic enough to hope for better fortune from you." He paused. Mallinson shifted his feet uneasily and adjusted the sling of his injured shoulder. Bathurst leant forward towards him and put a question with studied deliberation It was the question that he had put twice before to Bartholomew Savory. "Why did Roland Trevor cross the Atlantic, Mr. Mallinson?"

The man addressed rubbed his cheek with his left hand.

"Well, Mr. Mallinson?" murmured Anthony, with infinite persuasion.

Mallinson passed his unhampered fingers through his tawny hair as though in a quandary as to which way to turn. Then he burnt his boats and took his seat again.

"I've made up my mind that I'll tell you what I know, Mr. Bathurst—and all I hope is that I don't live to regret it."

Bathurst smiled grimly. "I'll join you in that hope, Mr. Mallinson. I'm all attention. Tell me first of the circumstances of the disappearance." Mallinson complied.

"Now retrace your steps."

"Trevor," went on Mallinson, "was in reality Roland Walsingham, the only son of Sir Joshua Walsingham. He had a row with the old man many years ago, and as a result of that cleared off to the States. Quarrelled over a girl, or something—I don't know the ins and outs of the case—and cut himself off from the old home entirely."

"One minute, Mr. Mallinson," said Bathurst. "Walsingham? Are you referring to the Lancashire shipowner who prospered exceedingly during the war?"

"The same man, Mr. Bathurst. He left my boss upwards of a quarter of a million, but I don't think he—Trevor, that is—knew anything about that till somewhere about July of this year. I guess it was some sort of sweet surprise for him."

"Why do you think that?"

Mallinson explained the matter as he had previously explained it to Eileen.

"Of course, you must realize that you enter the realm of conjecture there, Mr. Mallinson. You are simply basing your opinion on Trevor's manner when he returned from this journey or visit—or whatever it was. Remember, he told you nothing about his intended trip to England until the third week in October. A rather long interval, don't you think, to hold back news of such importance and—er—human interest?"

"Ask me another. You might figure it out to be so; but I can't tell, and remember, I'm just trying to tell you of my impressions. That's all they are."

"There's one thing," replied Bathurst somewhat offhandedly, but at the same time watching him closely; "we can check up a great deal of what you think by asking the Savorys. Trevor must have communicated with them regarding his journey to England."

"That's so," agreed Mallinson readily. "When I went with him down to Freyne to see Miss Eileen, the elder Mr. Savory explained all that to her."

"What did Trevor tell you in October—*exactly*?"

"That he wanted me to accompany him to England."

He made no mention to you then of Sir Joshua Walsingham, or the real reason that was bringing him over?"

Mallinson seemed uneasy but shook his head. "None whatever."

"When did he first tell you? To a day, if you can remember it."

"Not until the *Gigantic* got into Liverpool."

"Strange," meditated Bathurst. "Waiting months like that, and telling you at the very last moment. What prompted him to do that, do you think? Sort of eleventh-hour repentance?"

Mallinson shook his head.

"I think there was a reason why he let the cat jump then."

"What was that?"

"He had a warning letter when we arrived—when we got into Liverpool."

"Really? Now, this is most interesting." Bathurst leant forward eagerly. "Full details, Mr. Mallinson, if you please."

"That's the point where I slip up. I can't give you any. All I know is what Trevor himself told me." Mallinson paused and wrinkled his brows. "Let me think, now. He told me it was anonymous. . . . I can remember that . . . and contained a kind of warning. 'Warning' was the actual word he used. . . . yes . . . I'm dead sure of that." He paused again to reflect. "Then I asked him two or three what you would call natural questions to try to find out who had warned him or what it was he was being warned against . . . but he wouldn't tell me. Instead he told me of the Walsingham inheritance . . . who he was . . . why he'd come over to England." There was yet another pause. "He told me one other thing."

"What was that?" Bathurst's question came . . . rapid . . . insistent.

"That not another soul knew in the world. I was the only one he'd told."

Bathurst ordered a further supply of liquid refreshment, and for a moment or two neither man spoke. It was Anthony Bathurst who broke the silence.

"Tell me, Mr. Mallinson—that is, of course, if you can—when did Sir Joshua Walsingham die? Do you know? Did Trevor tell you that?"

"No—he didn't. And in the absence of any other knowledge I took it that the old man had rolled up quite recently. Anybody would have thought so from the way Trevor told me the story. But as it happens I *am* able to answer your question, but not from any information passed on to me by Trevor." He drained his glass, and Bathurst has told me since that he waited impatiently for the promised information. "Sir Joshua Walsingham passed out a matter of three years ago—April 1926. I heard Mr. Savory tell Miss Eileen when we went down to see her at the school."

"Why, then, was Trevor such a long time . . . ?"

"Shaking 'em down for the sugar?" Mallinson shrugged his broad shoulders again as he put the question. "I guess he knew nothing about that quarter of a million till that bright and sunny day in July I've told you about. That's my explanation of it all, and I can't find a better. If you can, I guess I'd like to hear it." He moved quickly, and evidently forgot for the moment his injured shoulder, for he winced with the sharp pain that his impetuosity cost him.

"What's the trouble?" queried Bathurst, nodding meaningly to the scarf that held the damaged limb.

"Shoulder," replied Mallinson laconically.

"What about it?"

"Strained."

"How did you come to do that?"

"Deck quoits," returned Mallinson. "When I think about that letter which Trevor got when we—"

Bathurst seemed to hear only the first portion of the man's answer. Ignoring the second sentence, he pursued the subject of the injured limb.

"If it's any good to you I'm pretty handy at first aid, Mallinson, and if it's only a question of a strain it's quite on the cards that I may be of some assistance. Is it the clavicle that's affected or the scapula? If it's a dislocation it's almost certain to be sub-coracoid. Sub-glenoid cases are rare, and sub-spinous very rare indeed. Let me have a look at it for you, will you?"

Mallinson shook his head decidedly. "Say, it's real kind of you to trouble, but there's no need. I've had advice, and it's going on quite all right. It's just an ordinary sort of sprain that will take time to mend, and I'm not worrying. But I thank you very much for the offer."

"Ship's doctor look at it?"

"Yes—although it wasn't really troublesome when I first did it. It seemed to get worse afterwards. Took two or three days to get real troublesome. These things are like that—I've noticed it before." He spoke coolly, and before he could realize his companion's intention Bathurst had moved forward to him quickly and shot out a hand. It caught Mallinson's forearm and held it for a space of a second.

"Hurt you if I do that?" he questioned.

"Like hell," said Mallinson, shrinking from the grip, and the beads of perspiration standing on his forehead; "seems to jar me all up the arm."

"Thought it would," returned the matter-of-fact Bathurst; "that shoulder of yours wants better attention than it's getting at present, and if you take my advice you'll see that it gets it. Don't monkey with it, Mallinson. It's a mug's game." He rose and changed the subject. "Eileen Trevor—where can I see her?"

Mallinson's colour came slowly back into his cheeks as he replied: "She's gone back to Freyne. Went back the day before yesterday, I rather fancy."

"Freyne?" echoed Bathurst. "She's at a school, isn't she?"

"Yes; it's in Sussex, so I'm told. My English geography is not too bright, I can tell you. Young Mr. Savory was my informant. They—he and his father—went down with me to see her when I first started the hunt for Trevor. She's a school-marm down there at a place called Freyne House."

"You're quite right, and I fancy I happen to know something of this Miss Eileen Trevor now that you've given me these additional details. Unless there are two girls on the staff there of the same name, the Press paragraph I read was right, and this girl's the well-known hockey player, well in the running for her International cap. Stout damsel."

A curious expression played momentarily on Mallinson's face before he shook his head. "Guess I know nothing of that sort of thing, although I did read something of the kind in the newspaper, too. I've never had much time for games and such like. Saw Babe Ruth once upon a time and was mighty disappointed. Think that's about the limit of my experience."

Bathurst looked at him fixedly. "I've a proposition to make to you, Mr. Mallinson. I want you to accompany me to Glebeshire. On our way down we will break the journey in town, go on to Freyne and pick up Miss Trevor. The idea that I've suggested to you may seem incredible and fantastic, but, anyhow, come and have a look for yourself at one or two things that I want to show you down there. What do you say?"

The man addressed perceptibly hesitated. "If you're thinking that your murdered man—Sutcliffe—is my boss Roland Trevor, you're bughouse, sir. Begging your pardon for being so explicit. Because it's impossible. All the same, if anything has happened to Trevor, I'd like to get the man who fixed it for him." His eyes gleamed with the earnestness of this spoken thought. "Yes, I reckon I'd like to get him—good and proper."

"If that's the case, Mr. Mallinson—if you're really sincere in saying that," put in Bathurst softly, "come with me to Northlynn and Raybourne, and one or two other places, and let me—"

Mallinson stuck out his jaw at the challenge. "What do you mean—if I'm sincere? I suppose you're thinking 'talk's easy', eh? I will come with you, mister, as soon as ever it's convenient to you, and I'll prove you're wrong."

"Perhaps," responded Bathurst; "and, on the other hand, perhaps not."

Chapter XXI
THE HOTEL IN GULLIVER STREET
(From the Rector's MSS. Continued.)

SOME TIME later, Anthony Bathurst, having seen Mr. Mallinson safely off certain premises described with a good deal of publicity as Crosby's Hotel, left his position of vantage on the opposite side of Gulliver Street and strode over to the hotel in question. The manner of his approach when he had entered immediately procured for him the presence of Mr. Crosby himself. Mr. Bathurst proceeded to explain himself and his errand with considerably more attention to detail.

Crosby nodded and, although obviously in a state of uneasiness, did his best to disguise the fact. He conducted his visitor into his private sitting-room.

"You know, of course, Mr. Bathurst," he opened, "that this matter of Mr. Trevor's disappearance is in the hands of the Liverpool police, and therefore anything that I—"

"No need to worry over that, Mr. Crosby," returned Anthony, "and when we get down to sheer facts you will find in all probability that I shall ask you no question that the Liverpool police haven't asked you already."

Crosby's reddish-brown eyes contracted a trifle, and he stuck out a rather determined jaw with a good show of resolution.

"I'd prefer that you didn't attempt to draw me, Mr.—er—let the issue be a straightforward one. As I said to you just now, I have passed certain information on to the police, and as a result of that—"

Bathurst intervened, and his smile helped to soften the interruption.

"Hear my questions first, Mr. Crosby, and judge me afterwards. You will then be able to see the truth of my previous remark to you."

Somewhat reluctantly the hotel proprietor consented.

"Very well, then. Get on with it."

"When did you last see the missing man—*yourself*?"

"On the morning of November eighth," he answered promptly, "in the coffee-room—about an hour after breakfast."

"Thank you. Now—about this other man Mallinson, who's left behind—did you notice him in the smoke-room during the evening of the eighth?"

"That sort of question is hard to answer—with any real certainty. Can't say as I did. Not now."

"He states that he waited for his employer in your smoke-room."

Crosby shrugged his shoulders. "Maybe he did. I can't remember now. I wasn't in the room much that evening; it's the night I see to my books. And the hotel's not too full. I told the police much the same thing."

"Did they seem satisfied?"

"Couldn't say; you're taking me out of my depth."

"I see. Now for another question. Mallinson states that he had a drink with you in this hotel that night—*last thing*. Is that statement true?"

"It is," replied Crosby sturdily.

"You can remember that?"

"Very well. We had two or three, if I remember right."

"What time would his expression 'last thing' signify?"

Crosby hesitated.

"Within a little. I don't want to pin you down to a matter of five minutes or so."

"Say half past twelve, then."

"As late as that?" queried Bathurst with some surprise.

"Mallinson was a guest staying on the hotel premises—I could supply him with drink after licensing hours—"

"Yes, I see that. That rather alters . . ." His face became very serious. "Mallinson, Mr. Crosby," he said with some softness, "has a strained shoulder. He carries his right arm in a sling. I'm curious to know if his arm was in that condition when he arrived here."

Crosby thought for some time before he answered. "There again I can't help you very much. I didn't see the two men on the evening of the seventh when they came here and booked their rooms. When I saw the missing man after breakfast on the eighth I can't recall Mallinson was with him." He paused and reflected. "No; I can't remember seeing him. But late that night, when I had that 'binder' with him, he certainly had the sling. Told me he had strained his shoulder or something on the voyage—playing deck quoits. Told me, too, that it hadn't troubled him much at first, but had grown painful afterwards."

"We can easily settle the question," put in Bathurst. "Send for the person whom they saw when they booked their rooms."

Crosby frowned. "Is it necessary—over so small a—"

Bathurst smiled sweetly. "Neither you nor I, Mr. Crosby, is in a position to measure accurately the value of *any* point—until we have all the information affecting it. Please send for your reception-clerk, and let me settle the matter."

Crosby, somewhat grudgingly, picked up the telephone receiver. "It's on the cards that the girl's not on duty at this minute. Anyhow, I'll see—if that will satisfy you." He spoke on the telephone. "Is Miss Harris there? Yes? Tell her to speak, will you? . . . Oh, Miss Harris, were you on duty in the reception office on the night when Mr. Trevor and Mr. Mallinson booked their rooms? You were? Leave somebody in charge then, will you, and come along to my office." He replaced the receiver. "The girl's coming up. You're in luck's way, for once."

A tap on Crosby's door heralded the entrance of Miss Harris. At a nod from her employer Bathurst smiled in her direction and asked his question.

"I wanted to ask you just one thing, Miss Harris." The girl turned a pair of bold, dark eyes on him and nodded engagingly. "When the two men Trevor and Mallinson booked their rooms here on the evening of November the seventh, can you tell me if Mallinson's arm was in a sling?"

Miss Harris shook her head immediately, and shook it, too, with undeniable emphasis.

"I can, sir. It was not."

"Certain?"

"Yes, sir. I am positive that I should have noticed it, if it had been. My job makes you quick at noticing things—if you know what I mean."

"Thank you, Miss Harris. That's all I wanted to know. Thank you, Mr. Crosby."

The girl turned to go out. But before she could reach the door, Bathurst called her back.

"Before you go, Miss Harris! When the rooms were booked, what was Mallinson's general attitude?"

"Attitude?"

"Yes. Let me explain myself to you more fully. Did he stand by and take no part, shall we say, in the conversation? Or did he make himself prominent—did he have a say in the matter? In other words—how did Trevor treat him?"

Miss Harris knitted her rather pretty brows.

"He had plenty to say, in my opinion! There was no hiding of his light under a bushel—by any manner of means. I'd vouch for that."

"Thank you again, Miss Harris," said Anthony Bathurst. "I think it will assist me considerably if I remember that."

The memory of the smile on Crosby's face remained with him for many days.

CHAPTER XXII
THE SECOND IDENTIFICATION
(From the Rector's MSS. Continued.)

BATHURST'S telegram (it was ruthlessly extravagant even for these days) had prepared me for whom we were to expect, and Michael and I met the party at Polchester with the primrose-wheeled Crossley. I thought it better to run them over to Raybourne in the car across country than to wait for the local connection on the side platform at Polchester and puff a steady way to Raybourne through the Linner Valley. Michael and I were on the main Polchester platform therefore when Bathurst and his party alighted from the Paddington express, and Michael at once caught him by the arm and told him what we had decided. I was glad that he showed signs of assent immediately.

Before the introductions had been performed I had, of course, been able to identify the various people whom Bathurst had brought down with him upon this strange errand to our countryside. The girl was a girl after my own heart, and let me say at once that Michael has always been said to have inherited both my tastes and my inclinations. Her laughing blue eyes, temporarily sobered by the reason that had served to bring her from Freyne to Polchester, quickly wrought havoc in the heart of more than one of us who were privileged to meet her then for the first time. The elder Savory was easily recognizable, and although his son Hector was approximately of an age with Mallinson, the "outdoor" man of the two speedily identified himself.

Bathurst introduced Michael and me all round, and we packed into the Crossley as comfortably as was possible. I noticed that Michael (the son of his father) arranged with Bathurst that he should continue to drive, and when I saw him escort Miss Trevor into the seat alongside of him I saw the *fons et origo* of the manoeuvre and chuckled to myself as I found myself fervently wishing that I were "x" years younger. I was seated between the two Savorys, and we, as a trio, faced Mallinson and Bathurst. I remember that I was agreeably surprised with Mallinson, while the two Savorys were just as I had expected them to be from the exercise that I had allowed my imagination. There was a healthy frankness about Mallinson's face that I found extremely attractive, and from the two North-country solicitors there emanated a cordiality and a polish that almost automatically put everybody at their ease.

"Mind your shoulder, Mallinson," said Bathurst, as the Crossley began to gather pace. "The roads round here, I have been told, are not exactly Class One, you know, whatever that may be. Unless, I believe, you happen to be in the neighbourhood of the local Mansion House."

Mallinson nodded understanding and settled himself firmly in his seat.

"Did Michael fix up for these gentlemen, Rector? Accommodation, I mean?" Bathurst asked of me.

"Yes; that's been attended to. He has booked rooms for them at the 'Four Flamingos'. It lies between the Rectory and Raybourne, and I can assure you they won't do better. Miss Trevor, if she will accept our hospitality, will come to the Rectory. It will be all the better for her presence. We shall be delighted."

"Good," returned Bathurst.

"Are we being driven straight to Raybourne now, Mr. Bathurst?" inquired Hector Savory.

"That's where Mr. Parry-Probyn's taking you, Mr. Savory. I want your help, you see, and I appreciate the kindness of your father and you in coming down here to give it to me. I'm well aware that time means money." He smiled in a sort of rueful reminiscence. "And when I consider the conditions of our parting after our first interview, my sense of gratitude increases."

Bartholomew laughed heartily at the aptness of the thrust, but quickly grew grave again. "We realized after you had gone that it was our duty to follow up anything that might lead us to Trevor—no matter how hopeless it might seem to be on the surface. He paused, and then proceeded: "Besides—it's our duty also to work with Mr. Mallinson here."

Something in his tone caught my attention, and I flung a quick glance in the direction of the man whom he had named. What did he mean exactly? Wasn't he too satisfied, I wondered, with Mallinson's bona-fides? Mallinson himself made a contribution that touched deeply upon what the elder Savory had just said.

"Guess it's up to every one of us to help all we know how. It's no good lettin' individual prejudices weigh in the matter at all—or even personal inclinations. If it's going to help—Peter the Hermit and Demosthenes have got to become as close as Bluepoints. And vice versa perhaps the very next day. That's how the job looks to me."

He pulled with care at the scarf that held his injured shoulder, and I spotted Bathurst cock his head at him somewhat critically—or so I thought. Mallinson seemed oblivious of Bathurst's scrutiny, and I noticed that he made a habit of glancing backwards over his right shoulder at the girl who was sitting next to Michael. Unless I were very much mistaken—and over these things, let me say, I am not only an intelligent observer but also an extremely discriminating judge—there was something of more than ordinary concern in his expression. There was something in it closely allied to admiration, and I registered the opinion that it wasn't altogether a bad thing that Michael's position and occupation prevented him from seeing what I had seen and which I continued to see. Certainly, things were promising well for the entry of more than one candidate to the courts of Love. The disused mines gave the elder Savory an amount of interest that he made no attempt to disguise, but Hector was frankly and openly critical of our scenery as the car made its way across country.

"Well, Rector," he said, turning to me with a smile that gilded the pill of criticism, "I must say that your countryside disappoints me—so far, that is. I've never set foot in your county before, although I've always wanted to, because, as you are probably aware, as far as we North-countrymen are concerned, it has a big reputation. As yet, however, I fail to see any justification for this."

His father took him to task, smilingly also.

"My dear boy," he urged, "wait. The Rector will be horrified at your barefaced treason. You don't want me to tell you that you don't judge a dinner by the *hors-d'oeuvre*. Hasten slowly. Wait till you're past the *entrée*, at least."

I waved my hand good-naturedly. I hope the adverb bears the stamp of truth, for I could see Bathurst was amused.

"If you stay with us any length of time, Mr. Savory," I said, with the best dignity that I could muster, "I have no doubt that you will revise your opinion. I have seen that happen with hundreds of people. You will be so entranced that you will erect a votive tablet to Glebeshire before you leave us. I am confident of it."

"Raybourne," said Bathurst, leaning forward to the window on his side, and pointing out into the distance at the town of the grey towers. "For the moment our destination."

Mallinson and the two solicitors looked ahead with some show of eagerness. Miss Trevor shared their interest, but there was a more definite shadow on her face now that the end of the journey was reached. The meaning of it was coming home to her with a greater significance and was being better assimilated.

Curgenven met us as soon as we arrived in the station yard. Bathurst had told me to instruct him as to the time of our arrival, and he at once drew him to one side for a short consultation. The inspector had news. "The girl in the bus *was* the girl who committed suicide. Jupp has identified her."

Bathurst listened and then asked a question. "Millington has them," I heard Curgenven answer. "Go and see Millington; tell him I sent you." Eventually he came forward to our group and I sorted the various people out for him, before following him to his room.

"As far as I can see, Mr. Savory," he said to Bartholomew, "although I've let him work on it, Mr. Bathurst's idea is on the verge of being absurd." He caught my eye and its occupant—displeasure—and immediately attempted to modify the adjective. "Or at any rate—something very much like that.

You can't get away from the fact that Sutcliffe had lodged in Verrinder—that's the village beyond Raybourne—for a matter of weeks. There may, perhaps, be a connection of some kind with your missing man Trevor—I won't deny the possibility of that—but beyond that I'm afraid . . ." He broke off and shook his head with all the pessimism at his command. And the pessimism of an inspector of police has always seemed to me to be comparable with the optimism of a sporting tipster—it's illimitable. The two Savorys expressed their approval of Curgenven's statement. Hector was particularly outspoken.

"Of course, Inspector," he said emphatically, "I am entirely in agreement with you. My father and I have insisted on the point that you have just made. It's elementary, after all, and we've told Bathurst so."

I went to Miss Trevor as she stood by Michael, and endeavoured to strike a note of cheerfulness, although I felt in my heart of hearts that the note would be proved to be, if not counterfeit, an evanescent one. While I was talking to her Mallinson joined us, and once again I saw the look of admiration flood into his eyes as he appraised the girl's looks and trim figure. A few remarks passed between us before the door of the room opened and Bathurst entered. Sergeant Millington followed on his heels. In his hands Bathurst carried various articles of clothing. He called to Mallinson, who left us and went across to him. I think everybody's mind sprang to attention.

"These clothes, Mallinson," we heard him say. "Can you identify them as belonging to Trevor?"

Mallinson went slowly forward, took the clothes from Bathurst's arms and held them up for his own inspection. The eyes of all of us were unsparing towards him. A look of something like relief passed over his face.

"I can tell you, sir," he said, "that as far as my knowledge goes this suit never belonged to the boss Trevor. I guess I know the wardrobe he brought with him across the Atlantic, and this suit wasn't part of that outfit. No, sir." He shook his head decisively. "It's English-made, you know," put in Bathurst. For a moment

Mallinson looked puzzled. Then his face cleared as Bathurst's meaning came home to him.

"You mean he might have had it made after he landed?"

Bathurst shook his head. "I don't, as it happens, but I expected you'd say that—and, of course, I admit it's a possibility. Still, the principal fact remains—you've never seen Trevor in these clothes?"

"Never," returned Mallinson; "never in my life." His certainty was unmistakable.

"Very well, then," proceeded Bathurst, "we'll leave it at that. Now have a look at this." He handed Mallinson a photograph. "That's the photograph taken here of Sutcliffe as he was found. Do you recognize it?"

There was no mistaking Mallinson's emotion now, although he screwed up his face as though seeking some point or feature that either was there and puzzled him or else that he found missing. At length he shook his head, though very slowly on this occasion.

"This isn't Trevor," he announced—but his previous emphasis and certain decision had vanished, and it was easy to see that his certainty, if not shaken, had been disturbed.

"Why not? Is it totally unlike him?"

"I wouldn't altogether say that, Mr. Bathurst. You see—I am puzzled. For one thing, Trevor never wore glasses."

Bathurst very quietly took a second photograph from the outstretched hand of Sergeant Millington.

"Now look at this, Mallinson," he urged softly, as he presented it to him. "Is this anything like Trevor?" As Mallinson took it I looked across and detected the wave of anxiety that surged up in the features of Eileen Trevor as she watched him. So much to her, evidently, meant this next answer of Mallinson's. It came at once. But the tones that delivered it were hoarse with emotion.

"This is Trevor," gasped Mallinson, "or, at any rate, Trevor's double. But how on earth he comes to be—"

"Thank you," intervened Bathurst quietly; "my theory then holds water after all." He walked to the window and plunged his hands deep into his pockets.

I watched him as he stood there—silently. Curgenven flung a glance of annoyance in his direction, and then turned to the two Savorys.

"Well, gentlemen," he asked, and there was an element of displeasure or even of asperity in his voice, "you've heard what this Mr. Mallinson says. Seems to me it's your turn now. What opinion can you give on the matter?"

The younger man shook his head in an expression of complete mystification, but his father found his tongue at length to answer Curgenven's question. He weighed his words carefully and spoke with the utmost deliberation.

"Since you've asked me, Inspector, I'll do my best to reply to you. I must, of course, accept Mr. Mallinson's statement as having been given to us in perfectly good faith. It's a certainty that he knew Trevor well. More than that—let it be noted—he is the only one amongst us here who knew him at all. Miss Trevor herself hasn't seen her father for very many years. I therefore accept Mr. Mallinson's identification as—er—true." He paused and considered his next sentence. "All the same, I share his amazement as to how Mr. Trevor comes to be down here posing as Sutcliffe while he's supposed to be on the *Gigantic* bound for England. I should like to hear Mr. Mallinson himself attempt to explain away my—er—difficulties. Then perhaps we shall find out that he has been mistaken after all."

Before Mallinson could reply Bathurst took a hand in the discussion.

"Let me express my sincere sympathy with you. Miss Trevor, on behalf of all of us." The girl nodded her acceptance—silent and dry-eyed. Bathurst then came back again to Mallinson.

"I, too, would like to hear your views," he said quietly—almost ominously, so it seemed to me—"perhaps an idea of yours might help to clear the air a little. Who knows?"

The man to whom the suggestion had been made chewed nervously at his upper lip. Then he shrugged his shoulders somewhat cavalierly.

"My dear sir," he said, "I'm just as much in the dark as all you gentlemen. I figure it out that there's some dark mystery here that it will take us a darned long time to get our hooks into; but take it from me, Trevor crossed on the *Gigantic* all right, and how he died here—God knows." His face was white with worry and anxiety.

Bartholomew Savory looked across at Bathurst, and his glance held a world of meaning. He translated it into words at once.

"Even so," he said, "we'll do our best to get at the facts, and I for one will leave no stone unturned to discover the truth."

"Thank you, Mr. Savory," interposed Eileen; "it helps me a lot to think that I have friends who will stand by me, because I need them now more than ever."

Savory turned and shook her by the hand, and I felt myself thrilling in response to the purpose that shone in his eyes.

Chapter XXIII
OLD ORLANDO
(From the Rector's MSS. Continued.)

IT WAS NOT until after breakfast the following morning that I had the opportunity to hear more. Actually it was Bathurst himself who came to me and gave me the information. I remember that I was writing at my desk when he came up behind me—almost silently.

"You'll pardon me, sir," he opened, "but I've been down to Raybourne this morning in the car, and I've taken the liberty of inviting Mr. Bartholomew and Mr. Hector Savory up here. I called at the 'Four Flamingos' on my way back and gave them the invitation in your name. They're coming up in half an hour's time. I want to ask them a question or two in Miss Trevor's presence. You don't mind, do you, Rector?"

I smiled. "Do as you like, my boy—my house, my son and I are separately and collectively at your disposal." I smiled again. "Poor things—all," I added, "but mine own."

"Thank you, Rector. It's extremely kind of you."

"Did you see Mallinson at the inn this morning?"
I asked. "Is he coming up here too?"

"He is not, sir," replied Bathurst; "for the very good reason that I shan't want him. Neither does the gentleman know that Mr. Savory and his son are coming up here to see Miss Trevor. As a matter of fact, Rector, I took particular pains this morning that Mr. Mallinson should know nothing of my visit or its purpose. Also, I have impressed on our visitors the necessity to keep silent about it."

I looked at him sharply. Before I could frame the question that had almost come to my lips, Bathurst rubbed his hands and then placed one of them on my shoulder.

"I regard Mallinson as a highly important factor in our problem, Rector. Indeed, I think I might almost describe him as the key to the situation, and I'm confident he hasn't told us all he knows. Don't ask me any more at the moment."

When the Savorys arrived they were accompanied by Inspector Curgenven. I made them all comfortable in my study.

"I've been following up one or two points," said the last-named, "since I saw you, and I first of all turned my attention to that shop at Northlynn. I thought if I concentrated on that I might be lucky enough to pick up something."

"Go on," urged Bathurst. "I'm interested. Any luck?"

Curgenven shook his head.

"Not much. Chegwidden's shop has been empty since about the first week in August. The man cleared out suddenly, so I'm informed, although everybody says business was pretty good. So good that his removal was in the nature of a surprise. The agents, Cave and Rattenbury, of Raybourne, who used to look after the property, report that the rooms above—two of them, there were—were reoccupied on October 9th."

"Yes," intervened Bathurst eagerly. "By whom?"

"By a Mr. Claude Sutcliffe," returned Curgenven gloomily. "They've described him to me—one of their clerks called on him, there's no doubt it's our Sutcliffe right enough—or Trevor, as I suppose I ought to call him."

"H'm," muttered Bathurst. "Doesn't get us very far, does it?"

"Half a minute. I got a specimen of Sutcliffe's handwriting. Brought it away with me, too." Curgenven's voice held satisfaction. "And I shouldn't call it the handwriting of an educated man."

"Why—is it so illegible?"

I chuckled at the aptness of the thrust, and the two Savorys laughed outright. The inspector held out a piece of paper for Bathurst's inspection. A touch of tolerant cynicism held the latter's mouth before he handed the slip over to me. I looked at the name—or, rather, at the signature that the paper contained. The "Claude Sutcliffe" at which I looked was certainly not in the hand of a scholar—but not, of course, on account of its illegibility. Rather was it crude and the letters angular, stiff and ill-formed. The man who had written it was not a master of his pen—unless, of course, the hand had been purposely disguised. Michael and Eileen Trevor came up and looked at it. As they did so the door opened and Mallinson entered. Bathurst frowned as the man explained his intrusion. Some of our conversation must have been overheard by him, for he took the paper and contributed a piece of interesting information—interesting to me, and so, I presume, to all of us. Bathurst however laughed it off as though it were commonplace and valueless.

"This isn't Trevor's fist," cried the American; "it's nothing like it!"

Eileen expressed agreement.

"Mr. Mallinson is right," she said quietly. "This is not my father's handwriting."

"It isn't the hand that either of you know, I agree, but you mustn't overlook the possibility of it having been disguised deliberately. Things are not always what they seem, you know."

"But why should my father disguise his handwriting, Mr. Bathurst? What reason could he have had for such a proceeding? It isn't as though he had anything to hide."

Bathurst looked her straight in the eyes before he replied, and the girl met his glance unflinchingly.

"I have every reason to believe, Miss Trevor, that your father never wrote it. Let us leave it at that for the time being. Mr. Savory," he said, turning to the elder solicitor, "we are told by Mr. Mallinson here that Trevor received a letter directly the *Gigantic* docked in Liverpool. As far as he can say, from what I will describe as second-hand knowledge, this communication was in the nature of a warning. Have you considered this fact at all in your own judgment of the case?"

"How—er—do you mean, Mr. Bathurst—exactly?"

"Well—if Trevor received it—from where did it come? Who sent it? There are two sides to a letter always, aren't there?"

Bartholomew inclined his benevolent old head. "Oh yes, I grasp your meaning. I have considered those points—but quite unsuccessfully. I must say that I'm completely in the dark. The inquiries that the Liverpool police made led nowhere."

"You can suggest nothing?"

"Nothing. I wish I could. I've puzzled my head several times over the same matter. So has my son here, but it's all a dark mystery to each of us."

"I'll ask you something else, then, Mr. Savory. What is the secret factor in the Walsingham inheritance?" Bathurst's face was keenness itself.

A kindly smile played on the elder Savory's lips. "Now you've asked me a question that I've been anticipating. And it's one that I can answer without any hesitation and without any difficulty. There is nothing whatever with regard to the Walsingham inheritance, as you call it, that is secret, extraordinary, or even unusual. Roland Trevor, or Walsingham, as I will call him in this connection, was old Sir Joshua's heir, and the only thing that can be described as at all out of the common in the matter is the fact that Roland was so long in coming forward to claim his inheritance. As a rule thousands of pounds don't lie about very long before they're claimed, and the claim is usually a pretty loud one that everybody can hear." The smile lingered on his features. "Does that help you at all, Mr. Bathurst?"

Bathurst shrugged his shoulders non-committally. "My next move is to Verrinder," he announced. "This afternoon."

"Alone?" queried Mallinson, with every sign of eagerness. "Because, if not, I should esteem it a—"

His offer was waved to one side, but courteously and with no tinge of resentment.

"You stay here, Mallinson, and look after Miss Trevor." Bathurst's smile was a happy accompaniment to the suggestion, but I'm afraid that Michael's ears and eyes found small favour for either effort. "Tell her about Tacoma, Mallinson," went on Bathurst. "There are a hundred things, at least, in that direction, to interest her, and you can do it better than any of us. There's nothing like firsthand knowledge of anything." With eyes twinkling with mischief he turned to the younger Savory. "Would you care to accompany me to Verrinder, Mr. Savory? I must make some move on behalf of the Glebeshire 'scenery'!"

Hector laughingly acknowledged the hit. "Too bad of me, wasn't it, Mr. Bathurst? But you'll have to excuse me turning down your offer, much as I should like to accept it. Although my father and I have been able to come down here with you, business can't stand still, you know, and we had our hands pretty well full up when we came away. Our afternoon is well mapped out, I assure you."

"That is so, Mr. Bathurst," added Bartholomew Savory, in corroboration of his son's statement. "Hector and I were forced to bring work with us. We couldn't have come if we hadn't done so, I assure you. If you want either of us, we shall be in our room at the 'Four Flamingos' all the afternoon."

Bathurst nodded. "I forgot you weren't here on a holiday." As he spoke, Eileen Trevor, accompanied by Mallinson and Michael, made her exit—the plea being a visit to my tropical garden, with its Cambro plants and masses of South American rhubarb, which Michael had extolled to her. At once Bathurst took advantage of Mallinson's absence. "It's quite all right, Mr. Savory," he explained to Hector. "I didn't want you with me specially—I just didn't want Mallinson—that was all. Understand?"

Hector laughed easily. "I understood before—only too well. There's something fishy about that fellow—my father and I have both felt it."

The three people who had gone out passed in front of the window, and I saw how Mallinson's eyes were fixed on Eileen.

It was an unusual interest, to say the least of it. I found myself wondering at it, and as I did so a terrible thought entered my mind. I strove to put it away from me, but certain words that it sometimes fell to my province to repeat burned relentlessly into my brain:

"The words of his mouth were smoother than butter, but war was in his heart; his words were softer than oil, yet they were drawn swords."

Bathurst prowled round Verrinder for an hour or so before he made any definite move. Mrs. Nuckey's establishment, which he did not enter, afforded him a certain amount of interest but not, let it be understood, from the standpoint of the scenic view therefrom. Curgenven had informed him that he had been through Sutcliffe's rooms at Mrs. Nuckey's with a small-tooth comb, and for the time being Bathurst was content to accept that and to abide by Curgenven's report.

Verrinder was a small place, and on the afternoon in question nearly all its inhabitants were either at work or inside their houses. The village green, with its encirclement of white posts, was deserted—the green turf looking dark, untidy, and almost dirty in the November dullness. Bathurst stood on the outskirts of the green and looked across at it. As he looked he turned things over in his mind. At the edge of the green, hard by the sign of the Quarryman Inn, was a rustic seat upon which a rustic sat. Although the afternoon was dark and the sky overcast, the weather nevertheless was moderately mild for the time of the year, and the old man took the air with evident enjoyment and appreciation. "Very possibly the oldest inhabitant," thought Bathurst, as he slowly approached him. "There are several, I believe, in every village."

Arrived at the seat, he raised his hat and gave the old man "Good afternoon."

"Good afternoon, zurr," came the reply. "It be warmish for the time o' the year. November ain't the pick o' the basket for months by a long chalk."

Bathurst agreed and complimented the ancient upon the charm of the village. "Suppose you've lived here a long time?" he concluded hopefully.

"Ay, zurr. Born and bred here, I was, and my father before me. And I bear a rare old Glebe name—if you're interested to know—that of Menhittet. I'm Nathaniel Menhittet, which was my father's name, too."

Bathurst extended the conversation step by step until they touched on the motor-bus murder.

"Dead man was supposed to have lived here in Verrinder, wasn't he?" inquired Bathurst.

"Lodged," corrected old Nathaniel, "up along at Widow Nuckey's."

"Did you know him at all—had you run across him in Verrinder?"

"No, zurr, but there's nothin' surprisin' attachin' to that. I'm not one that gets abroad a rare lot. Nice warmish marnens and afternoons you'll mostly find me on this zeat, but beyond that I'm a home bird." Nathaniel emitted a senile chuckle. "And a total abstainer. I'm a Wesleyan, and proud of it. Liquor to me is the devil's lubricant—the zlippery zlope of moral decline. When John Wesley came down to this part of the . . ."

His companion nodded, and the nod seemed to break into the continuity of Nathaniel's speech, for he left this history of the Wesleyan revival and got back to the main theme. "There's an old veller, though, that I know well who knew this dead man Zutcliffe. Proper old weasel he be, and up to every move on the board. Quite a character in his way. Born and bred in Verrinder, ran away to zea and knocked about in furrin' parts a rare lot. Name of Orlando Horton. His mother was supposed to have had Spanish blood or zomething like, which accounts for his outlandish baptismal name." Nathaniel let out a hoarse guffaw. "He's no Wesleyan, old Orlando—yon's his nightly Bethel now he's zettled down in Verrinder again." The old man gestured towards the Quarryman Inn.

Bathurst smiled and thanked him for his company. "Get yourself some tobacco, Mr. Menhittet, and when you smoke it, think of the stranger who admired the village of Verrinder."

It was half past seven when Anthony Bathurst entered the "Quarryman". The landlord who bore the illustrious name of Treloar, recognizing his quality, invited him into the "private room on the right, zurr". But Bathurst shook his head; if the "Quarryman" held his quarry, as he dared to hope, it would certainly be in the bar-parlour that he would run him to earth. A judiciously placed query amongst the company gathered there, and Orlando Horton—"old Orlando"—was pointed out to him. Bathurst edged quietly towards him, and, a conversational opening presenting itself, was soon on good terms with the man in question.

Orlando Horton was of middle height, thin and wiry, with sharp features and closely cropped grizzled hair. His eyes were alert, after the manner of the fox, and darted from object to object with extraordinary rapidity. He responded gallantly to the continued projections of Bathurst's generosity. Under the influence of the Glebeshire light ales, bottled in Polchester, Blackbrook and Oxbourne, he approximated eloquence. Gradually, as he had done with Menhittet, the donor of the feast skilfully directed the conversation towards the death of Claude Sutcliffe.

"I knew the man, zurr," declared Orlando, in conscious triumph.

"Knew him?" queried Bathurst, with a show of surprise. "But I thought—"

Orlando wagged his head oracularly. "When I say I knew him I mean that I had met him. More than once, too."

"Where?" questioned Bathurst.

"In this very bar where we're a-zitting now." Orlando laughed satirically.

"Really?" queried Bathurst. "Was he a constant visitor here, then?"

"Hardly that, zurr, but he got into the habit of droppin' in here of an evenin'. Outside the 'Quarryman' there ain't much for a man to do in Verrinder. Not every night he came, but every now and then, as you might say. Kept himself very much to himself, and hardly spoke to a zoul."

"How was it you got him to break the ice, then, Mr. Horton?"

Old Orlando grinned wickedly at the reminiscence. "Well," he answered, with a kind of malicious apology, "a lot of nasty-minded people wot attend plazes of worship might have said that I forced my company on him. Perhaps I did—the virst time—but after that he was always quite pleased to see me and have a yarn with me. A rare one for a talk he was. Very generous gentleman as well—very much like yourself. Thank you, zurr, I don't mind if I do have another." He wiped his old, thin-lipped mouth with the back of his thin hand.

"What was his business down here—did he tell you?" There did not seem much concern in Bathurst's question.

"No, zurr. I put him down as a gentleman with plenty of cash having a bit of a holiday. We get 'em down in these parts, you know. There's a man and a dog been stopping at one varm for months."

"How long was Sutcliffe in Verrinder—to your own knowledge—not from what you've read in the papers?"

"Vour or vive weeks. I'm pretty zure on that. He dropped in here several times afore I struck up his acquaintance. I remember zeein' 'im."

"Been abroad a good deal, hadn't he?" Although Bathurst asked the question carelessly, he watched Orlando very keenly as the old man replied to it.

"Well, zurr, since you've asked me I doan't mind tellin' you that I'm a little puzzled over that point." The old man drained his tankard with such delicate insistence that Bathurst made immediate arrangements for replenishment. "I zee the reports have it that Widow Nuckey says her lodger had been in foreign parts. The paper I zaw didn't give details as to *where* he'd been, but if you want the opinion of old Orlando, Mr. Zutcliffe hadn't been very far vrom the shores of old England. I'd like to be as sure of a vive-pound note as I am of that." Orlando Horton wagged his head again and the action served to give him the appearance of a fox contemplating a well-nourished Buff Orpington.

"Why are you so sure?" asked Bathurst quietly.

"I'll tell you, zurr. I've been all over this little old world. Australia, Japan, Africa, New Zealand, Canada, the States, South America—there's hardly a place you could name that Orlando Horton hasn't hit up against. I've drank the beer and cuddled the wenches in half the cities of the globe. I was in Patagonia, for example, a matter of seven years. Mr. Zutcliffe—he knew naught of any one of 'em." Orlando smacked his lips, warmed to his text, and lived again in the memory of his triumphs of liquor and lass. "Why, zurr, I was talkin' to him one night, and—and—"

"And what?" questioned Anthony. The name Patagonia was full of interest for him. What was he going to hear now?

"Well, zurr—more than one of his remarks was the very last thing in ignorance, zurr, if you know what I mean. No—Mr. Zutcliffe hadn't travelled very var—take it vrom me."

"Did he seem afraid of anything, Mr. Horton?"

Orlando laughed.

"That's another vunny thing you've asked me. He didn't *zeem* to be afraid, if you caught him off his guard as it were. Never zeemed to show no fear." He paused and sank his voice to a lower tone. "And yet, zurr, he once told me that he had enemies—deadly enemies. Enemies who might zeek his life. People, he zaid, who never forgot when an injury was done to them. Doan't you think that's vunny?"

Bathurst caressed his cheek. "Who were these enemies? Where did they come from? Did he ever tell you that?"

"No, zurr. Never."

"They weren't from Patagonia, by any chance?"

Orlando Horton stared at his questioner with undisguised amazement, and the hand that held his tankard shook visibly. Then he laughed outright.

"Patagonia," he repeated. "Never on your life, zurr. That man was never in Patagonia in all his born days. What made you ask that?"

"Well—they must have come from somewhere, mustn't they? And Patagonia's as good a place as any."

Orlando Horton rose to his feet. "If you doan't mind, zurr," he murmured, "I think I'll be getting down along home." He pushed open the swinging door of the bar-parlour and departed.

Bathurst smiled whimsically at his retreating figure.

Chapter XXIV
MORE SCENTS THAN ONE
(From the Rector's MSS. Continued.)

He was destined, however, to hear more of Claude Sutcliffe (deceased) before many minutes had passed. Another occupant of the bar-parlour of the "Quarryman" arose from his seat in the corner, crossed the granite floor, and touched his cap to the "gentleman from London".

"Your pardon, zurr," he opened, in the same soft burr of the West Country, "but I couldn't help a-hearin' a part of your conversation with old Orlando just now. I wasn't eavesdroppin', you understand, but as I passed by the two of you just now I caught one of your remarks."

"Well," said Bathurst, "that's all right—it's a public place almost, so that you needn't apologize. I shouldn't come here to exchange secrets. What is it you want to tell me?" He smiled encouragingly in expectation.

The man shuffled his feet awkwardly.

"Come and sit down here," said Bathurst in invitation, "and have a beer with me." The man obeyed. "Now," urged Bathurst, "tell me what you want to tell me. Take your time over it, if you think it will help you."

The man's heavy face drifted into a slow smile, and he sampled his beverage with the touch of an expert. "It's not a lot, zurr, but if you're makin' inquiries about the dead man on the bus, as I think you are—"

"Why?" queried Bathurst instantly.

"I zee you in Raybourne, zurr, this morning, with Inspector Curgenven, and put two and two together."

"I see. Go on."

"Well, I can tell you one thing about the dead man Zutcliffe that az fur az I know has never come to light. Leastways—not accordin' to the papers. A rather pecooliar thing too, zurr, when you come to look at it and think things over. See my meanin', zurr?"

"I shall be able to judge better when I learn what it is, shan't I?"

The man spoke quietly. "I am not a Verrinder man—or Raybourne, come to that. My name's Williams, and I'm a native of Northlynn. I lived in Northlynn till I was turned twenty-nine, and I'm the wrong side of sixty now. You may be thinkin', zurr, that that piece of information doesn't touch the point much—but it *does*. I know Northlynn like I know the inside of my own cottage, and I can tell you this: zomething I heard Zutcliffe say in this very bar-parlour one evenin' a few weeks ago told me that if he wasn't a Northlynn man himself *he was very familiar* with the place indeed."

"Surely he might have lodged there and picked up information from a native?" suggested Bathurst.

The man nodded grudgingly at Bathurst's question. "He might, but zomehow I doan't think zo. And I'll tell you why. Something he let drop gave me quite a different sort of idea. There's a little street in Northlynn that runs down alongside the 'Blue Boar' that's known as Gypsy Terrace. Its name has been changed, and fifty years ago it was called Catchpole Alley. In my young days it was always Catchpole Alley, but, of course, the old name has died out now, as you may guess, and I haven't heard Catchpole Alley mentioned for many a long year. No—not for years and years and years, till I heard Zutcliffe use it in here a few weeks ago." He paused, and then continued with sturdy independence: "That's why I think he's either a Northlynn man or has a strong bond with the place. It's little things like that that give folks away."

Bathurst's face grew very thoughtful.

"I think you may be right," he conceded after a moment or two's deliberation. "Many thanks for what you have told me. It may turn out to be of great value. Coming back to your point, though, I suppose you've never heard the name Sutcliffe in connection with Northlynn?"

Williams shook his head decisively. "Never, zurr. To the best of my belief, it's not a Glebeshire name. I can't recall ever having heard it down in these parts."

"My experience is the same as yours, Williams. I should say without any hesitation that it was a North-country name." Bathurst rose, ordered his companion another pint of beer, bade him good evening, and departed from the "Quarryman Inn". When he reached the Rectory, Hector Savory and I, with Michael and Eileen as a chorus, were engaged in a discussion of the whole case from every conceivable point of view. I found that the young solicitor inclined to the idea that the alleged voyage on the Gigantic wanted a good deal of investigation. Eileen was in strong agreement with him, and she was on the point of elaborating a certain theory, when Anthony Bathurst entered the room and joined us. I could see that his face wore a look of unnatural gravity.

"Where's Mallinson?" he asked at the first convenient break in the conversation.

"Out." It was Michael who replied to him. It seemed to me that Bathurst appeared relieved at the information. "Been out for some time," Michael followed up. "Savory told me. Why? Do you want him?"

"No, as a matter of fact, I don't, at the moment."

He turned to Eileen. "Is it imperative that you return to Freyne tomorrow, Miss Trevor?"

"I am afraid it is, Mr. Bathurst. As it is, it was awfully decent of Miss Darrell to give me the leave of absence that she did. I have had a lot of time off this term for hockey, besides the time I had in Liverpool. I simply daren't be away a day longer." She repeated the words that she had used to the elder Savory. "Now—more than ever," she added sadly. "I've no one in the world now, you know."

I think my expression checked the remark that I could almost see trembling on Michael's lips. After all, there is a time and place for everything, and there should be a fitness with regard to all things. A clown may adorn the theatre, but in the garb of his calling he offends one's finer senses in a cathedral. Savory assumed the position that Michael had desired to take.

"Don't say that, Miss Trevor. You can always count on both my father and me to help you in any way you may want."

With a flutter of the eyes, Eileen thanked him. Bathurst looked grave again.

"I appreciate what you say with regard to your work, Miss Trevor," he said. "All the same I—"

Eileen put her hand on his arm. "Please be frank, Mr. Bathurst," she declared. "I would very much rather you were. Why did you ask me in the first place? Don't you want me to go back to Freyne House?"

Bathurst looked her straight in the eyes, and the keen lines at the corners of his clean-shaven mouth were firm and set. "If you would prefer the truth, as you assert that you would, Miss Trevor, I should be the last to keep it from you." He paused to select his next words. "I should like you to stay here with your friends around you. However, I realize that you have your work in the world to do, and that it is not always convenient for any of us to do just what one wishes. When I—"

Eileen interposed, eagerly inquisitive. "Why, Mr. Bathurst? Why do you wish me to stay here—among friends, as you put it? What is your reason?"

"Because you are in danger, Miss Trevor. For all I know, in *grave* danger." The earnestness in his tone had its effect upon the girl. But she was a good plucked 'un, and as game as a pebble, and after the first shock of his statement had passed she kept her head up and her courage at high-water mark. All the rest of us who listened were impressed by Bathurst's voice and demeanour. There was no doubt that he thoroughly believed what he said. "I'm not sure, you see, in what direction the next attack will take place," he went on.

"Attack?" queried Hector Savory. "Do you mean that Miss Trevor is likely to be—?"

"I do not actually say that Miss Trevor will be attacked at once—although it's possible, and it is quite on the cards as well that when it does come it may be launched against your father or yourself." Savory stared in undisguised amazement.

"At least—that's how it appears to me," concluded Bathurst. Then he permitted himself a smile. "Still, forewarned is forearmed, you know, and that's a considerable comfort. When are you returning home?"

"We intended to go back the day after tomorrow. But in the light of what you've just told me I don't know whether we shall. Have you told my father?"

"No. My conclusions are only a few hours old and I haven't seen him since I formed them. I want you to tell him what I think. I have no doubt that he's a brave man and will face peril as pluckily as the next one, but I want neither of you to go out alone—even here in the Rectory grounds. And you, Miss Trevor—you must take every precaution too. Take a sturdy cavalier with you wherever you go. It won't be a difficult matter to find a man for that job. The Rector here will find you one if you're ever at a loss. Now, Rector, can I have your *ABC*?"

Michael dashed out with flushed face and returned with the book in question.

"What do you want, Bathurst?" I asked a little impatiently, for the whole business was beginning to get on my nerves and worry me.

"A train from Polchester in the morning," he answered with a half-smile; "not a motor-bus from Esting."

"Leaving us?" demanded Savory. "Wouldn't it be better if you stayed here until the danger is averted? If not for my father and myself—for Miss Trevor? She—"

Bathurst interrupted him, but very quietly. "I am taking a risk, I know. However, in life one has to take risks, and I fear there is no way out in this instance. I have every hope that I shall be successful. Miss Trevor!" The girl went across to him. "I want to arrange something with you before I go."

"Yes?" Eileen responded to his query. "I shall be ready when you want me, Mr. Bathurst."

"Where are you going, Bathurst?" asked Hector.

"London. I have an idea that London will tell me something about which I am very curious."

The younger Savory smiled. "That's a surprising answer to me, Bathurst, but I suppose the reason for that is that I haven't the 'flair' for deduction. I could have understood you being drawn to Northlynn or Liverpool—or even as far afield as Tacoma—but London. . . ." He shrugged his shoulders in an endeavour to convey more pointedly his failure to understand. It would be only fair and just for me to admit that I shared his mystification, and when Bathurst asked me last thing that evening if he could bring Eileen into my study I was as curious as an old village dame as to what his plans and intentions were. London hadn't occurred to me as holding any place on the map of our story. He wasted no time in telling us.

"Sit down here, Miss Trevor," he said, "and the Rector and I will fix one or two matters up for you. What train do you intend catching tomorrow?"

"The one just after lunch—from Polchester—two-seventeen I think it is. Young Mr. Parry-Probyn has offered to run me over in the car." The girl flashed me a bright and brave smile, and my heart warmed to her. Bathurst returned the smile. Not to be outdone, I followed suit.

"You can catch the two-seventeen," he returned; "but your ultimate destination will not be Freyne."

"But, Mr. Bathurst, I simply must—"

He turned and faced her. "When I discussed the question with you earlier in the evening I hadn't received an answer to a wire that I had taken the liberty of sending upon your behalf, although I had prepaid it. But it came twenty minutes ago. Here it is. Read it." He handed her the telegram. She took it from him, wondering, but endeavouring to control her amazement. "Show it to the Rector," he added, after she had read it. I read the message:

Pleased to grant extension of leave.—Price-Darrell.

"Believe me, Miss Trevor, I had the soundest of reasons for taking the course that I did. You must forgive me for what must appear to be an intrusion into your private affairs a little beyond the normal."

Eileen nodded slowly. "I am quite ready to believe you Mr. Bathurst, when you say that you are acting for the best." She paused a moment, and then proceeded: "And I am quite ready to place myself in your hands. What do you want me to do?"

He paced the room two or three times before replying to her.

"If I followed my inclinations I should ask you to stay here in Kirve St. Laudus with the Rector, but our inclinations are not always our best signposts, and besides protecting Miss Trevor and other people I have to lay Sutcliffe's murderer by the heels. You see, I can't forget that, and by moving you from here I may be able to do it. Haven't you *any* other friends, Miss Trevor? Can't you rake up anybody?"

The girl shook her head hopelessly at the request. "I haven't. I can't think of anybody."

"Forsyth," quoted Bathurst. "Harold Forsyth—the man whom your father mentioned in his letter to you that you showed me. The man to whom you were instructed to write. You couldn't very well go there, I suppose?"

Eileen shook her head again, this time with strong determination. "He's an absolute stranger to me, Mr. Bathurst. I don't know him from Adam. I couldn't and wouldn't contemplate such a thing as planting myself on him."

It was at that moment that I had a brainwave. I do sometimes, but Michael will tell you with little filial association that they are few and far between. I thought of my brother Charles and of his wife Elizabeth. I think I mentioned before, somewhere in the early stages of my narrative, that Charles was my only brother, whose address was "The Crofts" Mosforth Park, near Much Wenlock, Shropshire.

"I have it!" I cried in something like senile triumph. "I have a brother who has a wife. They are Michael's uncle and aunt—separately—not collectively. They have become so acclimatized to my fads, whims and vices that I can only believe they cherish sincere affection for me, incredible though it may seem. It's the only possible explanation. Their strong suit is Patience, and their telegraphic address Long-sufferingness. A word from me or from mine and they would give a subdued welcome to an Alsatian with hydrophobia." I saw my *faux pas* and hastened to make amends. I extricated myself somewhat clumsily. "Let alone to a charming young lady." Eileen threw me a glance of approval.

"Where does your brother live, Rector?" demanded Bathurst.

I told him. When he heard the address he showed signs of approbation.

"Excellent," he declared; "excellent. Couldn't be better, in fact. Suit you all right, Miss Trevor?" He turned and put the question to her.

"Yes—of course—it's a lot better in a way, although I don't like the idea of landing myself—"

"When can you make arrangements, Rector?" Bathurst put the question.

"Tomorrow," I replied. "Michael shall take Miss Trevor under his wing and deposit her with Charles and Elizabeth himself. I will give him instructions. 'He will be joyful in his glory and sing aloud upon his bed. Not only will he employ loud cymbals but also high-sounding cymbals'—and who shall blame him?"

Bathurst and Eileen laughed at my exuberance. In the midst of their laughter there came a tap upon my study door. I looked at Bathurst for instructions, I think, more than anything else. He thought for a second or so, then the tap was repeated—twice.

It was Michael, I felt certain, for there is an individuality about taps of this kind just as there is about knocks on the door, and I, for one of the company, knew my son's only too well. Bathurst eventually announced the invitation to enter. I was right. Michael came in, profuse with apology.

"I'm frightfully sorry, people, to interrupt you," he said, "but I've just heard something from Mr. Savory senior—Mr. Bartholomew Savory—that struck me as being decidedly interesting. He called up here specially about it. Can I let it off now, or is it . . . ?" He paused for an expression of our opinion. I glanced at Bathurst, who nodded his assent.

"Carry on, then, Michael," I declared; "let's have it."

"Well, Mr. Savory's been in Raybourne this evening having a look round, as you know. Hector stayed in to do some business, but his father thought he'd have a punt round. While he was out, he spotted our friend Mallinson engaged in a very deep conversation with a man in a motor-bus driver's uniform. He saw him pick this chap up at the depot and go into a public house with him. Old Savory went in behind them, and when they came out he came out too, close on their heels. Back they went to the bus garage, and after a time the driver chap cleared off. Mallinson either gave him money or a letter of some sort. As he cleared Savory took a chance and asked a newspaper boy standing on the corner what the man's name was. Who do you think it was? It was *Sturgess, the driver of the very bus on which Sutcliffe was murdered*. What do you think of that?"

Bathurst rubbed his cheek.

"Thanks very much for the information, Michael," he answered; "but on the whole I can't say that I'm very much surprised."

CHAPTER XXV
SUSPENSE
(From the Rector's MSS. Continued.)

ON THE following morning, not very long after Anthony Bathurst had left us, the elder Savory came up to the Rectory, asked for me, and put a very direct question. "Let me know this, Rector. Am I to tell Mallinson where Miss Trevor is going?"

I must confess that the question afforded me some little perturbation, and I am afraid that my face showed the fact. "I ask you, Rector," he went on, "because Mallinson has been to me and deliberately asked for the information. I understood from Bathurst when he told me what he had arranged that the matter was to be kept as—"

Here I interposed. "Wait a moment—I don't quite understand this," I said. "Bathurst's instructions to me were that only you and I (and, of course, our sons) were to have this information. Why should Mallinson even *think* that Miss Trevor is not returning to Freyne? As far as all his knowledge goes, the girl is going back to her duties at her school in the ordinary way."

"I know," said old Bartholomew, and the normal geniality of his face hardened, "and that's why this man's uncanny intuition and pertinacity frighten me. What does he know? How has he found out what he has? What was he doing with that man Sturgess last night? Eh, Rector? I'd give a thundering lot to know." He shook his head doubtfully. "I think it might explain a good many things."

I saw his point, and told him so. "What did you say to Mallinson when he asked you where Miss Trevor was going?"

"Put him off," replied Bartholomew with a laugh, "with all the evasiveness of a North-country solicitor, which is in no small measure, I can assure you. I've been at the game for too many years not to know how to do that sort of thing."

I told him then that I knew no more than he did.

He nodded. "Bathurst's orders to me were on all fours evidently with those he gave you, and I, for one, wasn't taking any chances."

"You did quite right," I affirmed. "If he asks you again, put him off again—'unto seventy times seven'. Have you told Curgenven about his meeting with Sturgess?"

"No. Do you think that I ought to?"

"Doesn't do any harm to keep these officials posted. I think I should, if I were you."

"Very well, then, I will! What's Curgenven's latest line of country?"

"Trying to trace Sutcliffe's movements before he came here—so Bathurst tells me."

"H'm. Some job, I should think," returned Bartholomew, "though, of course, the police are pretty clever at that sort of thing—they've got the resources, you see. Anyhow, I shall be seeing Curgenven this afternoon. I want to let him know that Hector and I are going back tomorrow evening. I promised him I wouldn't return to Liverpool without telling him." He came across to me, and seemed from the look in his eyes to be asking for my sympathy and help. "Rector," he said, "you heard what Bathurst said yesterday, didn't you? I can't dismiss it from my mind, although I've tried very hard to. My son and I are in danger from this unknown enemy. I feel it—I know it. We must get back to our work, however, and when the attack comes our assailant won't have matters all his own way, although—at the back of my mind—I have a feeling that I can't shake off that he will prove too cunning for us."

I shook him heartily by the hand with as much sympathy as I could muster. "Courage, Mr. Savory. We aren't alone. We have powerful allies working on our side. We have Bathurst and Curgenven, and—there is another comfort—Eileen is in excellent hands. Things might be a great deal worse." A sudden thought then struck me. "Tell me," I asked him, "did Bathurst say anything to you about what we were to do if anything happened down here? Plan of campaign, and so on?"

"No," he said wonderingly, "how do you mean?"

I proceeded to tell him that Bathurst had said that no matter what happened—except in situations that involved personal danger to anybody—we were to sit tight, watch points, and do nothing precipitate.

"Funny," he remarked. "I wonder why. Still, no doubt he knows best. Well, good-bye, Rector. Hector and I will pop in again before we go this evening—if we're alive, that is." He added the last statement with a grim solemnity. I tried to laugh off his pessimism, but the man was mentally shaken and very obviously not himself; and when he had gone and I began to meditate more closely upon what he had said to me, I found myself sharing his anxiety, and wondering, too, in which direction the first blow would fall. While I was thus employed, Mallinson was shown in to me by a flustered Emily. And I will say at once that nobody's manner could have been more cordial or courteous. There was no hint or suggestion in his tone to which I, or anybody else, for that matter, could have justifiably taken the slightest exception. Whatever else the man might be, he had the instincts of a gentleman.

"Pardon me, Rector," he said, "for troubling you, as I expect you are as busy as you can be, but you can guess that I am naturally concerned and interested in the matter that brought our little party south. I came up here this morning to have a chat with Mr. Bathurst. Much to my surprise, your maid tells me he went away this morning. Could you tell me when he's likely to be back?"

"I couldn't," I replied, and, strictly speaking, my answer was eminently truthful.

"Is he still at work on the Trevor case?"

I could see no reason why I should evade this question either.

"Yes—as far as I know. On the Sutcliffe case—that is."

"Aren't they one and the same? Where has Mr. Bathurst gone—can you tell me that?"

"There again I can't say." I was saying no more about that, so I was very careful to stop there. His eyes narrowed somewhat and I saw a glint come into them that I hadn't noticed before. But his approach was still perfect. I found myself admiring him for his restraint.

"You mean that you won't say, Rector? I understand."

"No," I replied. "Quite frankly—I mean exactly what I said. Nothing more and nothing less. I can't say—because I don't know. I can't have a better reason than that—can I?"

"I'm sorry, Rector! Please excuse my suggestion. I ought not to have made it." He paused, and I waited very patiently for his next move. I thought I knew what it would be, and my anticipations were accurate. "Could I see Miss Trevor?" he asked a trifle diffidently.

"She's out," I responded, "and I'm not sure when she'll be back."

"She's returning to Freyne this afternoon, isn't she?" His tone was anxious. We had now reached the cross-roads with a vengeance. I thought my best answer from all points of view was an affirmative, but I doubt if I shall be forgiven for an effort so *splendide mendax*. He nodded, and I saw his face change as though with doubting and perplexity.

"Thank you, Rector. I don't think I need trouble you any more, then." Stooping suddenly, he bent over me as I sat, and spoke in a low tense tone. Then he just as quickly turned on his heel and went out. Ten minutes or so after he had left me I had an astonishing shock. Without any preliminary warning, my study door opened to admit Bathurst, of all people. My face, of course, expressed my surprise, but he waved me back to my chair. "Why haven't you gone?" I gasped. "Seeing you gave me quite a turn."

"I'm going by the next train. Changed my mind. Anything happened this morning? You looked startled before you spotted me."

I told him of the events of the morning; of Savory's visit first, and then of Mallinson's. He heard me throughout the first story silently and with the keenest attention.

"So the Savorys suspect Mallinson, do they? Well, they're no fools, and it can't be wondered at. Go on, Rector."

Then I told him my second story, how Mallinson had come, and of the questions he had asked me.

"Wants to know Miss Eileen's whereabouts, does he?" He chuckled and rubbed his chin with the back of his forefinger. "Thought he might rise to that little move of ours. Things are progressing very nicely now. Go on again, Rector."

I came to the point where Mallinson had stooped down and spoke to me just prior to his departure. "What do you think he said to me?" I demanded of Bathurst. "He leaned over me *and actually accused the two Savorys of the murder. Fancy— accused them of being guilty of the crime of which they accuse him.*" I looked searchingly at Anthony Bathurst, to see the effect of my words.

"H'm," he conceded laconically; "things may be said to be getting interesting now—really interesting. Don't you think so, Rector?"

I stared at him again with some surprise; he seemed to have received my information so calmly. What did he know that was hidden from me? What had he been able to deduce from this tangle of events that had eluded me? I determined to put all to the test and to stake it on a series of questions.

"Tell me, Bathurst," I asked quietly, "is there any truth in any of this? Did Mallinson murder Trevor? Is Bartholomew Savory right? Am *I* right—for I may as well confess that I, too, suspect him?"

Bathurst shook his head. "Bartholomew is wrong, and you are wrong. Mallinson is innocent of Trevor's murder. I am certain of it."

"Innocent!" I declared somewhat incredulously, and the word seemed to cling to my lips, for I think I was frightened, and my next question was, as a result, a long time in coming. "Is Mallinson right, then, in the charge that *he* framed? Was Trevor murdered by the Savorys? How is it possible? I can't believe that such a—"

Bathurst intervened with a smile.

"Don't distress yourself, Rector. Mallinson's accusation is also devoid of truth. Roland Trevor was not killed by Bartholomew, by Hector, or by the twain. So now you're satisfied on both counts." He shook hands. "I'm going now, and don't breathe a word to a soul that I've been back. Four walls, Rector—and nothing else. I don't think I need go to London after all. Give me just a little longer and I'll read the riddle for you. But I'm forced to wait for something to happen. I want proof, you see. Good-bye."

The door closed upon him, and as I sat in my chair in front of my desk my hands trembled in front of me. What was to happen before he obtained the proof of which he spoke?

Chapter XXVI
IN THE NIGHT
(From the Rector's MSS. Continued.)

BARTHOLOMEW and Hector came in early that evening to recount their interview with Curgenven, as Bartholomew had promised, and as Michael had not returned from his errand to

Much Wenlock I invited them to stay to dinner with me. Emily could always rise to the occasion when necessary. The atmosphere of doubt, anxiety, and even of danger that was now definitely overhanging the case in general, and some of us in particular, seemed to have wrapped itself forbiddingly round my bones, and I clutched eagerly at the prospect of company that would relieve me of the spectre of comparative loneliness.

Dinner passed off very quietly. Bartholomew had told the inspector of the meeting he had witnessed between Mallinson and Sturgess, and, according to what he told me then at dinner, he found that Curgenven considered it to have a distinct significance.

"Between you and me, Rector," he added, leaning across the table towards me, "I shouldn't be surprised if our friend Mallinson doesn't attract special vigilance from the inspector from now onwards. I rather fancy that Sergeant Millington will be doing a little overtime for the next day or so. I'm pretty sure the job will fall to him."

I nodded agreement, for I knew that Curgenven was a man of assiduous care who took no chances. Hector Savory, however, took up the conversation and immediately struck a different note.

"We're all banking too much on a clean-cut issue. Wouldn't come as a great surprise to me if we were being hoodwinked all along the line." He sipped his sherry appreciatively. "An excellent Amontillado, Rector, which reconciles me to a great many of my doubts."

I suitably acknowledged his indirect compliment, and at the same time wondered where the gist of his remark lay. His father, I think, must have experienced the same feeling, for he put his difficulty into words.

"Hoodwinked in what way, Hector? Surely we know where we are now? Bathurst, at least, must. . . ." He paused and looked at his son.

Hector held his wineglass to the light and regarded its contents critically before he essayed a reply. When it came I was rather surprised, for I had begun to anticipate a somewhat different line of argument.

"Well," he said, "I'm inclined to look at it like this: Bathurst says to Mallinson, to all intents and purposes, 'This man Sutcliffe, who's been done to death down here, is your man Trevor.' Then he produces a photograph and says, 'That's so—isn't it?' What happens? Friend Mallinson, mark you, looks at the photograph—says, 'No.' Don't forget that fact. We were all there when the incident took place, and we all saw exactly what occurred. Then Bathurst fishes out photograph number two, and, lo and behold, Mallinson changes his ground and gives way!" He paused and drained his sherry. "And—for all we know—because it suited his book to do so. That's the point that's appealed to me for some time now."

I contested his conclusion rather vigorously. "Half a minute. Don't forget the question of the man's glasses. That was the point, if you remember, that caused Mallinson to shift his position. You mustn't omit that, you know."

"True," he conceded, "but very far from conclusive in my opinion. I should have preferred the identification to have been very much more—"

I interrupted him. "I have every faith in Bathurst, and I am content to leave it at that."

"So have I," exclaimed Bartholomew. "The Rector's absolutely right, Hector. Bathurst will see this affair through successfully. I haven't a doubt of it."

"I agree," returned Hector. "I am just as much impressed by Bathurst as either of you, come to that. All the same, I like to reason things out for myself, and certain things stick in my mind and I can't rid myself of them."

I rose from the dinner-table, walked across to the fireplace and poked the fire into a comforting blaze. Bartholomew rose after me and crossed to my window that looked out on to my garden in front of the house.

"By Jove, Rector," he cried; "it seems to me that we had better be moving if we want to get back to the 'Flamingos' tonight. There's a thick fog come up." I joined him at the window and looked out. It was as he had stated. There was a thick white blanket of fog that blotted out everything. It had rolled up from the Linner Valley, as was its habit at this time of the year, gathered ghostly strength as it swirled and swayed across the intermediate moorland, and now threatened to fold its icy power round Kirve St. Laudus.

"I can't let you go in this, Mr. Savory," I protested. "A fog like this in this part of the world is no joke, I assure you. Besides the inconvenience and hardship that would attend you if you attempted to get back, there would be a very distinct element of danger to you as well. You could very easily land yourselves in the Neddar Water, for instance. I must insist on your staying at the Rectory."

"It's awfully kind of you, sir," admitted Hector; "but it would mean giving you a lot of—"

I waved his contention aside. "Michael's away tonight, and so also are Bathurst and Miss Trevor. The fog couldn't possibly have chosen a better night for you; I will tell Emily at once to make the necessary arrangements."

Two hours more and the white wraith of fog had routed all opposition and reigned in indisputable monarchy. I could see that my two guests were sincerely grateful that I had relieved them of the hazardous journey back to their inn. Only a stout-hearted person would have ventured forth under the conditions that prevailed. The comfort and comradeship of the red, flickering flames from my fire cheered our conversation and assisted materially to shut out from our minds the white abomination that crept and stalked in stealth outside. At half past eleven I ordered my two companions "something hot with a slice of lemon in it", and shortly afterwards saw them to their rooms. Before I turned in myself I put an Old Carthusian scarf round my neck, crammed a hat on my head, and opened the front door.

The fog was now worse than ever, and as soon as the door was opened the white hosts of the invader poured greedily into the hall. I hastily drew back from them, closed and bolted my door and followed my two guests to bed. I mention this incident and the conditions that prevailed at about eleven forty-two that evening in view of what was destined to happen afterwards.

I suppose that it must have been about an hour later that I was first disturbed. Usually I am a very sound sleeper, but in all probability the unusual events of the day had affected me mentally and rendered me perhaps a trifle abnormal. Anyhow, my bedroom is directly above my study, and each room looks out on to the garden and on to the gravelled path that leads round past the shrubbery to the other part of the house. The house faces due south, let me observe, and the exotic growths that I am able to rear in my garden bear excellent testimony to the fact.

In the first place I was awakened from a light restless sort of slumber by what I felt certain was a step on the gravelled path below my bedroom window. I lay awake for a second or so and listened intently. But I could hear nothing. Just as I was beginning to think that my imagination had cheated me, there came a curious clicking sound which caused me to sit bolt upright in bed. The realization of what it was came to me in a flash. Somebody was attempting to enter my study downstairs—perhaps had already succeeded! Secretly wishing that Michael and Bathurst were much nearer at hand than they actually were, I slipped on my dressing-gown and a pair of golfing brogues that I always kept handy. Just about to switch on the electric light, I stayed my impulsive hand—reflecting that in a campaign of this nature darkness and silence must be my strongest allies.

Closing the door quietly, I tiptoed along the corridor until I came to the door of the room in which I knew Hector Savory was sleeping. I tapped on it very lightly, to receive no answer. A second tap proved equally fruitless. Then I tried the handle. Much to my relief it yielded to my pressure at once, and I cautiously entered the room. From his breathing I judged that Hector Savory was asleep, but, luckily, it didn't take me very long to waken him. At the third gentle shake of his shoulder he opened his eyes.

"What the . . . ?" he grunted, and then, seeing me, he seemed to come to full consciousness "What is it, Rector? What's the trouble?"

I told him hurriedly in as few words as I could find. Sliding from his bed instantly, he prepared himself to accompany me. The result was that within a space of about three minutes since my first alarm, we were noiselessly descending the staircase together. The door of my study that opened on to the hall was open a matter of a few inches, and at the foot of the stairs I halted my companion and put my finger to my lips for silence. It occurred to me that whoever was inside the room had opened this door that now faced us out of regard for his own safety—in order, no doubt, that he should better hear anything that might be going on in other parts of the house, or the approach of anybody coming down the stairs.

As we stood there at the foot of that staircase, all sorts of ideas flooded my brain; but the one that eventually stood out from the others clearly and vividly, as it were, was the idea that our midnight visitor was employing his time going through my private papers. I didn't know why, but I reasoned thus. There were no articles of value in my study whatever—unless you include five or six "pots" for rowing that I had collected years ago on the Isis—and the only thing of possible interest to anybody was my big desk. If he were at work on this, as seemed to me likely, it was then quite on the cards that his back would be towards us as we entered, and we might conceivably be so placed strategically that we might have a chance of taking him by surprise.

I beckoned to Hector to follow me as I tiptoed stealthily to the door that stood ajar. He did so. Holding our breaths, we craned our necks for a few inches round the edge of the door. What I saw made my heart leap into my mouth, and I caught Hector by the sleeve of his dressing-gown to prevent him crying out. A man was seated at my desk. From his movements he appeared to be searching for something, as papers, documents and certain books were being taken, looked through hastily, and then replaced just as quickly. Although the man's back was towards us as I have stated, there was something about his build and figure that was curiously familiar, and when I saw the sling that held his arm I knew my suspicions were correct.

I turned towards Hector, and in reply to my unspoken question his lips silently framed one word. The word was "Mallinson!" I nodded in tacit agreement, and as I did so the figure that had been crouched over the desk rose, as though under the influence of a sudden impulse, and strode silently to the french doors through which he had previously made his entrance. Within a second he had vanished into the white mistiness of the night. Simultaneously, almost, Hector Savory dashed across the room with the obvious intention of pursuit, but once again I laid a restraining hand upon his arm. As I did so he turned on me, troubled and anxious.

"Why, Rector? Let me go after him. Think—what I may be able to discover now may lead to much!"

But I shook my head in dissent. Bathurst's instructions came back to me clearly and forcibly. "Do nothing precipitate, Rector. Sit tight and watch points unless the situation spells personal danger to any one of you." I couldn't see that it did that. I therefore continued to hold him back.

"Let him go, Hector," I declared. "We are at any rate in a better position than we were. We have now definite reasons for suspecting Mallinson, *but he is unaware that we have seen what we have seen*. This gives us an advantage that we might immediately lose if we went after him and let him know that we had witnessed tonight's little episode, to say nothing of the virtual impossibility of catching him in weather like this."

Hector Savory nodded. "That's common sense, Rector. But what the blazes was the man after in here? Any idea?"

"Frankly, I haven't," I replied, and walked to the desk where Mallinson had been so recently busily engaged. As far as I could see, nothing had been taken. None of my private drawers appeared to have been forced or even to have been tampered with. They were all locked and, apparently, on closer inspection, there had been no serious attempt made to break open any part of the desk. The various papers and books which we had seen

Mallinson examining seemed to have been put back in their places in fair order, at least, and, as far as I could judge without a detailed check, there was none missing. "Can't make it out," I exclaimed at length; "but we'll go back to bed and sleep on it. Whatever it is, there is one thing: we shall have something interesting to tell your father in the morning."

Hector grinned in anticipation. "Right-o, Rector. I'll get back to bed, then, although I don't suppose I shall get much more sleep tonight."

I followed him up the staircase, and in my own case his forecast with regard to sleep would have been very true. I lay awake all the rest of the night, and Hector Savory's query hammered and hammered at my brain. What on earth was it that had brought Mallinson to my study in such a manner and at such a time of night? Try as I would, I could find no answer that satisfied my intelligence.

Chapter XXVII
THE CAMPAIGN DEVELOPS
(From the Rector's MSS. Continued.)

WE TOLD Bartholomew of the events of the night at breakfast next morning, and I don't know which of us was the more eager to spin the yarn. The old man shook his head gravely in his expression of commiseration with me, but at the same time owned up to a certain feeling of gratification that his feelings with regard to the *bona fides* of Mallinson had so quickly received such corroboration. After all, he had ample justification. I could not find it in my heart to blame him. There is scarcely one of us, travellers through this Vale of Frailty, sufficiently strong of character to withstand always the devastating temptation of the triumphant "I told you so!" I have known archbishops succumb to its seductiveness.

Soon after breakfast the two Savorys left the Rectory for their inn refuge, and they made the occasion one for bidding me good-bye altogether.

"I don't suppose that there will be time for us to see you again today, Rector," said Bartholomew, as he shook hands with me; "as you know, we intend to get home again as soon as we can. There's a convenient train, so Hector tells me, soon after midday. So here's saying good-bye, sir, and many thanks for all your kindnesses."

I thanked them in return, and putting on a heavy overcoat accompanied my visitors to my front gate that opened on to the Raybourne road. The fog had gone—completely—and, for late November, it was a glorious morning. As I watched them swing along to the inn that had afforded them temporary hospitality, and then turned back to the house, I wondered when we three should meet again—in thunder, lightning or in rain! As it happened, my wonderment was but short-lived, as I had the answer in just over the space of an hour. A ring at my bell brought me quickly from the preparation of my next Sunday's sermon, and I answered the ring myself—not, I am very much afraid, in the sweetest of tempers, for inspiration was already fugitive. Hector and Bartholomew Savory stood on the threshold. Before I could express my surprise at seeing them there so unexpectedly the elder man spoke.

"Can we come in for a moment, Rector? We've news for you."

I made them comfortable and prepared to listen.

"I've come to reciprocate, Rector," announced Bartholomew, "and to return your compliment of this morning. For now *I* have a song to sing-o! While we were here with you, our bedroom at the 'Four Flamingos' has been turned over very much in the same way as your study."

I stared at him in amazement. What had they in unison with me to attract this undesirable attention? What did we share, save our common purpose?

"Anything missing?" I asked.

"As far as we can see," he confided, "nothing. There was nothing of value in the room. What could there be? All the same, Rector, it's—disturbing, to say the least of it, and we thought, Hector and I, that it was best that you should know what had occurred."

"Naturally—naturally," I agreed. "I wish Bathurst were here. He would probably be able to make more of it than we."

Hector Savory carefully wiped the glasses of his pince-nez with a silk handkerchief.

"He's right," he asserted. "I must give him his due. Bathurst is right in what he predicted. He said the blow might fall on any one of us. This business seems to me to be a very likely preliminary." He spoke despondently.

When they left me they approximated definite anxiety, and Hector's depression seemed to have communicated itself to his father. However, my normal duties occupied my time for the rest of the day, and I put the Sutcliffe mystery as far away from my mind as I could. After all, there were other things in my life than this wretched murder.

Michael's return in the late afternoon, of course, brought it back to me. We exchanged our stories, he first. Nothing startling had occurred either to him or to Eileen on the journey to Shropshire. Everything had gone according to plan, and my letter to Charles and Elizabeth had proved a complete passport for Eileen's immediate welfare. In fact, from what Michael told me, my good brother and his better wife were far from being discomfited at the turn of events which had brought them so unexpected and charming a visitor. Indeed, Michael thought they were secretly overjoyed to take a hand in the game, as Charles himself had put it. Eileen had been received with all the honours of a fairy princess, and had already made a complete conquest of their hearts.

Michael had, before leaving "The Crofts", impressed upon her the imperative necessity of taking the utmost care of herself. He had repeated to her Anthony Bathurst's warning and injunctions, and was assured in his own mind that Eileen thoroughly appreciated and was fully alive to all the possibilities of the situation as it was developing. "For two pins, Father," Michael concluded to me, "I would have stayed up at Uncle Charles's with her. But as my instructions weren't to that effect I've come home to you. 'Orders is orders.'"

I nodded approval of his action, and then proceeded to tell him my story of all that had taken place at the Rectory since he had left Kirve St. Laudus with Eileen. After that, I informed him of the affair in the Savorys' bedroom at the "Four Flamingos".

"By Jove, Guv'nor," he said, when he heard this last piece of news, "things are getting hot, what? Bringing the battle to our own doorstep, aren't they? What are they after, in the name of all that's wonderful?"

"I can't enlighten you, Michael," I confessed. "I wish I could, but, as Hector Savory said, it's all of a piece with Bathurst's anticipations. When he comes back he may be able to throw light upon what seems impenetrably dark to us now. We will continue to live in hope."

"But what on earth could Mallinson have wanted from you," Michael insisted, "or from the Savorys, come to that? These latest developments have got me whacked to a frazzle, and it's no earthly good me saying that they haven't."

Interesting and perhaps thrilling as the situation had now become, a matter of but two hours more served to intensify these conditions, and Michael was destined to receive yet another shock which left him (and me) in a state of even greater bewilderment than ever. I had been reading my evening paper for some little time after Emily had brought it to me, when my eyes encountered a headline that made me (in the "argot" of the present day) "sit up and take notice". It and the lines below it ran as follows:

SUPPOSED BURGLARY AT WELL-KNOWN SOLICITOR'S

I read the paragraph that followed below with the keenest interest.

The Liverpool police were informed early this morning on the telephone that burglarious entry had been made last night into Loxteth Chase, West Loxteth, a house on the outskirts of Liverpool and the residence

of Mr. Bartholomew Savory, the eminent solicitor practising in Lordship Street, Liverpool. Mr. Savory, together
with his son, Mr. Hector Savory, is at the present moment
away on important business in the South of England, and
the information concerning the burglary came to them
from Reynolds, Mr. Savory's butler, who is in charge at
Loxteth Chase during his employer's absence. It is not
known at the time of going to press what loss Mr. Savory
has sustained, but the Liverpool police are anticipating
effecting an arrest before long, and are at the same time
nursing a hope that this last affair may shed some light
upon the recent strange disappearance from the City of
Liverpool of a Mr. Roland Trevor. Up to the moment all
the efforts of the police to achieve a satisfactory solution
for this gentleman's disappearance have signally failed.

I pushed the newspaper over towards Michael, and strove
to collect my thoughts. "Read that, Michael," I said, prodding at
the column with the stem of my pipe. "Where on earth are we
getting to now?"

Michael obeyed me, and I saw the amazement creep into his
eyes as he read.

"Seem to have deserted our doorstep, Michael, for somebody
else's," I declared, with an attempt at jocularity.

"Well, there's one thing, Guv'nor," he returned; "we're learning things, at any rate. Seems to me we're up against a gang of
some kind. There must be more than one man in it. It's stark
plain that if Mallinson did the jobs here he couldn't have done
the one up there. You simply can't get away from that. No man
can be in two places at once."

"Barring, of course, that he's a bird," I replied profoundly.
I hope that in the circumstances Sir Boyle Roche will pardon
the flagrant plagiarism. No other reply appeared possible. Here
my story will cease for a time and another pen will take up the
narrative.

Chapter XXVIII
THE FIRST OFFICER OF THE "GIGANTIC"

When Anthony Bathurst left the Rectory of Kirve St. Laudus for his unknown destination, he carried a letter in his pocket that he had received that morning and of which even the Rector himself had no knowledge. But Sir Austin Kemble, the Commissioner of Police, had responded to a request from Mr. Bathurst as rapidly and as willingly as he had done many times before. To be more explicit, Mr. Bathurst had put forward an inquiry to Sir Austin concerning the actual terms of the will of the late Sir Joshua Walsingham and a further inquiry with regard to a certain marriage certificate, and the answers that had come to him from Sir Austin had afforded Anthony Bathurst considerable satisfaction. So far from opening up a situation that presented new difficulties, the first of these answers coincided rather with certain ideas that were already beginning to take possession of Mr. Bathurst's mind, and it enabled him to regard the future development of the affair with a considerable amount of complacency.

The terms of Sir Austin's letter decided Anthony Bathurst to call at the picturesque village of Northlynn en route for Polchester, and it would have occasioned the ordinary observer perhaps justifiable surprise if he had followed Mr. Bathurst to that part of the village of Northlynn that occupied his particular attention—the burial-ground attached to the Parish Church of St. Philip. One fragment of his conversation with Orlando Horton's friend of the Quarryman Inn seemed to him to hold a great significance, namely, that gentleman's strong conviction that Sutcliffe undoubtedly had Northlynn associations.

Mr. Bathurst methodically toured the twisting paths and grassy ways that led to and round the tombstones, conscious that the family history of many an English village may be gleaned, in part, from that hallowed portion where the "rude forefathers of the hamlet sleep".

The churchyard was ill tended and far from beautiful, but half an hour's careful investigation yielded the incontestable fact that, as far as the monumental records went, no Sutcliffe rested there—in peace or otherwise. Anthony Bathurst was undeterred by that, as he had anticipated something of the kind, but not one of the names that he had been half prepared to find was to be discovered either, and he was forced at the end of the period named to assess his visit as fruitless. But when an investigator is in the position of being short of data that when gleaned would complete his case, he is bound to neglect nothing. Information when collected must be classified and tabulated. It must be garnered and husbanded, to be taken from the storehouse of memory and used when the appointed moment comes. Mindful of this, Mr. Bathurst made certain notes affecting the human harvest that lay in Northlynn churchyard, and then entered the church itself. Within a few seconds he found himself facing a mural brass "sacred to the memory of Joseph Wyndham". He read the further inscription with strong satisfaction, left the church, and turned in the direction of Polchester to catch his train.

There was a lot of light let into the problem now, and Anthony's heart was considerably lighter. On the occasion of this, his second visit to the City of Liverpool within the space of a few days, he intended to do one thing (amongst others) that it had been impossible for him to do the time before. Inquiries had elicited for him the information that the *Gigantic* had docked a couple of hours previously. An official at the offices of the White Star Line listened sympathetically with ear inclined to Mr. Bathurst's suggestion and gave him an answer that he considered in the circumstances eminently satisfactory.

"As a matter of fact, sir," the man said, "you're in clover, as it happens. The first officer of the *Gigantic*, Mr. Dalrymple, is actually in the building at the present moment, and it's quite possible that I could arrange for him to—"

A generous movement on the part of Anthony, quickly perceived by the official, translated this possibility, through the territory of probability, to the region of certainty, and within a very short space of time he found himself in conversation with Mr. Dalrymple.

The first officer of the *Gigantic* was a fine-looking man of middle age, with a firm, clean-shaven mouth that carried the lines of humour, strong features, black hair and dark eyes. He listened to what Mr. Bathurst had to tell him, and regarded the two photographs that Mr. Bathurst placed in front of him with interest and perhaps some little amusement. Anthony pointed to the two men separately.

"They're my two passengers," Dalrymple said, "without a doubt, although I don't know that I saw very much of them on the voyage over from New York, but I certainly remembered the two names Trevor and Mallinson, when you mentioned them. I made up a Bridge 'four' with them one evening in the first-class saloon, but beyond that particular evening, and what I may call a natural conversation that arose from us playing cards together, I don't think I said more than a dozen words to either of them during the whole of the voyage. They weren't at any table, you see. I invariably dined at another table."

Mr. Bathurst carefully considered the first officer's statement. Then he put a question to Mr. Dalrymple that the latter thought rather surprising and distinctly irrelevant.

"Who was the fourth member of your card party, Mr. Dalrymple? Can you remember?"

The first officer knitted his brows. "Yes," he asserted, "I think I can answer that for you; it was a gentleman named Stapleton."

A thrill of satisfaction passed through Mr. Bathurst's mind. This was better and better! Everything fitted!

"What was Mr. Stapleton by profession?"

"A clergyman who had had a holiday in the States for reasons of health," responded Mr. Dalrymple with a smile. "Vicar or something of a small parish somewhere in the West of England, but for all that a man who liked his game of Bridge and his spot of 'Scotch' with the best of us. A man, too, whom everybody on the *Gigantic* thoroughly respected. In fact, there wasn't a more popular man on the ship."

"I see," agreed Mr. Bathurst gravely, before he shifted to another point of attack. "I'll come back to Trevor and Mallinson for a moment. Were they strongly familiar?" he queried.

"Familiar?" reiterated Dalrymple queryingly. "I don't quite—"

"Let me explain better what I mean. Did they address each other by Christian names, for example?"

"I couldn't answer that," replied Dalrymple. "As I told you just now, my conversational acquaintance with them was very limited. I simply knew that they were Trevor and Mallinson, and very little else. Stay, though . . . The first officer of the *Gigantic* paused, in an obvious attempt to recall something that was temporarily fugitive.

"What is it?" demanded Mr. Bathurst hopefully. "Thought of something?"

Dalrymple smiled and shook his head. "I don't know whether it will come back to me, but I've a hazy sort of recollection that I heard Mallinson call Trevor by a name of some kind when I was playing cards with them. Now what was it?"

Anthony let Dalrymple think without interruption. He had always found this silent policy pay far the best when confronted with similar instances in the past. The face of the first officer cleared in a smile of triumph.

"Don't worry," he said; "I thought I should get it if I thought long enough. I'm damned slow, but moderately sure. The name was 'Horton'. I distinctly remember hearing Mallinson call Trevor 'Horton'. 'Arthur Horton'."

This was far from the answer that Mr. Bathurst had expected. For all that, he permitted a smile to play over his features when the understanding of the name came to him.

"Will you be in Liverpool, Mr. Dalrymple," he asked, "during the next few days?"

"No, thank heaven. The Lord deliver me from Liverpool and all its works! I'm going home tonight. I'm only a poor ruddy sailor, but nothing's going to stop me. My home is at Harlow, in Essex."

"Would you leave me your address, then?"

"Certainly. Why not? I haven't a card with me, but if you will write it down . . ."

Anthony removed the top of his fountain-pen in preparation, to exclaim somewhat disappointedly: "I'm short of ink—run dry! Perhaps you would be good enough to write it down for me."

"With pleasure," Dalrymple consented. Less than an hour later Mr. Bathurst sat in his room at his hotel and surveyed the name and address of the first officer of the *Gigantic*.

> COLIN ROWBOTHAM DALRYMPLE,
> *"Langlands",*
> *Harlow,*
>   *Essex.*

It was not the first time that he had seen that handwriting. The ornamental flourish of the "D" in Dalrymple, with its sweeping circular stroke at the top, gave him the clue that he wanted almost immediately. The handwriting was the same handwriting as that on the racing programme that had been found in the dead man's pocket. "*S, T, D,* and *M,*" he murmured: "all of them."

Chapter XXIX
THE BLOW FALLS

Mr. Bathurst boarded the London train at an obscure village station the existence of which had never even entered his dreams. The porter's news that the train for which he waited carried a restaurant car had reassured him exceedingly and caused him to anticipate his approaching journey with a much greater zest. On the whole, he was feeling very satisfied with the way that the case had gone. Since leaving the Rectory of Kirve St. Laudus he had taken three definite strides towards a successful conclusion. This conclusion would be brought very near to hand if the testing of one piece of evidence which he was bringing back from the North turned out to be satisfactory.

Upon his arrival at Polchester, he was fortunate enough to find a local train for Raybourne waiting at the side platform, and his luck still held when he entered the Raybourne police station. Inspector Curgenven, in company with Sergeant Millington, was there, and he listened attentively to the statement that Anthony Bathurst made to him.

"I knew the Wyndham family," he declared at length, "or perhaps I should say I knew *of* them. They were fairly prominent in Northlynn during my father's time, but I don't fancy that there are any of them living in Northlynn now. I think they cleared out. Of course I could find that out for you, if it's important. With regard to the other question that you raise, I can let you have the glasses that were found on Sutcliffe, if you think it will help you to have them."

"Thanks, Inspector," replied Mr. Bathurst cheerfully. "I am optimistic enough to cherish the idea that it will." He became confidential. "I am about to essay a trifling experiment in comparatives, Inspector, and if my efforts are attended with the success that I anticipate, you will be able to lay your hands on the man you're wanting—which will be a distinct feather in your cap, Curgenven. Don't forget that."

"It sounds all right, Mr. Bathurst, but your mention of feathers and caps makes me think of chickens and accountancy and such things as false analogies—I read that last word in a detective story two nights ago, and it's stuck in my mind ever since."

Bathurst smiled at the inspector's note of dubiety, and he turned on his heel.

"Well, your pessimism may be well founded, Curgenven," he declared as a parting sally; "we shall be in a position to see, I think, in a very short time from now. But remember this: if I'm right in my prediction of a moment ago, what will happen will stick in your mind a bit longer."

Michael and his father were at dinner when Anthony got back to the Rectory, and, of course, he had to hear from the former, with infinite patience, of the successful depositing of Eileen Trevor at Charles Parry-Probyn's place near Much Wenlock.

"You were insistent that she should exercise extreme care?" demanded Bathurst.

"You bet I was," returned the young man. "Eileen's as safe there as a coin in the Bank of England, or as a letter in the Post Office."

"An unfortunate simile, the latter," said Anthony dryly, "but I know what you intended to convey. Have you heard from Miss Trevor since you left her at your uncle's?"

"Yes," replied the Rector, "we heard by this evening's post. She wrote to me, as a matter of fact. Just a line, thanking me for the trouble I had taken and saying that she was all right. The letter was apparently written and posted yesterday evening. I was rather surprised that I should have been the selected recipient of her correspondence. I should have thought that that honour would have been reserved for Michael, but there you are, you never know—history records similar instances, and Miss Trevor has excellent tastes. We have it on unimpeachable record that 'the first shall be last and the last first', and I can quote to you also in support of my statement the historic stone that the builder refused, but which nevertheless, in spite of this setback, became the headstone of the corner."

Michael accepted his father's pleasantry with good grace, but Bathurst's mind was so set upon the imminent urgency of this problem that the Rector's banter found him perhaps less responsive than usual.

"Just a minute. Something I *must* know," put in Anthony. "Where's Mallinson these days? Seen anything of him lately?"

"Seen anything of him," repeated Michael, with a shade of dangerous meaning; "I should just think we have. Ask the guv'nor if you want the whole story."

The Rector of Kirve St. Laudus smiled benevolently as he peeled his banana, for it was a fruit that he loved exceedingly.

"Are not banana and guava, fruits of the Indies, greater than all the fruits grown of Albion?" he asked mockingly. "What was that you said, Michael?"

His son repeated his previous statement.

"Oh, about Mallinson's midnight visit to my study? I forgot for the moment, Bathurst, that you were unaware of that."

The Rector proceeded to relate to Anthony what had happened, and how he and Hector Savory had watched the performance and held their hand.

"I take it, Bathurst," he added, "that we did right, in view of the instructions you gave me upon leaving?"

Bathurst looked very grave when he answered the Rector's question. "Yes, sir, I think you did. I am very glad that you did. I want Mallinson to remain free—absolutely and unrestricted to do as he likes. If he thinks we are watching him, or that he is being spied upon in any way, that fact may hinder us rather than help us."

"Good," said the Rector. "It is comforting and consoling to reflect that one has taken the right course. By the way, Bathurst, there is something else that I must tell you. I understand that Mallinson repeated his little performance here at the 'Four Flamingos'."

"Oh—how was that?"

"Went through the Savorys' bedroom, I believe, very much as he went through my desk. So Bartholomew came and told me. Mallinson's a man who evidently believes in doing all things thoroughly and nothing by halves."

"Did the Savorys lose anything, do you know?" asked Bathurst.

"Don't think so," replied the Rector. "As far as they could tell they seemed to have been as fortunate as I in that respect, but I see from the paper that a similar occurrence has taken place at their house in Lancashire." He regarded Bathurst with a glint of amusement showing in his eyes. "How did you fare on your visit North? And what do you make of all these attempted burglaries?" he questioned.

"I got on extremely well, Rector, as I think you will see before very long." The words had scarcely left Anthony Bathurst's lips when Emily, the Rector's maid, entered the dining-room. The reddish envelope of a telegram showed somewhat flamboyantly on the salver that she carried in her hand. The Rector took up the envelope with a frown of perplexity. The frown deepened as he read the message, and both Michael and Anthony sensed immediately that the news he had received had perturbed him.

"What do you make of this, Bathurst?" he inquired, as he tossed over the flimsy form. "I confess that it disturbs me considerably."

Anthony noticed that the hand that held the telegram was shaking with emotion. What could have transpired to upset Parry-Probyn so thoroughly? He read the message:

Sorry to hear your bad news. Miss Trevor leaving immediately.—Charles.

It had been handed in at Much Wenlock, and the sender "Charles" was, of course, the Rector's brother, to whose care Eileen had been entrusted. Michael, white-faced and anxious, came at once to Bathurst's side.

"What does it mean, Bathurst?" he asked in a low voice that he endeavoured to keep as steady as possible.

"It means only one thing, Michael," came Bathurst's answer. "I told you that there would be another attack, and that I didn't know upon whom it would fall. Miss Trevor is in imminent danger. Perhaps even now we may be—"

"What?" demanded Michael. "You don't surely mean—?"

"I mean that we may be too late to help her." His face assumed that grim, set look that has boded ill for many a criminal. "But we'll trust not. She shan't go under without a struggle." He looked at his wrist-watch.

"There's no train before the morning, Bathurst—if that's what you're thinking," warned the Rector.

"I was afraid of that, sir. See to the Crossley for me, Michael—do you mind?—and be prepared to leave in a quarter of an hour. In the meantime, I want to telephone."

"I'm coming too," said the Rector; "wherever your destination is."

"You're not," said Mr. Bathurst; "you're staying here. This is a job for Michael and me." The rest of the sentence he whispered to Michael. "Oh, and bring your revolver, laddie, will you?"

Chapter XXX
THE PERIL OF EILEEN

It was something of an eerie sight at the door of the garage when Michael urged the big primrose-wheeled car from its resting-place. It was a very dark night, with little moonlight, and Bathurst had to employ his torch to assist the rapid and smooth working of the operations. The Rector of Kirve St. Laudus, who had come out in the wake of the two men, felt yet another twinge of apprehension when he heard Bathurst's next question to Michael. "Revolver all right, Michael?"

"O.K.! I've got it here." Michael patted his pocket.

"I trust," intervened his father, "that you will not be forced in any circumstances—"

"Leave him and that to me, sir," broke in Bathurst without ceremony. "If there's any shooting to be done at sight, I'll do it. But Michael may yet have to protect himself. We are not commanded to love our neighbour *more* than ourselves."

He referred to a large ordnance map that he took from his overcoat pocket.

"I'm going across country, sir—as far as possible, that is. It's nearly ten o'clock now, and I think I can get through to Exeborough by five o'clock tomorrow morning. What do you think? There we can pick up the Northern Express. But I've got to drive in the dark nearly all the way—don't forget that."

The Rector nodded. "You're making for—?"

"I'm not sure, sir! But I think your brother's place. I must, you see. It seems to me to be the only place where I can make sure of picking up any scent at all. However, I'll think things over. Get in, Michael."

Failing to observe the Rector's outstretched hand in the darkness, Bathurst got in and took the wheel, and the big Crossley glided out and away.

"Other way, Bathurst," corrected Michael, as the former turned the car at the Rectory gates.

"No, not yet." Bathurst was laconic.

"What do you mean—not yet?"

"The 'Four Flamingos' is our first place of call. I want to get there before they close. We shall only just do it. It will probably save us a lot of time, and, as I told you just now, we haven't a moment to lose. I don't like the look of things at all, Parry-Probyn. Don't talk to me until we're on the Exeborough road. I want to think."

Outside the inn of the quaint sign, Bathurst swung out of the car quickly and threw open the door that led the way to the unpretentious inn parlour. Michael followed him without any loss of time. To the somewhat slovenly lad who came forward to greet them Bathurst rapped a quick order. "Tell your guv'nor I want a word with him at once. Say that it's very urgent." The lad shambled off up the stone passage towards the public bar. Anthony drummed impatiently with his heels on the stone floor whilst he and Michael waited. But it wanted a very few minutes to ten, and Treliss, the landlord, did not take long to obey the summons that the lad had delivered to him.

"Yes, gentlemen, what are you wanting me for?" Bathurst went straight to his point.

"That gentleman you have stopping here—Mr. Mallinson, by name—is he still here?"

Treliss shook his head. "No, zurr—he be gone. Went away a couple of days ago—a little time before the two Mr. Savorys went."

"Did he go in a hurry?"

"What do you mean by that exactly, zurr?" Treliss smiled a broad smile. "He went off quick and unexpected-like, but he settled his bill all fair and square, if that's the point you're a-gettin' at."

"As I feared, Michael," said Bathurst; "we're late."

"Seemed to be settlin' down in these parts, too. I was fair surprised to lose him." Treliss was never a disciple of reticence. "Gettin' quite chummy, he were, with lots of the locals. Had old Orlando Horton in here the other night from Verrinder. Fair character, the old man is—I give you my word. He won't like 'Quarryman' beer after tasting mine."

"Good night, Treliss," interrupted Bathurst, "and many thanks. I'd stay for a while, but you'll be wanting to close, and I shall hear you saying, 'Time, gentlemen, please!' if I'm not careful."

He was silent when he re-entered the car, and for a long time Michael respected it, as he had learned to do. The car travelled well and the monotony of the journey through the darkness was relieved more than once by Bathurst stopping and alighting to read the directions on a signpost by the aid of his electric torch. After a time, and under the influence of the motion of the car, Michael fell asleep. It was intensely cold, and Bathurst tucked the thick travelling-rug round his knees and drove on. The boy could do with all the rest he could get.

When Michael awoke it was to find himself being driven through the streets of Exeborough, and to hear the clock of St. Alban's Church in the main street striking five. The street lamps were still alight, with their glasses showing the white finger-prints of King Winter, and Michael shivered in his seat as he came back from the land of slumber to the courts of wakefulness. And as this emotion passed through Michael, so also a similar feeling seemed to be passing through the town. The trams were crawling and clattering from the depot, and the workers whose industry made an early demand upon them were flitting with shadowy figures along the streets to the various hives that were destined to harbour them until the evening. From small eating-houses there came the smell of frying bacon. To Michael's surprise Inspector Curgenven was already on the platform of Exeborough station when they arrived there. This was certainly a contingency that he had not anticipated.

"Good morning, gentlemen. Come this way, will you? I've ordered hot coffee and rolls for you in the station-master's room, and there's ample time for you to enjoy your breakfast. Millington gave me your message, Mr. Bathurst, and I've made arrangements about your car. Where have you parked it?"

Bathurst told him, and thrust his hands into the deep pockets of his heavy travelling coat—thinking hard. "Where are we bound for?" continued the inspector.

Some seconds passed before Anthony replied.

"Frankly, Curgenven, I'm in considerable doubt. I've changed my mind, I think, since I left Kirve St. Laudus. If I play carefully, and cover every step and every inch of the ground, I *must* lose time—which is the last thing I can afford to lose. I've done a lot of thinking while I've been driving, and I've come to the conclusion that I must take a risk. God send that my judgment is happy. If not . . ." He stopped abruptly, and a shrug of his shoulders pointed his sentence.

Curgenven gave it rapid interpretation. "You think Miss Trevor is in danger?"

"I *know* that Miss Trevor is in grave danger." He was silent once more. But before the inspector spoke again, he went on: "By the way, Curgenven, I conducted that little experiment of mine in comparatives that I foreshadowed to you, with eminently satisfactory results. I only hope that this next one of mine will prove as successful. We're going to Liverpool—I've made up my mind."

"Liverpool?" queried Michael. "Not to my uncle's, then?"

"No," replied Bathurst; "although it's on the cards that we may have to retrace our steps and work back there. That's the risk which I indicated just now. But at the moment my trump card is Crosby's Hotel! Crosby's Hotel in Gulliver Street."

Chapter XXXI
ON MALLINSON'S HEELS

THE TRAIN ran to scheduled time, and it was a few minutes past four when the three men alighted on the platform of Lime Street Station, Liverpool.

"There's a decent hotel at the top of Regent Street." It was Michael who volunteered the information.

"That's good news, but I'm booking no rooms yet awhile, Michael," protested Bathurst. "I must make sure of our ground first. We're travelling light, besides—so it doesn't matter a great deal. You and Curgenven stay here for a moment. I'm going to ring up Crosby's Hotel. After that we can make our arrangements."

He was soon back to them, and, perhaps for the first time since the primrose-wheeled Crossley slipped swiftly away from the garage at the Rectory of Kirve St. Laudus, his face showed signs of the strain that had been imposed upon him.

"So far so good," he encouraged them. "We're not beaten yet. The risk I took in coming straight here has been justified. Mallinson is at Crosby's Hotel. I've just spoken to Crosby himself. Our man has been out since breakfast this morning, and according to Crosby returned about an hour ago. Now, Curgenven, this is where you come into the cast. I want a man to watch that hotel and also to have a fast car at his disposal. I want a second man to keep in constant touch with the first, and who can communicate with us at our hotel at a minute's notice. I'm pretty confident that tonight will see the finish of this ghastly business, and that, if we play our cards properly, Mallinson will lead us to Miss Trevor. Can you manage all that for me, do you think?"

"Where shall we be, Mr. Bathurst?"

"Derbyshire's Hotel, Regent Street. Mr. Parry-Probyn and I will get along there now and fix things up. I suppose you won't want a hot-water bottle?"

Curgenven grinned. "Very good, Mr. Bathurst. While you're doing that I'll pop along and arrange those matters of yours with the police."

The three men dined at six o'clock in a private room, and Michael subsequently smoked cigarette after cigarette in a hopelessly futile attempt to steady his nerves and distract his attention from what was to come. He found these periods of inaction far more trying than the heat of the struggle, no matter what danger the latter might possess. Every sudden noise startled him and caused him to scan the faces of his two companions with swift anxiety. Nearly two hours passed in this way, but soon after the clock on the mantelpiece had struck eight there came a tap upon the door, and at Bathurst's almost simultaneous invitation a waiter entered.

"Inspector Curgenven?" he inquired of them.

"I'm your man," replied Curgenven at once. "What is it?"

"You're wanted on the phone, sir; I was asked to inform you. In the manager's private room on the floor below."

Curgenven wasted no time and returned to them within two minutes.

"Mallinson has just left Crosby's hotel," he reported. "So far he is on foot, and we have two men in the car trailing him easily. One of them will report at once if there's any change in his movements."

"Where was he making for? Did your man say? In what direction?"

"East," returned Curgenven.

Michael jumped to his feet under the stress of his excitement. "I shan't be able to stand this much longer, Bathurst. How long are we to sit here doing nothing? Can't we—?"

Bathurst restrained him.

"We are *not* doing nothing, Michael. On the contrary we have established communication to which we shall hold on."

The words had scarcely left his lips when the waiter who had come before put his head round the door. "'Phone again, sir," he said to the inspector. "Urgent, too. according to what was said."

Curgenven raced down and raced back. "Come on," he announced. "Things are moving, and so are we—now. One of our men reports that Mallinson is at Fiske's Garage, Palatine Street. He's engaging a car, and according to the man who 'phoned me the people there know him as a previous customer. I should say he's well used to dirty work, because he's evidently hired a car from them before. We're to get round there as quickly as we can in our car. My men will contrive to leave a message for us."

"Come, Michael," cried Anthony. "The waiting game is over. You're going to feel better now, boy. And see that that revolver of yours is handy. Mine may not be enough."

They were away from the hotel with incredible swiftness, and their chauffeur, whom Curgenven had requested to be especially chosen for his knowledge of the country adjoining and of the city of Liverpool itself, brought them to within a hundred yards of Fiske's Garage in Palatine Street with rapid efficiency. The inspector dropped from the car, and simultaneously almost, as he made his way to the establishment, a youth came forward to meet him The latter touched his forehead.

"I was told to tell you by the other gentleman that you were to follow on to Kenyon Moss. If there's any alteration he'll let you know. You're only a matter of about three minutes behind."

"Right," acknowledged Curgenven. He slipped a coin into the lad's hand, ran back to the waiting car, and instructed the chauffeur accordingly. The latter digested the information, leant forward from his driving-seat and explained the position. Curgenven listened attentively.

"From what our driver tells me," he said to the others, when back in the car again, "we're bound for the ironworks and collieries part of the county. He says that between Liverpool and St. Helens there lie several of the principal mines in Lancashire."

"I hope to blazes we pick up our man before very long," confessed Bathurst. "I shall feel much more comfortable then. He mustn't give us the slip. If he did, I should never forgive myself."

Michael jerked his head back towards the driver. "Tell this fellow to step on the juice. I feel much the same as you—only more so."

For a quarter of an hour they drove in silence, and then an exclamation from Curgenven broke the spell.

"There's my man in my car," he cried, "not more than two hundred yeards in front! You can bet Mallinson's not very far in front of him. Look out—my chap's slowing down."

Bathurst picked up the speaking-tube and spoke to the driver.

"Crawl up to the car in front, and see if they want to communicate something. Don't pass it on any account."

A moment later the first police-car turned to the left and ran for a few yards down a side road. Bathurst's car followed suit. The driver of the first car stopped, alighted and came to speak to Curgenven.

"Our man's only about a quarter of a mile in front, sir," he announced. "He's making for Kenyon Moss. I managed to get in the garage when he hired the car and I heard him instruct the driver. He's been there before, for he described the actual place that he wanted to old Fiske. Now my difficulty's this: if I keep behind him I'm afraid he'll spot before very long that he's being followed. What do you say to us taking another route across country that I know well and getting there before him? My car's much faster than the old bus he's hired; old Fiske doesn't let his best stuff out to roam around the Kenyon Moss district, and I'm driving a Bentley."

"How far is this place Kenyon Moss?" Bathurst put the question incisively.

"About thirty-four miles, sir. Through Dyer Green, Peerstown, Gibbonsbridge, Smurthwaite and Barton Fell."

Anthony shook his head. "Keep straight on, then. I can't afford to risk any more. A young girl's life is in peril. Keep picking the man up without getting too close, and we'll do the same behind you. If anything goes wrong, signal at once, and for heaven's sake be careful!"

The two big cars swung away again, and they were through Dyer Green before Michael noticed the first diminution of pace. The country through which they were now passing lay close to the Lancashire and Staffordshire Canal and was black and forbidding in its appearance. Ironworks, railway sidings and mine shafts dotted the landscape, and there seemed to be nothing else visible for miles round. The cars pressed on, and Bathurst, now by no means free from anxiety, looked at his wrist-watch. It was close on ten o'clock, and, judging from the pace at which they had travelled, he felt that they must be nearing their destination. Suddenly the car commenced to sway and jolt and eventually came to a standstill. Michael began to fume, but before he could express himself in words the driver came to the door and opened it.

"We're on the edge of the Kenyon Moss district, Inspector, and the car in front reports that the chap we're after has got out of his car and is going ahead on foot."

"How far ahead is he now?" called Bathurst curtly.

"About three hundred yards, sir—no more. He's round the big bend you can see up yonder. That's why I pulled the cars up here."

"Has he left his driver in charge of the car, do you know?"

"Yes, sir."

"How are we going to circumvent him, then? It will mean us making a detour." Bathurst moved his foot carelessly and kicked something on the ground. "What's this?" he cried. "Where are we?"

"That's an old disused fish-plate, sir. You'll find plenty such round here. Fish-plates, old rails and rivets. We're close to the old Talisman Mine, you see, once one of the most important coalmines in England, but abandoned now."

"You men take the cars off the direct route and stand by with lights out," ordered Anthony. "You and I, Michael, and Inspector Curgenven will go forward at once. Spread out and move slowly. Get as much cover as you can when you pass Mallinson's car, and when you locate Mallinson, if either of you do before I do, hold on where you are and pass the word along as quietly as possible. Have your revolvers handy, and remember that I've a powerful electric torch if it should be wanted. It's as dark as hell."

Bathurst did not exaggerate in his last statement. There was little moon, and Michael moved forward with an inexplicable sense of impending danger. The loneliness and darkness of this abandoned place seemed more frightening of themselves than any actual peril could ever be. They rapped themselves round him and chilled his very soul.

"Hist," came in a low voice from Bathurst to his left; "be careful—Mallinson's car on the move—coming this way, too."

He saw Bathurst and Curgenven drop on their faces and commence to wriggle forward—so he did likewise. The manoeuvre proved successful, and they crawled forward for another two hundred yards or more. It seemed to Michael that he was travelling downhill nearly all the time, and when they came to a halt he looked behind him and could see the downward line of pathway that he had traversed. From a hiding-place behind a line of scrub-like bushes they could see in front of them a kind of clearing or open space, in the middle of which yawned the black aperture of the abandoned Talisman Mine. Old boards lay scattered round the mouth of the pit, and Michael found himself wondering for what they had been used.

It was a little lighter here, and a raw, cold wind was now blowing in their faces. Suddenly Michael felt his arm gripped. It was Bathurst—who was sniffing at the air. A familiar, domestic, and altogether delightful smell met Michael's nostrils, and he inhaled it gratefully. It was that pleasurable scent of burning tobacco. Bathurst put his finger to his lips and stabbed with the forefinger of his other hand towards a biggish bush thirty yards or so away to the left—a bush which commanded better than any other the downhill slope that trickled its serpentine way to the mouth of the mine. As the wind blew the twigs of the bush apart a figure could be seen crouched there, intent on the downward road to the shaft. Michael recognized it at once, and the beating of his heart responded to the recognition. It was Mallinson, and Michael noticed with a start of surprise that he had discarded his sling.

Chapter XXXII
IN THE NICK OF TIME

AFTER WATCHING Mallinson for a moment or two Michael looked away and saw Bathurst beckoning him. He obeyed the obvious request and edged towards Anthony, wondering what the trouble was. Bathurst put his mouth right against Michael's ear and spoke in a very low tone.

"Follow me as quietly as you can," he whispered, "and mind the loose stones. I'm going to skirt round to the mouth of the mine—on the opposite side to this. I've got an idea."

"What about leaving Mallinson?" Michael whispered in reply.

"I've told Curgenven what I'm going to do and where we're going. He'll stay over this side and keep an eye on Mallinson. It will be all right. Come on."

Bathurst sidled away noiselessly, and Michael slithered after him. There was much more cover in the region for which they were now heading than their previous position had held, for the abandoned accessories of the old mine were scattered in profusion round the near approach to the shaft, and their shapes and shadows made patches of blackness all round. More rivets and fish-plates, rusted and corroded railway lines coloured with the tints of disuse and rottenness, and heaps of old, worn-out sleepers bore witness to the fact that close by had been a siding connected with the mine, but which had been removed in parts and was now in a complete condition of abandonment. It was very dark in the region for which Bathurst was making, and the heaps of rubbish on the ground caused it to appear darker still—so much so that Michael had sometimes great difficulty in picking out Bathurst's figure as it moved in front of him. Several of the boards that he had been able to distinguish before from his position in the bushes now lay near at hand.

Bathurst stopped, and Michael quickened his pace and moved up to him. "Can we be seen here?" he asked.

Bathurst shook his head. "Don't think so. It's so hellishly dark. Keep in the shadow of that pile of old sleepers."

"What are all these boards for?" queried Michael. "To cover the mouth of the mine."

"Why have they been moved, then?"

"That's a question I asked myself just now, Michael—when I first saw them. I kept on asking myself. The answer is—to further a devilish enterprise."

The colour ebbed from Michael's face when he heard the words—and he snatched at Bathurst's arm.

"What do you mean? Don't tell me that—"

"Quiet, Michael, please," returned Bathurst, interrupting him. "Listen!"

Michael strained his ears. The noise of the engine of a car gradually came to him. He listened attentively. It was coming from somewhere in front of them, from some point along that road which they themselves had travelled. No sooner had he realized the truth of this conjecture than he saw the headlights of a car glimmering away in the distance. They grew brighter and brighter as the car, without any appreciable slackening of speed, commenced to descend the long, sloping pathway that gradually dropped down to the mouth of the mine on the farther side of which they were. To his utter amazement the car showed no signs of stopping, but came on and on. Bathurst's exclamation of horror jerked him back to immediate action.

"Quick! These boards, Michael. Up with them! Give me a hand, quick! It's a slender chance, heaven knows, but we must take it."

Michael divined his intention and clutched feverishly at the long board that lay nearest to his feet. In a second they had raised it on its end and, as it swayed to its full height, pushed it gently to fall over the black yawning pit.

"God send it doesn't jump or fall short, Michael." With straining eyes they watched it crash over the lip of the shaft, shift a foot and jump a little, and—hold!

"How far has the car still to come, Michael?"

"It's about half-way down the long slope now. For God's sake be quick, Bathurst!"

"Impossible to get round in time. Another board—quick, man, quick!—and as close to the other as we can get it!"

A second board was raised to its towering height in the same manner as its predecessor, and Michael felt the muscles of his back almost tearing to shreds under the strain. This time it fell dead on a wet patch of ground, with a heavy thud, shivered twice, as it were, and held.

"Now, Michael, after me—quick!"

Bathurst raced round the edge of the mouth of the mine in the direction of the oncoming car, which seemed now to be travelling much more slowly. Michael, always fleet of foot, was but a few yards behind him. They had covered only a short distance when the off-door of the car opened, and to their utter amazement a dark figure took a flying leap out. As he did so two other figures broke away from the clump of bushes to the left and ran with all their might across the clearing towards the car. Suddenly one broke away from the other and hurled himself at the prostrate figure of the man who had jumped from the car. The other man who had dashed out from the bushes ran on with incredible swiftness after the now slowly moving car.

He overtook it but a hundred yards from the black mouth of the mine, leapt on the running-board, and through the opened door pulled the body of a girl from the back of the car. He bent down for a moment before flinging her out on to the ground, but Michael's heart came clean into his mouth when he realized the inevitable end to it all. The driver of the car tried to rise from his seat by the wheel, but the man who had jumped on the vehicle forced him back with merciless strength on to his seat as the car ran towards the yawning edge. Michael, sickened at the sight, could watch no longer, and put his hands across his eyes. By the mercy of Providence, however, which staged one of its oft-recurring miracles of divine benevolence, the car ran straight for the two boards which bridged the mine with such narrow frailty. They held the car's weight for a palpitating part of a moment. Short though it was—it was just enough!

The man on the running-board turned, leapt back-wards with the strength and ferocity of despair and hurled himself into safety. The car swayed for a second, left the meagre bridge, and then ran smoothly and mercilessly into Eternity! Man and vehicle toppled into the black pit with a tremendous crash, and there came back from the depths a muffled roar as they struck the invisible bottom. Then there seemed to float over the scene a devastating quietness and all was silent once again in the Talisman Mine . . . Away in the darkness a dog barked. . . .

"See to Miss Trevor at once, Michael," cried Bathurst. "Curgenven's snared one of his birds all right—I saw him put the bracelets on him—and the other gentleman here needs my attention."

Michael needed no second bidding to the task assigned to him, and Anthony ran towards the man who had just looked so closely into the eyes of the Angel of Death. It was Mallinson. He picked himself up awkwardly and lurched forward towards Anthony—white and shaking.

"I guess I'm all right, Mr. Bathurst, and so I think is Eileen. She seems to be in good hands. But we cut it rather fine, didn't we?"

Anthony shook him warmly by the hand. "I certainly shan't contradict you on that point. But I never tumbled to their devilish game until it was almost too late, and my plans nearly went astray. You're a very brave man—I should have been helpless without you. Also, I'm proud to have met you."

Michael called to him from the darkness, and they turned at the sound of his voice.

"She's coming round; she's only fainted—the best thing that could have happened in the circumstances."

"She was bound and gagged on the floor of the car," explained the man who had saved her. "I was only just in time to release her and throw her clear."

"Come and let her thank you," said Mr. Bathurst. "I'll introduce you."

Michael stared as he heard the statement. What the blazes was Bathurst talking about? Mallinson and Miss Trevor knew each other quite . . . Then he heard Bathurst speaking again. The words came to him dimly out of the darkness.

"The man who saved your life, Miss Trevor! Or as I prefer to put it, your father, Sir Roland Walsingham. You owe him a greater debt than ever."

Chapter XXXIII
WHAT HAPPENED IN THE PLANTATION

ANTHONY BATHURST paused and gazed back into a patch of black shadow.

"And here, if I mistake not," he continued, "comes Curgenven with Mr. Bartholomew Savory. One more, and our little party would be complete. What a pity Master Hector left it too late to bring off his little jumping act, as performed with such success by his father. Delays are proverbially dangerous!"

He stopped again, and his cynicism turned into a mood of cold gravity. "Perhaps, after all, it was as well. The greater criminal will meet with the greater punishment, which is entirely as it should be. For the father—death with a crawl; for the son—death with a pounce." He shrugged his shoulders. "A pair of pretty scoundrels. Take Miss Eileen and Michael up to your car, Sir Roland, will you? I'll stay behind a moment or two and arrange things with Curgenven." He turned and looked at the murderer whom he had taken, and there was cold horror in his eyes. The man shrank from him.

The Rector of Kirve St. Laudus pulled the big chesterfield up to the fire.

"We may as well be as comfortable as possible after an excellent dinner such as we have enjoyed, with its creatures of root, fruit, flesh and wine. Who is going to allay our curiosity first—you, Bathurst, or you, Sir Roland? The cigars are on that small table, Michael—unless our guests prefer cigarettes."

Anthony Bathurst looked across to Walsingham. "I think, perhaps, if Sir Roland tells us his part of the story it will help you all to understand my narrative better when my turn comes."

Walsingham laughed, and Michael Parry-Probyn pulled Eileen a little closer to him on the big settee with a gesture of proprietorship.

"I'm quite ready to fall in with Mr. Bathurst's suggestion," agreed the tawny-haired baronet. "I guess that having paid the piper, as one might say, he's well entitled to call the tune. I'd tell that to the world." He lit his cigar with deliberation. "After all—I don't know that I've such a tremendous lot to tell you as you might imagine. But I'll do the thing properly and start at the right place—the beginning! Over twenty years ago I quarrelled with my father, and the bone of contention was the usual one—a girl. Sorry, Eileen, to describe your sex so ungallantly—but you know what I mean. The old man and I had a hammer-and-tongs row and I cleared out—to the States—with the girl who became your mother. He said so many unforgivable things to me before I left, that I hardened my heart against him after the manner of Pharaoh, and swore I'd finished with him for all time. I didn't desire to hear from him again, or to communicate with him at all, and when your mother and I, Eileen, had a very narrow escape in the big railway disaster in California in 1909, when a great many of the dead were so burned as to be unrecognizable, I didn't trouble to contradict a report that she and I had perished. I changed my name to Trevor and started a fruit farm at Tacoma, and when Eileen here was about five I sent her to an English school. When my wife died and the farm prospered, I just lost interest in most things outside my business and was content to jog along without worrying about the Old Country at all. As far as I knew my father was a poor man and the chance of inheriting riches from him never entered my head."

"One minute, Sir Roland," put in Bathurst. "When your father died you were advertised for in both English and American papers. How was it you never saw an inquiry for Sir Joshua's heir?"

"I never saw a British newspaper, and took only a local Tacoma one. The first intimation of my inheritance came to me most unexpectedly. I was on a trip to Puget Sound in July last when I ran across a very old friend from my home district—a man named Forsyth, who had been at school with me. To cut a long story short he was amazed to recognize me, as he had counted me dead years before. He was in the middle of a tour round the world for a holiday, and spotted me from a peculiar scar I carry on my forearm. As I got it through burning myself very badly in the school lab. when he and I were doing a 'stinks' experiment, you can figure out how it was that he spotted me for a dead certainty. He told me of my father's baronetcy, death, and fortune, and also how I had been sought for as the sole heir to a little matter of two hundred and seventy-three thousand pounds." He paused for a moment and knocked the ash from the end of his cigar.

"You may or may not believe me, gentlemen—but I'll tell you that I hesitated for a week or so about coming home to claim it. Anyhow, it's perfectly true. Eileen's future, however, eventually decided me, and I wrote to the Savorys in July and to her in August, acquainting them all of my intentions.

"I wasn't anxious to leave the farm for a month or two, owing to pressure of business, and I also wanted a little time to think things over. In October I communicated with the Savorys again, and told my chief assistant, a man named Mallinson and a man whom I liked, that I wanted him to accompany me to England. I wanted companionship badly, and I thought Mallinson would give it to me better than anybody I knew. He had been with me long enough to understand my whims and fancies. I didn't tell him all the news. Just a rough outline; but he guessed there was money in it—I'm sure of that." Walsingham stopped again and broke into a laugh. "I think the idea tickled him rather—he started to call me Arthur Orton, after the notorious Tichborne claimant."

Anthony Bathurst smiled with him. "I knew that; the first officer of the *Gigantic* told me—although in his case he failed to establish the proper connection." Walsingham went on. "Well, Mallinson and I crossed on the *Gigantic* and reached Liverpool on the seventh of last month. Note now what happened directly we docked. A letter was delivered to my cabin, and try as I would I was unable to trace who had brought it. The contents had been typed and were in the form of a warning message. Remembering it now after the lapse of time, and after all that we have been through since, the letter read something like this:

> *"If you wish to live to enjoy your inheritance keep a still tongue in your head and confide your movements and intentions to nobody. Do all your business yourself and unaccompanied.*
>
> *"A friend.

"The words 'yourself and unaccompanied' were heavily underlined."

"To whom was this addressed?"

"To me, Bathurst. I thought I made that clear."

"Yes—but to the name of Trevor or Walsingham? You were very reticent when I tackled you before."

"Oh—Trevor. I'm sorry I didn't see your point."

"Thank you, Sir Roland. Go on, please."

Sir Roland continued: "Well, it was then that I made my big mistake. I confided in Mallinson—fully. We had fixed up at Crosby's Hotel, and on the eighth I made my plans. That warning I had received worried me just a bit, and it struck me that there might possibly be something in it. I determined to visit the Savorys at their private house instead of at their office. I thought that their house out at Loxteth would be much less likely to be watched. I disappeared after breakfast and arranged with Mallinson to meet him that evening to go together to Loxteth Chase. I was armed with the necessary documents and certificates to establish my claim, and we each carried revolvers, for I considered that if there were a rough house or anything of the sort two fists with shooting-irons would be better than one."

Walsingham stopped, and the hardest of hard looks came into his eyes before he proceeded.

"We were on foot, and our way lay through Loxteth plantation," he continued, "which in one part goes down sheer to the edge of the River Stroath, which is, as you probably know, one of the lesser tributaries of the Mersey. It was very dark, and I was walking a few yards ahead of Mallinson. Besides being dark it was darned lonely—we hadn't passed a soul for a couple of miles. The time, I should think, would be about a quarter to eight. Suddenly I heard a clicking sort of noise behind me, and turned instinctively. Gentlemen, if ever I saw murder in a man's eyes I saw it in Mallinson's then. Black murder! His revolver was drawn, and he was taking careful aim at me. I flung myself to one side like a streak of greased lightning as his finger pressed the trigger, but the hot searing pain through my shoulder told me where his bullet had gone home.

"I fell to the ground, and as I did so I realized that I had one chance of life, and one only—a slight one at that. I shammed dead—played 'possum'. My treacherous gentleman approached me, turned me over, satisfied himself that he had finished me, dragged me towards the slope, rifled my pockets of all documents and means of identification, took my revolver, put his revolver in my hand, a letter in my pocket, and finally gave me a hefty kick which sent me headlong down the sloping bank to the dark water of the Stroath below. I had the sense to let my body relax and roll onward. I knew it was too dark for him to follow my rolling body all the way to the water's edge, so I pulled up a few yards from the brink, caught hold of a big stone, and heaved it with a splash into the water."

Eileen clutched Michael's arm, and her shining eyes were eloquent testimony to her admiration for her father's resource and intuition.

"Go on," she half whispered.

"I listened attentively for a few minutes, but could hear nothing. So I took careful stock of myself and my position. First of all there was my shoulder. I stopped the bleeding as best I could, and it seemed to me that the bullet had gone clean through, which was all to the good. Then I read the letter he had shoved into my pocket. Here it is. Read it, Bathurst. Read it out."

Sir Roland pulled it from his pocket. Bathurst took it and obeyed.

> *"I have determined to take my own life. My employer, Mr. Trevor, has found me out, and there's nothing ahead for me but dismissal, disgrace, and perhaps prison. It would take me years to repay the money I have stolen. Good-bye all.*
>
> *"James B. Mallinson."*

Sir Roland went on at once. "In an instant I saw through his little game. *I was to commit suicide as Mallinson! He was to appear armed with my credentials as Sir Roland Walsingham!* And who would be the wiser? Even if he had known of Forsyth's existence, by the time Forsyth came back from his world tour he could be miles away, with a hell of a lot of my money. And Eileen and Savory hadn't any real knowledge of me at all. At the hotel where we had slept the evening before I doubt if anybody knew t'other from which. We were just Mallinson and Trevor together, and either, as far as England was concerned, could be accepted as the other."

Bathurst nodded agreement.

"I realized that only too well. There was just one difficulty, though, he might be put in—as far as I could see. Trevor's signature. Yours."

"He knew it well, and I've no doubt had practised copying it many times."

"I'll come back to the point later—if Miss Trevor doesn't," returned Anthony. "What did you do next?"

"I decided to return to Crosby's Hotel and await events. All that I had to do, it seemed to me, was to reappear from the dead and spoil friend Mallinson's little game. I went back to Gulliver Street, fixed up a sling for my arm, together with an explanation, had a drink with Crosby last thing, said nothing to anybody, and waited for my erstwhile right-hand man to reappear in all his counterfeit glory. To my utter consternation and amazement he never turned up! I hung on there—not knowing what to do—but just thinking things over. Then an idea came to me. *Was the warning genuine after all?* Had he walked into a plot and to a death that was meant for me? Then I thought of my daughter Eileen, down at Freyne, and of her possible danger as the heiress after me.

"That brought me to a quick decision. For the time being I would continue to wear the identity that Mallinson had attempted to thrust upon me, for nobody knew me definitely as Trevor. In this direction—if the real Trevor lay low—might lay safety for me, and—what was even more important—safety for her. So, as Trevor's friend and companion, I called upon the Savorys, to discover if possible if the real Mallinson had been to them in his masquerade. When they told me no I detailed the story to them as I had amended it to suit the new conditions, and we three resolved to acquaint Miss Trevor with the entire facts. I wired to Eileen and prepared her for our coming. It was safer than writing, because she had had a letter from me in August and I couldn't have Mallinson's fist bearing too strong a resemblance to Trevor's."

Eileen leant forward to him with an expressive gesture. Her failure to understand was something very obvious upon her face.

"But I had a letter from Mallinson, telling me that my father—"

Sir Roland interrupted her with a laugh. "Had met with an accident! I know. You sprang that on me when I came to Freyne and I had to pretend that I had sent it. Don't you remember? What is more, I had to be pretty quick on the uptake over that. Mallinson, of course, wrote and posted that to you before he tried to murder me. It was necessary to his plan. He was so confident of success that he sent it off beforehand. It was to have the effect of keeping you quiet long enough for him to feather his nest, or, rather, *my* nest," he corrected.

A gleam came into Anthony Bathurst's grey eyes. "That letter helped me immensely."

The rector observed and smiled at his enthusiasm. "'Who is as the wise man?'" he quoted, "'and who knoweth the interpretation of a thing? A man's wisdom maketh his face to shine'."

"Bathurst's wisdom made many things, Rector," intervened Sir Roland. "We went to the police—the Savorys and I—as you know—with our stories, and the police ran up against a dead wall everywhere. Really, Bathurst, I think this is where you should come in, for I confess there are many things that still are hopelessly dark to me. How did Mallinson become Sutcliffe? When I think of that my brain does a whirl and refuses to function."

"I agree with Sir Roland," declared the rector. "Take up the parable, Gamaliel, and we others will assume the authentic and historic attitude. I shall assume it with some degree of proper and pardonable pride. Indeed, I think I might be allowed a kneeling position, for if it hadn't been for me playing the organ after evensong on 'Stir-up' Sunday, this affair would have ended on a higher note of tragedy even than on which it opened." He turned to Michael and Eileen with a whimsical smile. "Please remember, you two young people, that you owe the presence of Bathurst in this affair to me. In fact, Michael, my skill in the selection of persons is equal to your own. Which is very high praise, Miss Eileen, I assure you."

Chapter XXXIV
ANTHONY BATHURST UNTIES THE KNOT

ANTHONY BATHURST smiled across at Eileen and accorded her a little bow.

"I agree with the rector," he said, "in the matter of that last statement. So much so that I think the compliment is entirely mine. I would never desire to be rated higher." He selected a cigarette from Sir Roland's proffered case and lit it contemplatively. When he started his story he had become grave again.

"It is when I reflect upon this affair as a whole that I realize how one clue, and one clue only, served to help me to link up the events that had occurred—seemingly unrelated—in two counties. Two counties as far apart as Glebeshire and Lancashire. If I hadn't chanced upon that one piece of evidence we might have . . ." He broke off and shrugged his shoulders with a gesture of resignation.

"I knew that a murder had been committed, but the dead man's identity had been so cleverly concealed that I fear it would have been next door to impossible to have brought his slayers to justice without this piece of evidence to which I refer." The rector interrupted. "Do you mind if I try to follow your reasoning, Bathurst—or, rather, to attempt to anticipate it?"

"Not at all, sir. Go ahead."

"The clue of which you are now speaking was the photograph. I am well aware of that. But beyond that actual statement I am unable to travel."

"You are right, Rector. But I saw more in that photograph than you did. Do you remember the expressions 'Geoduck for ever', and 'The Lifting of the Ban'?"

The rector nodded, and Sir Roland's eyes betrayed their admiration, for he at least saw Bathurst's direction. The last-named continued: "The geoduck (which on the photograph we saw written as GeoDuck) is a large edible clam peculiar to the shores and mud flats of the Western States. In Great Britain they are usually called gaper-shells, but the learned know them as *Panopea generosa*. They weigh from six to ten pounds and burrow vertically several feet into the mud—breathing when they get there by means of extraordinary siphons generally misnamed necks, which just reach to the surface. Hunting these strange creatures provides sport for hundreds. The moment the nose affair is lifted and poked above the sand, a spear is stuck into it and then the hunter digs down into the sand very rapidly until he comes to the shell. Now mark my words. There has been a fifteen-year ban on geoduck hunting—*a ban which was lifted on July fourteenth last at Tacoma.*

"The shore of Puget Sound was crowded on that particular Sunday, and from that photograph I knew that I had safely arrived at Tacoma as my starting-point, or at any rate close to it. The dead man had a Tacoma or Tacoma district association! *So had the man who had disappeared from the City of Liverpool!* Now let me retrace my mental steps to the finding of the body. A theory came to me early on that the man was meant by his murderer *to be identified as somebody else*. I considered that more than one feature pointed to it, and eventually I struck something that definitely made up my mind for me."

He turned to the rector and Michael. "You will remember that Doctor Wilcox, although not a skilled oculist, was able to see from the doubly-concave glasses worn by the dead man that they had been made for a person with an unusually myopic left eye. The body, as we saw it, however, was entirely *innocent of a single wrinkle or mark round the corners of the eyes*, some of which at least are *inseparable* from short sight, because the sufferer screws the eyes up in order to see the distant object with a greater degree of clearness. Also there was no such mark from the eye to the ear as horn-rimmed spectacles invariably leave. If the face be pale the mark is red. If the face be tanned the mark is white. I experimented on myself with the actual glasses. But in the case of the dead man there was no mark at all. This body, I said to myself, is a substitution."

"Oh—good," muttered Eileen under her breath, and at the sudden eulogy Anthony Bathurst rubbed his hands. "Yes—the body was *not* the body of the man who habitually travelled on top, although it was meant *to be identified* as his—the man who endured drenching rain, although a martyr to muscular rheumatism so acute that he was unable to shave himself! Of course—because he knew that the dead man would have *a growth of hair* when found, and Mrs. Nuckey would see it. She never identified *Sutcliffe*! She identified the *combination of externals* that she knew in him so well and which she was prepared to find when she came! Horn-rimmed glasses, the man's coat, his unusual hat, and the unshaven chin. There they were—each one of them. For he was dressed exactly as Sutcliffe.

'Where had the change been effected? That was my next problem. It must have been after Lanning somewhere. Could it have been brought off somewhere during the stoppage in Northlynn? Did the mud on the seat and the top rail indicate that a man had stood on them? Was there any window, for instance, that overlooked the top of the vehicle so closely that the body could have been lowered in the fog on to it while Whitehead cowered from the rain upon the platform? I remembered that wonderful clue of the master detective Holmes—'points and a curve, Watson'—that led to the body on the top of the train, and I also recalled how narrow were the Northlynn streets. As a matter of fact, Rector, let me tell you, I was walking the other day in Northlynn on the pavement near the 'Blue Boar', and the way was so narrow that an occupant of a car stopping alongside me almost knocked me over as she pushed open the door.

The rector nodded. He had endured similar incidents. "Well, we re-ran the journey, as you know, with the substitute cast, and there was the empty shop at Northlynn with its window-sill ready made for the murderer's purpose. On the left-hand side of the bus, mark you—the side that Mr. Hector Savory, in his character of Sutcliffe, always chose! What I found in the room behind the window-sill pleased me greatly, for the various marks that were noticeable on the dead man had all, to my eyes, postulated a condition of duress or of imprisonment even before his actual murder. Consider these points: the wounds on his wrists were more like tears than cuts, and such as I had once seen upon a man who had attempted to wrench himself free from handcuffs that bit into his flesh. When I saw this I examined the body further for corroborative support. It was there! There was a mark on his palate where the gag had been forced upwards into his mouth, and there was also a stain on the lapel of his coat where food had been spilled when he had been fed by his captors with his hands useless."

Bathurst stopped and selected another cigarette. As he did so the rector broke in again.

"I am curious, my boy. What was the smudge on the back of the overcoat?"

"It came from the window-sill of the shop when his body was dragged over."

The rector nodded. "I see. Go on, my boy."

"The evidence of the room all fitted the theory that I had formed. The man had been strangled. Wilcox had likened the job to a Thug outrage—and there was an elastic band very similar to the bands that the Thugs so often use. There were also the rough appliances for eating and drinking, an enamel mug and earthenware plate, and there was a length of clothes-line. A valuable adjunct towards enforced captivity! The sofa bore marks that a reclining man's feet might well have made, and the faint scent of hair-oil on the head-rest made me more confident still that the dead man had lain there before his murder. I put my-self into his position—both physically and mentally. If I had wished to communicate with the outside world, how could I have done it? Remember—Mallinson was handcuffed and perhaps tied as well. Could he have pushed anything into the spaces of the sofa in any way? How? I considered carefully, and this is the conclusion to which I came: he might have been able to use his mouth and teeth, for there is no doubt that there were occasions when the gag was removed.

I tried it as well as I could, and I determined to search that sofa very thoroughly before I came away. And I found the Tacoma photograph!

"By infinite patience in the use of his arms and teeth, Mallinson had worked up his coat to his mouth, pulled the card from his breast pocket—using his teeth, of course—turned over flat on his stomach, and pushed the photograph into its hiding-place. It had softened at the corner from the flow of his saliva. A little thing, Miss Eileen, for your life to rest on, eh?"

"By Jove!" said Sir Roland. "But I suppose you're right, though. Just fancy! Your next step was, of course, Liverpool?"

"Yes, Sir Roland. There had been a postcard, if you remember, Rector, postmarked 'Poole'—but that marking was only the version of Mrs. Nuckey. 'Pool', what that lady really saw, was the termination of Liverpool. And there was another statement that she had made that intrigued me exceedingly, as the ladies say. She said that Sutcliffe hinted at enemies hailing from Patagonia, and that he spoke of them as being of small physique! But the Patagonian native is the very reverse of small—he is a remarkably fine specimen of manhood. Sutcliffe was a *liar*—why? Was he deliberately creating enemies to explain the murder that was to be staged in the near future?"

The rector cut in yet again. "Stop a minute. Bathurst. Why Patagonia?"

"I can even explain that, I think, sir. Whilst at Verrinder he had made the evening acquaintance at the local hostelry of one Orlando Horton—globe-trotter—who told our friend Hector Savory yarns of Patagonia, and I suspect that in the telling he gave the natives that were his companions nicknames that were products of inversion. You know what I mean—in the same manner that we call a huge chap 'Tiny'. Sutcliffe—or Hector Savory, as I had better call him now—fell for that in his ignorance, and committed the error in conversations with Mrs. Nuckey afterwards."

"It's feasible, certainly. Now for when you arrived in Liverpool."

Bathurst smiled.

"There were at least three people, I thought, whom I might find it profitable to watch closely—the two Savorys and the man we knew as Mallinson, and when I found Hector wearing pince-nez my pulse quickened and my interest in him began to develop. When I discovered that he knew that the dead man was supposed to have been in Verrinder *five weeks* before the murder, it developed still more. I got them all down to Kirve St. Laudus, as you know, *to watch them*, and gradually a second idea began to form in my brain. Was this man Mallinson who was with us all he pretended to be? Two things began to stand out very clearly. Hector's disinclination to walk abroad in the Raybourne district, and Mallinson's unusual interest in you, Miss Eileen."

Sir Roland's eyes twinkled. "You don't miss much, do you?" he said.

"I try not to," replied Bathurst; "but I'm afraid I'm not always too successful. My visit to Liverpool served to confirm the suspicions that I was now beginning to entertain concerning the identities of 'Trevor' and 'Mallinson'. Who was there, I argued, to identify whom? They registered at Crosby's Hotel as Mallinson and Trevor, but who knew, as Sir Roland has told us, t'other from which? They weren't there long enough to be known by their respective personalities. Why shouldn't 'Mallinson' be 'Trevor'? The letter supposed to have been sent by Mallinson to Trevor's daughter didn't seem too genuine. 'An accident.' 'In hospital.' 'Don't write to him.' All beautifully vague! I began therefore to reconstruct the crime mentally, convinced by this time that the Savorys were implicated, and putting aside for the moment the question of motive. That would show itself in time. When they realized that the Walsingham heir had been found they plotted to kill him. I fancy that the elder Savory had arranged the details. Roughly, this was the manner of the murder: the dead man was to be found miles away from Liverpool with a ready-made identity, which Hector was to manufacture during the few weeks beforehand. The dead man's companion must not have the slightest idea that his employer had been murdered. By the way, Sir Roland, had they your photograph?"

"Yes. I had sent them a copy of the same one that Mallinson had with him. We had several of those taken."

"Exactly—and once again it wasn't plain which was you and which was Mallinson. You were each much of a height with Hector—they could see that, and plans were made for the false identification. It was pretty certain that if Hector did a certain routine habitually the substituted corpse would be hailed as his. That it was anything to do with you would never be dreamed of. Northlynn was selected for the scene of the crime for a very good reason. Trevor was to be decoyed from the docks and brought hundreds of miles south, so that there could be no possible linking up with Liverpool. The message he received was, of course, from the elder of our pair of scoundrels. If he did as Bartholomew warned him to, and transacted all his business secretly, it would serve to divert all suspicion from the idea that he ever could have met the Savorys. Trevor would disappear! When Mallinson, the pseudo-Trevor or Walsingham, turned up, after his attempted murder of his employer, this is what happened: Hector, already at Verrinder near Northlynn, received the 'O.K.' postcard from his father. Mallinson—believed to be the Walsingham heir—was decoyed from Loxteth House by the elder villain and brought to the room over the empty shop of Northlynn. And the stage was set for the murder."

"How was it done, Bathurst?" queried the rector.

"Getting him there? On a pretext, I should say, of formal identification as Sir Roland. No doubt there was a plausible story all ready to hand." Michael leant forward with perplexity in his eyes.

"But why Northlynn? How was it that they—?"

Bathurst's answer was ready and rapid. "Bartholomew married a Northlynn girl many years ago—Nancy Wyndham by name, who's been dead some years—and he knew Northlynn like a book. An acquaintance of old Orlando put me on to that. Told me something Hector had said about Northlynn in an unguarded moment. As a result I had the old man's marriage certificate looked up. When I found the family name of his wife inside Northlynn Parish Church I knew I was home."

"Bartholomew bought Chegwidden's shop in August, I suppose?" The question came from Sir Roland.

"He did—under another identity—because its proximity to the road had caused the idea that he eventually carried out to germinate in his brain. Paid Chegwidden a good sum to get out. He knew the shop well and knew also how the buses stopped outside for quite an appreciable time. But he had reckoned without one point."

Anthony Bathurst paused, and a whimsical smile played round his lips.

"Yes?" invited the rector.

"The shop had been used for the frying of fish with the concomitant 'chips'."

"Well?" said the rector.

"The odour—clings," suggested Mr. Bathurst.

"I'm afraid I don't—"

"It permeates clothing, sir—once it gets hold it is almost impossible to remove—and they weren't sure how long it might be necessary to keep Mallinson there. The shop had been used for frying fish for so long that all the rooms and cupboards were impregnated with the smell. The smell that might be detected on his clothes must on no account lead back to that nest of murder at Northlynn. All fish-shops on the route might be suspect unless an authentic identification was forthcoming. So Hector *chose* for his lodgings at Verrinder *another* shop used for this same—er—sinister trade. Mrs. Nuckey's. So that things might fit—do you see?"

"Devilishly ingenious," was Sir Roland's expressed opinion.

"What were they waiting for?" inquired the rector.

"A night with a thick fog. Bartholomew knew that they came nightly in the Linner Valley at this time of the year. Don't you remember the previous experiment? On the previous foggy night, when Sutcliffe didn't return to Mrs. Nuckey's, he got from the bus-top into the room at Northlynn and stayed there. He tested the possibility. It's quite simple—I did it myself. Arrangements had already been made regarding his tenancy. Mallinson was eventually murdered by the pair of them about eight o'clock on the fatal night, and dressed in what appeared to be Hector's clothes. They had had, of course, a complete duplicate suit in the room ever since Hector arrived. Hector walked to Lanning Arch, boarded his usual bus, the weather made it absolutely certain that he would have the top to himself, and at the Northlynn shop he stepped into the room, and the body was dragged or pushed over the sill, with the appropriate ticket in the turn-up of the trousers. Next morning they vacated the premises, which had been empty but for them. Hector, of course, had now resumed his own identity."

"What was the motive, Bathurst? My money?"

"Yes, Sir Roland. They were very deeply involved. Both embezzlement and fraudulent conversion. You will find that they have dug very deeply into the Walsingham estate, I can assure you. When the heir was found so unexpectedly, they could hear their bell tolling. It meant 'finis' for them. That was why I used your daughter as their decoy. In the first place her existence was a surprise and a shock to them. They must have ground their teeth—they were *in statu quo*—there was another claimant for the money that was so vital to them. When I sent her to Shropshire I baited the hook, and I knew they would make the attempt from there. Then I could bring the crime home to them."

Bathurst turned to the rector. "Remember how I warned them against themselves? When Sir Roland here invaded your study to find your brother's address, and then disappeared, I felt that he had obtained it, and when the time came would lead me to Miss Eileen-—I had immense faith in him. Where did you pick up the trail. Sir Roland?"

"I came in and overheard Michael say, 'My uncle's in Shropshire'—you know how I actually found the full address. Sorry, Rector; hope I didn't do any serious damage. I posted straight up there, made Much Wenlock, and within two hours of getting there had the luck to see the Savorys go by in a big car. How did they get you, Eileen?"

"I got a 'phone message that the rector had met with a serious accident, that I was to break it to his brother, and meet Mr. Bathurst's car outside Shrewsbury station in two hours' time. When I got there, of course, they were there. They said Mr. Bathurst had been delayed and had sent them to meet me, and I believed them. I was quite unsuspecting. I was chloroformed in the car and taken to Loxteth House. They kept me there. The rest you know." She shuddered at the reminiscence of the horror through which she had passed.

"I was on your track all the time, Eileen—and on theirs, too. I saw you enter the car at Shrewsbury and followed you in another. But I lost your car in Liverpool. Anyhow, I guessed where you were, and I felt that no serious harm would come to you while you stayed there. They couldn't risk it. The dirty work would have to be done elsewhere. But I took no chances however, and when they discussed the end they had planned for you, I was behind a curtain in Savory's study not six yards away from him. I heard the entire plan. If it had come off, another, and the last Walsingham of all, would have disappeared—so they thought— for your body would never have been found. The old Talisman is dark and deep. But the plan miscarried, thank God."

Sir Roland rose and shook Anthony Bathurst's hand, and the latter, rising, crossed to the window.

"I have two questions to ask," complained the rector, "before my mind finds the peace that it deserves. One of you, Bathurst, and one of Sir Roland. Yours first, Bathurst. How did that racing programme come to be in Mallinson's pocket?" His eyes twinkled as he put the question. "Bit of a poser for you, eh?"

Bathurst was unruffled. "No, sir. The explanation of that is excessively simple. On the voyage over Sir Roland and Mallinson helped to make up a Bridge four. Remember, Sir Roland?"

"That's quite right. With Dalrymple, the first officer, and an old clergyman. What was his name? Let me think. I've got it— Stapleton."

"Well, Dalrymple, whom I've met, used an old racing programme of his own for scoring purposes, and it passed in some way to Mallinson, who after the game kept it. I rather fancy that the murderers stuffed it into the pocket of his new suit purposely. It might serve to confuse the issue even more, you see."

"Thank you, Bathurst," said the Rev. Parry-Probyn. "Now you, Sir Roland. Why did you ransack the room at the inn and afterwards a room at Loxteth House?"

Sir Roland denied the soft impeachment. "Not guilty, Rector. Yours was my maiden and sole effort at ransacking. Try somebody else."

Anthony Bathurst blew a ring of smoke in the direction of the ceiling. "As a burglar, my dear Rector, I am quite accomplished. Even though Sir Roland here gave me the example and the impetus. I was anxious to lay my hands upon a pair of glasses or pince-nez constructed to remedy an exceedingly myopic left eye. My first attack on the Eighth Commandment was unrewarded, but Loxteth House proved more fruitful. A man usually keeps a spare pair at home. Hector Savory was no exception. The pair that I 'won' coincided exactly with the horn-rimmed pair found on the dead man. Is there anything else?"

The rector shook his head. "Although I realize," he replied, "that your answer concerning Sir Roland's accusation of the real murderers was strictly and literally veracious, I am nevertheless a little hurt. Still—we will consider the book closed." His smile drew an answering one from Anthony.

There is only the last scene of all for me to describe. So writes the rector. . . .

Michael pulled Eileen to his side.

"Do you know," he half whispered, "I was frantically jealous of Sir Roland when he came down here. Didn't like the way he looked at you. Thought he was in love with you, or something like it, and resented the idea like blazes. Wasn't I a priceless ass?"

He temporarily relinquished the lilies and languors of speech for the roses and raptures of action. Miss Walsingham surrendered to his kiss.

"That wasn't too bad, sweetheart, was it?"

Eileen playfully wiped her lips with the corner of her handkerchief.

"If that's a fair sample of the future," she declared, "it occurs to me that he's going to be much more jealous of you than you were of him. With a good deal more cause, I fancy." Her eyes sparkled.

"I'm all for the cause," whispered Michael.

"Then there are two of us," confessed Eileen.

THE END

Printed in Great Britain
by Amazon

55459605R00126